BITS AND PEACES

(short stories)

BITS AND PEACES

(short stories)

MITCHELL GRAYE

Other than the story titled "You Know Why?" identified as a true story, all stories in this book are works of fiction. Names, characters, places and incidents are products of the author's imagination or are used fictitiously. Any resemblance to actual events or locales or persons, living or dead, is entirely coincidental and not intended by the author.

First Edition: October, 2014

ISBN: 1500573515
ISBN: 978-1500573515
Library of Congress Control Number: 2014913055
CreateSpace Independent Publishing Platform
North Charleston, South Carolina

DEDICATED TO:

A TIME WHEN NO PEOPLE ARE JUDGED BY:
THE COLOR OF THEIR SKIN;
THE WAY THEY PRAY;
WHERE THEY'RE FROM;
WHO THEY LOVE:
WHAT THEY OWN;
TO WHOM THEY'RE RELATED;
OR WHO THEY KNOW.

BITS AND PEACES

<u>Section I</u> – Consisting of six fiction stories.

<u>Section II</u> – Comprising seven stories narrated by a fictional Mitchell Graye. In each case, the narrator meets an unusual person, and the story is driven by that character and the narrator's interaction with him or her. The first story takes place in the 1980s when the narrator was a businessman, and subsequent stories occur during different time periods beginning when he was a *writer wannabe,* then an unknown writer, successful writer, and very successful writer.

<u>Section III – Essays and Nonfiction</u>

SECTION I

FICTION

PRACTICING

The pink rubber ball goes high in the air, almost touching the leaves of a tree, then falls back into the little boy's baseball mitt. He tosses it up again, his straight blond hair swaying with the motion. Again, the ball drops down into the pocket of his mitt. Out of the corner of his eye, he sees his second-grade classmate, a girl with curly brown hair.

The girl, wearing a short blue dress, is standing twenty paces away, watching the boy's athletic exhibition. He tosses the ball higher in the air and moves three steps back to catch it. The next toss spirals in an even higher arc. He runs five steps to his left, snags it in the webbing of his mitt, and half glances over to the curly haired girl. It's confirmed. She's still watching.

He tries an overhand toss that shoots the ball into a branch high up in the tree and it quickly plummets to the ground. The boy turns, scoots five paces, and catches it on the second bounce. They finally look at each other. Her body shifts slightly from foot to foot.

Not sure what he should be doing, he stays his new ground and, with serious intent, tosses the ball up again, though not quite as high. She follows its flight. He catches it easily and, with attempted camouflage, makes her appear in the corner of his left eye. Now what? With great nonchalance, the ritual is repeated two more times.

Finally, "How did you learn to catch?"

His eyes stay on her as his chin slants downward toward his chest. One more very short toss in the air. "My dad taught me."

"Oh." Her eyes focus straight at him. "Girls don't catch like that."

"Ah-ah." He pounds the ball into his mitt.

"Do you like my dress?"

"Uh-huh."

She smiles. "Do you think I'm pretty?" Her head tilts slightly to the side.

"Yeah." The boy looks at his sneakers and fiddles with his mitt.

"You wanna sit with me when we have milk and cookies today?" she chirps as her knees move closer together.

"Okay," he answers and then lightly tosses the ball in the air and catches it.

"See you later."

"Yeah. See you later."

The girl with the curly brown hair turns and prances away. The blond-haired boy tosses the ball higher in the air than before. Then higher. And higher and higher and higher.

JOEY, ALL TIME SLUGGER

When I was seventeen, I didn't know how valuable a lesson it would be when Joey showed me that where a person lives in his own mind can matter as much as, or more than, his real condition.

It was in the schoolyard back in the fall of 1963 that I first caught sight of Joey pushing his middle-aged body around third base. After he crossed home plate, he took a little note pad out of his pocket and wrote something in it. To my surprise, he then picked up the bat and took the batter's stance at home plate.

Teddy, the chubby, freckled kid from my math class, pitched the softball to Joey, who hit it to right field. Steve picked up the ball at the short fence next to the basketball hoop, then pegged it over the head of the second baseman, allowing Joey to head for third base. When Richie kicked the ball into short left field, Joey bounded around third base, crossed home plate, and made another entry in his notebook. He took off his Yankee cap, mopped his lined brow, then ran his hand through his graying brown hair.

At that moment, I was behind the five-foot wire fence in front of the two wooden benches that comprised the first-base dugout. I walked over to Billy, who lived in my apartment building just down the block.

"Hey, what's with this guy?"

"He's trying to break Babe Ruth's lifetime home run record." (This was 1963, prior to Hank Aaron and then Barry Bonds becoming the owners of that record.)

"In softball batting practice?"

"Yeah. He's a nut. The guys are having fun with him."

"How many *home runs* does he have?"

5

"Six hundred and eighty-something. He had six hundred and forty-something when he got here this afternoon."

"How old is that guy?" I asked.

"I don't know. Forty-three ... forty-six, ya think?"

"Yeah," I nodded.

A few minutes later, Joey came barreling around third base, crossed home plate, then came crashing into the gate while the ball sailed high into the backstop fence. He pulled out the notebook and dug the pencil out of his pocket. I strolled nearer to him while he recorded another entry.

"How many you got?" I asked?

"Six hundred and eighty-seven," he said with a childlike grin that showed large spaces between his upper row of teeth. "I'm gonna break Babe Ruth's record today."

"That would be seven hundred and fourteen. You're gonna do that today?" I looked at him doubtfully.

"Uh-huh." Sweat streamed down from his curly hair. "That's my dream. I'm gonna break it."

"But you don't gotta do it today," I said, thinking to myself that this guy is going to have a heart attack. And that wouldn't be amusing.

"I wanna do it today." He grinned again. "It's my dream. 'Scuse me. I gotta go get in the batter's box."

"Hey, what's your name?"

"Joey," he called over his shoulder as he picked up his bat. He turned back to me and, with a loud, childish speech pattern like my friend's kid brother, repeated, "My name is Joey."

I acknowledged with a short wave of my hand.

Joey stepped up to the plate. On the first underhand pitch, he grounded the ball toward third base. Nobody was playing third and the ball rolled down the left-field line. Ricky jogged over to the ball, juggled it, then threw it over the second baseman's head as Joey was chugging into third base. He made the turn and crossed home plate. Out came the notebook and the pencil. He walked over to me.

"Six hundred and eighty-eight," he declared, still panting and his chest heaving, causing me further concern.

"Hey, gimme that. I'll keep score for you," I said.

"Okay. Here." He handed me the notebook and pencil. "Hey, what's your name?"

"Uh, Ralph ... Ralph Kiner."

"The Mets announcer?"

"That's right."

"Really?"

"Yeah. I'm gonna announce the home run that breaks Ruth's record."

"Great!"

Joey got up at the plate and hit a blooper into short right field. The ball rolled down the foul line and kicked around the fence while Joey dashed around the bases. I made six entries in his notebook.

"Way to go, Joey. Six hundred and ninety-four," I called out to him. He smiled and waved to me, then got back up at the plate. The next pitch was lined into center field and Joey soon crossed home plate.

"Hey, Joey. That's seven hundred. You're getting close."

Three pitches later and Joey hit number seven hundred and fourteen, tying him with Babe Ruth's lifetime home run record. His face was dripping, and he was panting. I was getting worried that he'd have a coronary right then. I was thinking that I should have made that last one the record breaker.

"Joey, that's great. You tied the record. Why don't you go home now and come back tomorrow and break the record. I'll be back tomorrow to announce it. I'll bring a camera and take pictures."

"No, Ralph. I gotta break the record now. I'm visiting my parents today. Tomorrow, I'll be back at the home. I have to do it now. You gonna announce it like the TV play-by-play?"

I was reluctant, but I was also getting a clearer picture of Joey's circumstances. "Yeah. Okay. I'll announce it. This is the big one," I said, swallowing hard and hoping I was doing the right thing.

Joey took his stance at the plate. I picked up a stick from the ground and held it in my hand like a microphone and moved right behind the batter's cage so he could hear me.

"Joey steps up to the plate. He's going for the lifetime home run record. The pitch from Teddy and Joey swings … it's a blast to center-field. It's over Steve's head and bounces to the fence. Joey's digging for second … he's steaming for third. Steve picks up the ball and fires to the infield. Joey rounds third. Here comes the ball. Here comes Joey … and he beats the ball! He beats the ball! Joey breaks the all-time home run record."

I'll never, ever forget the triumphant look on Joey's face when he crossed home plate. His reality was the only reality and, clearly in his mind, he had broken the all-time home run record. The guys picked him up and carried him around the infield. Joey pumped his arms in the air as tears streamed down his face. I turned away for a moment to wipe a few tears from my own eyes.

Minutes later, a big gray van pulled up to the curb just outside the fence and a uniformed man and an older woman got out. Joey took a few baseballs out of a duffle bag. He signed them and tossed them to the guys on the field, then waved and got in the van.

That day, back in 1963, Joey showed a seventeen-year-old boy that people are capable of creating their own reality and influencing their own degree of happiness for better or worse. And since then, when life got tough, I'd think of what I learned from Joey, the all-time home run king.

SLEEPING WITH THE ARTIST

The crowd thinned out in the subway exit as people chose the east or west staircases to the street. Philip's aggressive gait as well as his expensive blue pinstriped suit and coordinating silk tie set him apart from the other commuters. He was at the bank of elevators in his office building a few minutes later, and acknowledged the young man at his right.

"Good morning, John."

"Good morning, Sir."

They got in the elevator, Philip pressed the button, and the door closed behind them.

John stared straight ahead, and then glanced at Philip out of the corner of his eye. *Wonder what he's going to do today,* John thought. *Probably thumb through some papers to prepare for a big meeting. Everybody will be watching and waiting for his decision about some megadeal while he sips coffee from a fancy china cup. At twelve o'clock, he'll probably be entertained at some fancy restaurant by big-shot bankers. And some good-looking women in the group will flatter and fall all over him. Then, who knows what for the evening. I wonder if he even knows what I do in the company.*

Philip looked over at John from the corner of his eye. *Wonder what he does when he leaves the office at night,* he thought. *Probably meets his buddies at a bar, then goes to a dance club. Doesn't actually look that tired. Maybe he goes right home to an apartment he shares with a sweet girlfriend who just finished art school. She sells some of her paintings, and also works as a museum tour guide to help pay her half of the rent. Last night, they had a modest dinner she prepared from scratch. They talked about their dreams and ambitions, passionately made love, and then held each other in the dark before drifting off to sleep.*

The elevator proceeded upward. Philip turned to the younger man.

"So, John. How are things going in the marketing department?"

"Very good, Sir."

"Glad to hear that. Not making you get home too late, I hope."

The elevator door opened on the fifty-third floor, and Philip nodded to John to exit first.

"Have a good day, Sir."

"Same to you, John."

Philip walked through the hallway toward his corner office a bit slower than usual. "Good morning, Barbara," he greeted his assistant, then hung up his suit jacket in his closet, sat down at his desk, and glanced at his calendar. He slouched, paused a moment, then called out, "Barbara, please cancel my ten o'clock meeting."

"But Philip, I thought that meeting was very important," she called back. "And that's such short notice. They might be on their way already."

"Well, try. And cancel lunch with those boring public relations people with their phony conversations." He rolled his eyes and thought, *if someone else was in this job tomorrow, they'd forget my name.*

* * *

John placed his jacket on a hanger and hooked the hanger over the top of the partition wall of his cubicle. He turned on his computer and saw nearly twenty emails sent to him since leaving the previous night. He opened the first few, but had trouble concentrating and welcomed the interruption by Brian, his co-worker in the next cubicle.

"Hey, how'd it go?"

John shook his head. "She doesn't get it, or just doesn't give a crap. I told her straight up that I'm fed up with babysitting her three-year-old brat while she comes home all hours of the morning."

"Good. And what'd she say?"

"She said that's what her job requires. I told her she ought to quit being a stripper and get a regular job. So she gets pissed and yells that she's not a stripper. She's an exotic dancer."

"And that, my good man, makes you the envy of all the guys."

John slouched in his chair and thought to himself that the last time she stripped for him was two months ago. "Really? You know what?" he said to Brian. "I'm going over there at lunchtime and getting all my things out of her place. And before I leave, I'm gonna tell her she'll be needing a babysitter beginning tonight. I'm outta there!"

YOU'RE THE ONLY ONE WHO KNOWS

Michael Damsky was asked to attend a meeting with his boss, Kelly Barber, the company's controller; and her boss, Dennis Murphy, the vice president for finance. The agenda was vaguely described as being special assignments.

Michael, having worked at Great Brands for twenty-one years, assumed that if what's past is prologue, special assignments would mean a great deal of overtime hours and interacting with people outside the financial-related departments in different ways than customary. But then again, the past might not be a predictor inasmuch as Murphy had come from outside the company less than a year earlier, and he hired Kelly to be controller just seven months later.

Eleven on the dot, Michael walked into Dennis Murphy's office. Murphy was seated behind his large desk and Kelly Barber sat opposite him in a guest chair.

"Good morning," Michael said upon entering. "I understand I'm invited to a meeting here at this time."

"Yes, that's right," Murphy answered as Kelly turned to face Michael. "Why don't we sit at the conference table," he said, indicating the eight-seat rectangular table in the corner of his office. Murphy picked up his phone, punched in four numbers, and a few seconds later said, "Waiting on you," in a low but firm voice.

Seated at the table, Michael waited to hear about the special assignments. Elizabeth Green walked into the office with a quick step, step, step.

"Sorry I was detained," she said, looking toward Murphy. "Where would you like me to sit?"

"Anywhere."

Michael pondered her presence since she was associate director of human resources, and wondered whether the meeting was going to be about a financial project related to the employee pension plan or health care plans.

"Michael, we're here to tell you that there's going to be a reorganization of the finance department," Murphy began. "Kelly, you can proceed."

"Right. As Dennis said, we're reorganizing the finance department. As a result of the reorganization, your position is being eliminated."

"What? I'm being fired? For what reason?"

"You're not being fired for *cause.* Your job is being eliminated as a result of the reorganization to be more efficient and cut down on costs."

Michael glanced over at Murphy. Then back at Kelly. "And my staff? They'll report to you?"

"They'll report to Mark."

Michael turned to the associate director of human resources and said, "She means Mark Robels, the guy she hired two months ago to fill a brand-new position she created after being here for only three months." He paused. "It just so happens that Mark worked with Kelly at their mutual prior employer, which I know because I googled him and confirmed the nepotism with people at that company.

"Why exactly are you here?" he asked, leaning toward Elizabeth Green. "Is it to see to it that this passes some kind of legal criteria? Or is it to put some kind of priest-like HR blessing on it?"

Elizabeth's face flushed. "I have papers for you, Michael. Some of them have to do with your options regarding health insurance at your own cost, your 401(k) plan … and your severance agreement."

"How much is my severance pay?"

"The company is offering you six month's severance pay if—"

"Offering? Meaning it's negotiable? Upward."

Elizabeth looked to Dennis and Kelly as though wishing one of them would pick up from that point in the discussion. "I'm sorry, Michael, but *offering* in this context means in exchange for you signing the agreement included in these papers. The agreement states, among other things, that you will not sue the company due to the termination of your employment. You should read it closely. And you should have a lawyer read it. The offer is good for twenty-one days, so it must be signed and returned within that period."

"One day for each year I worked for the company?"

"That's a coincidence."

"And if I don't sign it? No severance pay?"

"Yes."

Michael's eyes darted around the room at the three of them. "Is there anything else on the agenda of this meeting about special assignments?"

"No, that's it," Dennis answered.

"Then I'll go."

"You can't go back to your office," Kelly said.

"What do you mean I can't go back to my office?"

"We don't want you to do anything with your computer, touch anything in your desk, or speak to anybody," Kelly replied.

"First of all, Miss Controller, you should be familiar enough with the company's internal procedures and controls by now to know that I'm not able to wire cash funds outside the company, nor am I an authorized check signer. In fact, I don't even have access to blank checks. As for not speaking to anybody, I want to say good-bye to some people. Yes, I will tell them I've been fired; I mean that my job has been eliminated due to the reorganization. It's definitely not appropriate for me to be sent directly to the elevator, and give people the impression that I've been dismissed for doing something dishonest."

"You could make copies of company financial records via your computer," Dennis said.

Michael stared at him. "And how do you know I haven't already done that every night? You don't know. Do you? ... I'm going to say good-bye to my friends," Michael said, turning and walking out of the office.

* * *

Michael exited the elevator in the lobby and walked over to Walter, the security guard for the prior eight years.

"Hey, Michael. Headin' for an early lunch?"

"No, Walter. I'm leaving the company and stopping to say good-bye."

"Really? When are you leaving?"

"Right now, as I leave the building."

"So fast?"

"That's how it is sometimes."

"I'm not happy that you're leaving, and I think there's more I don't like about it."

"Not for you to investigate."

"I'll miss seein' you around."

"You'll find someone else to break your balls. I'll miss your jokes and your ugly puss, too. You enjoy and take care of those grandkids," Michael said, reaching out his right hand and grabbing Walter's.

"God's speed, Michael."

He walked the length of the lobby to the doors leading to the street, stopped and turned around. One last time, his eyes roamed the lobby he had entered and left for twenty-one years, and then walked through the revolving door to the street.

It was still not quite lunch time, and Michael wondered what he should do next. Go home? Not ready for that. Find a lawyer? Not ready for that either. Besides, he had twenty-one days to sign and return the agreement. He really wasn't hungry, but there was a small place a few blocks away where he'd often eat lunch when he was by himself. He decided to stop by for a few minutes.

Michael walked down the two steps from the street level to the Rainbow Diner. Not many customers seated yet. As he got to the counter, George popped his head from below the take-out counter where two orders were waiting for pick up.

"Michael, how you doing? So early? You wanted to get here before today's specials are gone?"

"Actually, I'm not really hungry."

"What's that about? Oh, 'cause it's too early. You stopped by to say hello? Elias," he called to the kitchen, "step out front a minute. Michael stopped by to say hello."

Michael felt his shoulders sag.

"Hi," Elias called out, walking through the kitchen door.

"Actually, you two, I didn't come by to say *hello*. I came to say good-bye."

"Why good-bye?" George asked.

"Well … because I'm being transferred."

"Transferred to where?"

"Chicago."

$$* \ * \ *$$

Michael walked down Fifth Avenue with no particular destination in mind, and without observing anything other than the changing of the *Walk/Don't Walk* signs on the corners. Within twenty minutes, the streets were packed with people despite the wide sidewalks running alongside the display windows of fashionable Fifth Avenue stores.

Michael's seventeen-year-old daughter, Heather, expressed ambitions to attend the Fashion Institute of Technology and have a career in the fashion industry, though her most immediate ambition was to pass her road test and obtain her driver's license. Nineteen-year-old Gregg had just returned from his freshmen dormitory after finishing his first year at Columbia University, where he was aiming for an engineering degree.

At Forty-Second Street, Michael began paying more attention to his whereabouts and turned west toward Sixth and then Seventh Avenue, on the way to Pennsylvania Station where he could get a Long Island Railroad train home. At Seventh, he looked across Forty-Second and noticed a Tad's Steak Restaurant. *Haven't eaten in a Tad's in something like twenty-five, thirty years*, he thought. *Wonder what they charge these days.* When he was a college student, he paid $1.99

for a steak with garlic bread, baked potato, and a salad when buying dinner before an evening class. He crossed the street and peered inside Tad's window. There was a line of four people waiting. What the heck. He was then both tired and hungry. The sign indicated a price of $13.89. He entered and waited his turn.

"Steak or hamburger?" a guy with a big fork in his hand asked Michael as he reached the front of the line.

"Steak."

"How you like it? Rare, medium, well-done?"

"Medium-rare."

The guy swung a partially cooked steak from a pile of slabs on his right onto the center of the grill sitting over the streaking flames. Michael soon had his steak and was glad to sit down at a table six rows behind the cashier. He cut and chewed until half the steak was eaten, then leaned back and looked around. His mind went years back to when he was working hard to do the best he could in college; his biggest problems had to do with getting through class and his worries were whether he could get an "A" instead of a "B." His mind flashed over the years from college to the previous year—before Murphy became vice president and chief financial officer and then hired that know-nothing politician controller.

Now that he wasn't so hungry, the steak didn't taste as good as the early bites, or as good as when he was a college student. He had expected that sitting and eating in a Tad's Steak Restaurant would give him a sense of comfort, but that didn't last. A couple more bites of steak and Michael got up from the table and headed out the door.

It was twenty minutes before two o'clock when he reached the escalator on Thirty-Fourth Street taking him down to the Long Island Railroad waiting area, including the dozens of fast food places, bars, shoe shine stands, newsstands, bookstores, and so on. The next train to his town would depart in forty-three minutes and then again every hour thereafter. He looked around. No need for a shine. Already ate, and read today's *New York Times*. He went into the sports bar.

"What'll it be?" the bartender asked.

"A light beer."

"Coors okay?"

"That's fine."

The bartender pulled a bottle out from below, wiped it down, and popped the cap. "That'll be four dollars."

Michael put a five-dollar bill down on the bar, took the beer, and walked to the side of the bar with it. *Where'd the custom of tipping the bartender for popping open a bottle of beer begin? Maybe I should apply for a job like that—no deadlines, no work to take home.*

He nursed the bottle of Coors for nearly an hour and noticed that his train had left ten minutes earlier. That's when he decided that he wasn't going to take any train until the one that would get him home at the usual time.

* * *

Donna Damsky was in the kitchen, checking on the chicken in the oven, when she heard her husband's car pull into the driveway. Not long after, she heard the front door open and slam shut.

"Donna, I'm home."

"Hi. I'm in the kitchen."

Michael first went to their bedroom, took off his jacket and tie, walked into the bathroom to wash his hands and face, then went to Donna and gave her a kiss.

"How was your day?" she asked.

"Life in corporate America. And your day?"

"Life in an underfunded American hospital. This patient needs this, that patient wants that, the doctor said they can't have it. A family member complains that their father isn't getting enough care, and the hospital doesn't have the money to add back the two nurse's aide positions temporarily cut three months ago."

"And the ride to and from work?"

"The best twenty minutes of the day," she answered.

"The kids home?"

"Gregg went into the city, and Allie is over at Megan's house, studying with her friends."

"*Studying* with friends," Michael repeated. "Right."

"I hope you didn't have chicken for lunch."

"No,"

"What'd you have."

"Tuna sandwich."

After dinner, Michael joined Donna in the den to watch "Dancing with the Stars."

* * *

Next morning, Michael put on a blue suit, yellow shirt and blue tie, kissed Donna good-bye, and left the house to catch the 7:42 train to the city, as he'd done nearly every day for more than twenty years. He carried his workbag in one hand and the *New York Times* in the other as he stood at the station platform waiting for the train to arrive. He looked around, noticing many of the same familiar faces of mornings' past, nodding acknowledgment to those who had marched a long distance with him on that same road. Michael chose a seat by the window that morning, and watched the sights of all the neighborhoods the train passed through—sometimes with blank stares, sometimes with thoughtful recollections.

He got off the train at Pennsylvania Station at 8:32, and walked the steep flight of steps from the tracks to the busy shopping arcade level. Michael had no plan after reaching the top of the stairs. He could go to the Statue of Liberty or a Broadway show, or some other thing that tourists do when New Yorkers are scurrying around the streets or meeting in their offices. Too early. He started to head into Au Bon Pain to sit down with a cup of coffee and the *Times*, then realized that other commuters from his neighborhood, arriving on later trains, might view him through the window sitting back and not rushing to his office. He stopped, turned in the other direction, and took another flight of steps up to the level of the Amtrak trains. Michael found another Au Bon Pain sixty paces from the top of the stairs, ordered a coffee, selected a table at the back, and spread his newspaper across it.

By nearly ten o'clock, Michael was tired of reading the newspaper. *Time to read the agreement,* he thought, and opened his workbag. He first pulled out copies of several Great Brands' financial papers that he'd printed out days earlier when he'd been trying to figure out why the numbers didn't reconcile, then sorted through his bag and found the papers given to him the day before by Elizabeth Green. He located the severance agreement and read it slowly, then read it again.

Effective May 21, 2013, blah, blah ... Employee will receive severance pay equal to six months' salary in one lump sum within one month after signing and returning this agreement ... blah, blah ... Employee agrees that he will not sue the Company, any of its officers, directors or employees, blah, blah ... Employee agrees not to disclose to any person other than his attorney or immediate family members the amount of severance received or the existence of this agreement, blah, blah ... If not signed within twenty-one (21) days from the date hereof, the Company has the right to rescind any or all terms of this agreement, blah, blah ...

And so why can't I tell anybody the amount of my severance pay, or even the existence of the agreement? Michael wondered. *What's the point of that? Because it's so lavish? It's not.* He could take the easy and sure route, and take the six months' severance pay, equal to one and one quarter weeks' pay for each year he worked for the company. Or should he sue? A more emotionally gratifying route—if he wins. On what grounds? Age discrimination, having just turned the age of fifty? Nepotism? Being assholes? He concluded that he would invest some money to consult a labor lawyer.

* * *

Gregg slept extra late, having come home in the wee hours of the morning after his night in the city with friends. It felt good not to have worry about any classes, term papers or exams. His summer job would begin the following week, and that would end late nights during mid-week. He was in the kitchen, popping an English muffin in the toaster, when the phone rang.

"Hello."

"Hello, can I speak to Michael, please? This is Andy Walton calling."

"He's not home. This is his son."

"Oh, Gregg. As I said, this is Andy Walton. I'm a friend of your father's from Great Brands. I feel like I know you from all the years your father's talked about you."

"Hi. I've heard him mention your name often."

"How is he doing? Is he taking it hard? I imagine it's hard on the whole family."

"Uh ... he seems to be okay," Gregg replied, sensing right away that his father didn't share with the family something that happened.

"Well, tell him I called on behalf of a group of us, and that we want to be supportive."

"I will. I'll definitely tell him. It's nice of you to call."

The English muffin popped up in the toaster. Gregg sat frozen in a kitchen chair.

* * *

It was 1985 when Michael graduated from New York University, located in Greenwich Village where its urban buildings largely surround Washington Square Park. Perhaps it was not merely a coincidence that he took the subway from Pennsylvania Station to West Fourth Street, then strolled over to the park and sat on a wooden park bench to be enveloped by the trees and the past. Since Michael attended college, some newer and taller buildings had been added to the perimeter of the park, as well as within his sight a couple blocks away. *It doesn't appear quite the same*, he thought. *But neither do I. Boy, the students sure look young.* It was a balmy day, and Michael decided to pick up a sandwich and drink from a shop across the street, returning to settle at another park bench. The sandwich balanced in his lap, and the drink on the bench by his side, he ate slowly while his eyes and mind drifted here, there, and everywhere.

A tattered man shuffled over, sat down several feet from Michael, and heaved a big cloth bag between them, letting out a soft "Whew" as something in the bag made a clonking thud as it hit the bench. Michael attempted to politely ignore the activity and sounds. The man looked at him, straight ahead, and then back at him.

"You a professor or somethin'?"

"No, I'm not."

"How come you're wearin' a suit and a tie?"

"That's what I wear every Monday to Friday."

"What're ya doin' sittin' here in the park, dressed all fancy like you *are* a professor?"

"I felt like coming here today to look around. I graduated college here a long time ago … NYU."

"I know it's NYU."

"And what are *you* doing here?" Michael turned the tables on him.

"I live here."

Michael turned his head directly toward the man so that he made eye contact, and gave him a questioning look.

"It ain't my address. Can't get my mail sent to Washington Square Park. I live here during the day."

"Then you actually live somewhere else … where you sleep."

"Sleep wherever I can," the man explained with a laugh.

Michael forced a smile.

"You got it now. Right?"

"Yeah, I got it. You're homeless. I kind of thought that, but I didn't want to be rude and assume it."

The tattered man looked squarely at Michael for a few seconds. "Thank you. Sorry if I'm bothering you, mister. You were eatin' and thinkin'."

"I was. That's okay. What's in this big bag? Your stuff?"

"Yup. All my belongings. Everything I own."

"Seems heavy to drag around with you all the time."

"Can I leave it with you? Ha, ha," he laughed, hitting his knee.

"Guess not," Michael replied with a grin.

"What's in your bag, there?"

"In here? Mostly, it's a contract."

The tattered man looked at Michael without understanding.

"It's a severance agreement. I got fired from my job yesterday. My company is offering to pay me a certain amount of money if I agree not to sue it for firing me."

"You can do that? You can sue someone for firing ya?"

"Sometimes. If you've been discriminated against for no good reason."

"Well, hot damn! I never knew that before."

"You ever been fired?"

"How you think I got where I am, livin' outta this bag? I was let go from a small factory when its business got slow, let go from a restaurant when its business went down, and got fired from a warehouse 'cause stuff was missing and they needed to blame someone. Money ran out, and I lost my apartment. Had a good job before that in a factory. Nine years. But they moved everything to Asia... Thailand."

"You have family anywhere? Any kids?"

"Nah. Never had any kids. No woman ever foolish enough to marry me," he said with a half laugh. "That's a good thing in the end. Wouldna' been cool, me and a missus and two kids, all draggin' bags full o' our belongings around the street." He paused and turned his face away from Michael, and looked straight ahead. "Only people I got are my two brothers, Johnny and Aaron. They live in Orlando."

"Can Johnny or Aaron help you ... what's *your* name?

"Curtis."

"Mine's Michael."

"I'd reach to shake your hand, Michael, but I know people don't want to touch a homeless guy."

"Well, if I weren't eating my lunch, I'd shake your hand. I'm germophobic just before and while I'm eating. So, back to Johnny and Aaron. They can't help you, Curtis?"

"They don't know about my situation."

"How long have you been homeless?"

"Almost two years."

"And your brothers don't know?"

"They got their families. Got their own problems. Johnny's forty-six, Aaron's forty-three. And I'm fifty—the big brother."

"Your brothers don't know where you are and can't reach you? Probably think you're dead."

"I got a phone."

Michael flinched. "Where does the bill get mailed?"

"It's one of those pay-as-you-go phones. I found it."

"Found it?" *As in found it on a Radio Shack store shelf?* Michael wondered.

"Really. Someone left it on a bench a long time ago, along with a handful 'o those cards to add minutes to the phone—six cards for eight hundred minutes each. Okay, I didn't turn it in to a cop to give to some lost and found. The guy that lost it wasn't gonna go to the cops to claim it 'cause I'm willing to bet all of those refill cards that it was one of those drug dealers that hang around here all the time. Can you see one of 'em walking into the cop station, sayin' *Hello, Mr. Policeman, I'm here to pick up the phone I lost. You know the kind of phone that can't be traced?*" Curtis laughed, smacking his hands together.

"I guess those eight-hundred-minute cards will last you a while. Eventually, though, you'll use up the minutes."

"I collect soda cans and bottles … and we don't talk long. You don't believe me? Call my number. You gonna hear the phone ring in my bag. Call 646-555-1818. Go 'head. Go on."

This matters to him, Michael thought, as he pulled out his phone and Curtis repeated the number. He dialed and soon heard the ringing of a phone in Curtis's big stuffed bag.

"See? I told ya. I'm Curtis Williams. I'm poor and homeless, and a sorry specimen, but I ain't a liar, and I ain't a thief. I'm an honest man."

Michael smiled and looked at him, deciding that Curtis, no matter his situation, was truthful. "You know what, Curtis? I believe you. I do."

Curtis returned the smile. "Thank you."

"I understand your pride, not wanting to tell your brothers. But only up to a point. It's your family. Your *brothers*."

"You *think* ya understand, but ya can't really. They're my *baby* brothers," he added, and tears slid down his cheeks. "Sorry, being a weeping child. They got others that need caring, and I don't. Me ... I should be able to help them."

Michael didn't know what to say, and was quiet until he finally came out with "You really are tough on yourself."

"Maybe. What about you? You only been fired one day. Why'd they fire you?"

"The excuse was that it was part of reorganizing the company. I think it was to give another guy my job. Someone who worked with my boss at another company."

"He wanted someone who'd be on his side no matter what. Cover his ass, huh?"

"*Her* side. My boss is a woman. But yeah."

"Maybe the new guy's doin' her."

"Your mind is in the gutter ... but, could be. Never know," Michael said with a forced chuckle. "I'm curious about something. Why do you think you were the person accused of stealing the stuff from the warehouse? Hope you don't mind my asking. Do you think it had to do with you being black?"

"Ya know, not everything bad that happens to a black guy is 'cause he's black. The factory I worked at for nine years wasn't moved to Thailand 'cause I'm black. And when I was laid off from the restaurant, a white guy was laid off before me. At the small factory, me, a white guy, and another black guy were laid off at the same time. But, yeah, I was fired from the warehouse 'cause I was black. It'd figure that the black guy did the stealing. Know what I mean?" Curtis asked, looking straight at Michael.

"Yes, I do."

"But not just any black guy," he continued. "There were two other black guys working there. The boss picked this black guy 'cause he figured I knew who really was doin' the stealing ...and he was right!

I did know. It was him. So how would anyone believe me about the boss stealing after he fired me for the stealing? They didn't. The son 'o bitch had it figured. Got rid 'o the guy he was afraid of and didn't have to answer any more questions from the office about missing stuff."

Michael sat still and rewound in his head everything that Curtis had just said.

"Got rid of the guy he feared," Michael repeated. "Were you arrested?"

"Nah, I wasn't arrested. There was no proof I stole anything. 'Cause I didn't."

Michael thought back to Curtis's emphatic declarations about being an honest man.

"The boss woulda been stupid to call the cops. If they investigated stuff close enough, maybe he could go to the clink. Fired me, tells the big boss he got rid 'o the problem quiet-like, and he's off the hook."

"Your boss was a real two-bit dirtbag."

"You got that right. I gotta live with the result. What's the army call that? Collateral damage?"

"What would you like to do about it? I mean if you had a chance."

"You mean revenge?"

Michael nodded.

"I wouldn't shoot him, or nothin' like that. But if I could make trouble for him I sure would. But I'll never be in a position to. Maybe your boss got rid 'o you 'cause you know somethin'."

"There's nothing I know that could get her or her boss in trouble. They fired me together."

Curtis laughed. "Maybe you don't know you know. Maybe you don't know, and they *think* you *do* know."

"You've got a creative mind, Curtis. What are you doing living in the park? You could've written detective stories. I think if they thought I knew something bad about them or the company, they would've done something different than just let me go and give me severance pay."

"What's your family think about it all?"

"Um," Michael hesitated. His eyebrows rose and his lips squeezed together. "Actually … you really want to know?"

"We're talkin' about it. Unless you don't wanna say."

"I haven't told them."

"Haven't told them what?"

"About being fired."

"You kiddin' me. You are kidding me."

"No, I'm not kidding. I'm really not."

"How come?"

"Why have I dressed in a business suit early in the morning and taken the same train in from Long Island? Just to hang out in a coffee shop at Penn Station and then come down here to talk to you?"

"Damn! Why man?" Curtis asked. Why're you doin' all that?"

"I guess I haven't come to terms with it yet. I'll tell them soon. I can't keep up this charade long. Unlike you. You could probably keep up the charade for months and months. Maybe even two years."

Curtis laughed from his belly on up. "You're good, Michael. You're good."

"You're the only person on this planet that I've told," Michael said. "You're the only one who knows."

* * *

Michael, Donna, Gregg, and Allie sat around the dinner table that night enjoying Donna's pot roast.

"Isn't this nice?" Donna said. "All of us having dinner together with Gregg home from school."

"And Allie not being off at someone else's house making believe she's studying," Michael added, winking at his daughter.

"My friends and I *are* studying when we get together for a group study session, Daddy."

"She learned that one from me, Dad. It's not all her fault. Product of her environment."

"How was your night in the city?" Michael asked.

"Good. We had fun."

"What does that mean?"

"Dancing. Bars."

"Like school," Michael kidded his son.

Gregg laughed. "No, not like school. Nobody had to get up for class," he quipped. "I'm staying home tonight."

"Pooped out?"

"No. I could go for doing something physical. Maybe the gym. Or … Dad, do you still have the baseball glove you used when you gave me infield practice and you played first base for me?"

"It's buried somewhere in my closet—as a souvenir. I wasn't fifty then."

"You're still in shape. I'll go easy on you."

"Okay. If I can possibly find my glove."

"It's on the second shelf in your closet," Donna said.

Michael looked at her with a fake smile.

Father and son arrived at the same baseball field they used to practice at years earlier. Michael slowly took in the field—the bases, the pitcher's mound, the backstop behind home plate. He cajoled Gregg into letting him take some time to do some stretching because he's not the same age and can't just pop on the field and start throwing, and bending to scoop the ball from the dirt.

"You ready yet, Dad? It'll be time for breakfast soon."

"For that I'm gonna throw you grounders that'll make you eat dirt before you can pick them up."

"Try it."

Michael tossed grounders to Gregg's left, and to his right. Fast, then slow ones, making him charge in. Tossed them in the air behind him, then short pops in front of him. Gregg cleanly handled nearly all of the tosses and fired the ball to his father at first base. Michael thought that Gregg purposely challenged him with throws in the dirt, just as he challenged Gregg with grounders far to his right. Michael waved Gregg in after forty minutes.

"Had enough?" Gregg asked.

"I didn't want you to get hurt and not be able to report for your job next week. You still got it, kid. Handled everything cleanly," Michael said, putting his arm on his son's shoulder.

"I had a good teacher ... You still handle the throws good."

"Yeah, for an old man."

"You're not an old man."

"In some contexts, people see a fifty-year-old guy as old."

"Dad, can I ask you something?"

"What is it?"

"I haven't said anything about this to anybody else. And I wanted to ask you while we're alone."

"Well, what is it? What do you want to ask?"

"Earlier today, when I was the only one home ... there was a phone call. It was from Andy Walton, your friend from work."

Michael felt himself gulp. "Yeah?"

"He said he was calling to see how you're doing. Asked if you're taking it hard? And that he was calling on behalf of other friends, too. That they want to be supportive."

Michael flushed, feeling stupid and embarrassed. He rubbed the back of his head with his hand, and exhaled.

"I didn't say anything to Mom."

"Gregg, let's go sit down."

They walked to the benches behind the dugout fence.

Michael fessed up to being let go from Great Brands. And to pretending to go to work each morning.

"I don't understand why you did that, Dad."

"I've been having a hard time accepting what's happened, and wasn't ready to talk about it," Michael responded, seated next to Gregg on the bench of the third base dugout. "And I also didn't quite know how to announce it to you guys. This kind of thing never happened to me before. I was embarrassed. Of course, not as embarrassed as I am now."

"Dad, you've always told me not to be down on myself about how something turns out if I tried my best. And remember what you said when I didn't get picked to play on the high school all-star team because Jon Hecky was picked based on popularity?"

"Remind me."

"You told me that losing to a stacked deck in a poker game has nothing to do with how well you played your hand."

"I said that?"

"Yeah, and I always remembered it."

"That was pretty smart."

* * *

Seven days after being fired, Michael sat down in front of his lap-top computer to begin drafting the first résumé he'd prepared in more than two decades. Though he'd seen many résumés submitted for positions in his department, how to begin his own was perplexing. Procrastinating, he chose to first check his email inbox. There were the usual nuisance messages reminding him of final chances for the best offers from more than a dozen merchants. But there was also an email from Elizabeth Green, the associate director of human resources. He clicked on her message: *Dear Michael, Please call me regarding revisions to be made to your agreement.*

Thank you, Elizabeth.

Michael knew he wouldn't be able to concentrate on his résumé after reading that message, and reached for the phone.

"Hello, this is Elizabeth Green."

"Elizabeth, this is Michael Damsky. I received your email."

"Thank you for calling, Michael. I'm sorry if my message sounded mysterious. What's up is that there are two changes that are going to be made to your agreement."

"Two."

"Yes. The first change is to recognize that you've been with the company for a really long time, devoting a significant portion of your career here, and your termination is due to a reorganization. Considering all that, and the present tough job market, the company has revisited the amount of your severance pay."

"And?"

"It will be twelve months' pay instead of six. I'm sure you're glad to hear that."

"Yes, under the circumstances."

"The second change is the inclusion of a confidentiality clause which was mistakenly left out of the agreement given to you."

"It's in there. It says I can't tell anyone other than my lawyer or my family about the contract or the amount of my severance pay."

"Yes, that is already included. But in addition, you may not disclose anything about the company to other parties in any way. Not verbally, in print, or otherwise."

"What's anybody worried I could say?"

"I'm not a lawyer, Michael. There's a cookie cutter clause that they want included that wasn't before. So those are the changes. I assume that the *two changes* will be okay with you. How would you like me to send the revised agreement to you?"

"Um ... send it by email attachment. I expect that the twenty-one day clock will start over."

"Okay."

"And I expect that there will be an accompanying email attachment that will be a signed letter from Dennis Murphy stating that the severance agreement offer is revised as you described."

"I understand."

"When will that happen?"

"Today or tomorrow."

$$* * *$$

Three days after his conversation with Elizabeth Green, Michael walked into the old world charm of the lobby of 230 Park Avenue for an appointment with labor lawyer Mark Vicarro. Michael brought copies of the original severance agreement, as well as the revised version doubling the amount of severance pay and adding the confidentiality clause that read, "*Employee shall not disclose any confidential information about Great Brands, Inc. or its subsidiary companies, its directors, officers or employees. For purposes of this agreement, "confidential information" is defined as any financial data or other data that is not available to the public, and "disclosure" is defined as including, but not limited to, verbal, written or electronic communications in any form to any person, group or form of media. Breach of this confidentiality requirement at any time in the future will require that Employee return the full gross amount of severance pay paid pursuant to this agreement, prior to deductions for income and social security taxes withheld."*

Michael strode out of the elevator on the thirty-first floor, rounded a corner, and walked into Office 9132.

"Hi, I'm here to see Mark Vicarro," Michael told the pretty blonde receptionist.

Vicarro, a dark-haired middle-aged man of average build came to the reception area to greet Michael and escort him back to his office. The lawyer sat in the chair behind his desk and invited Michael to sit in one of the guest chairs opposite him. Michael observed the surroundings. It was a good-sized office, though not pretentious, and the many files piled on the small conference table made it look like a lawyer's office.

"So, let's get to you and your old company," Vicarro said, pulling a notepad in front of him. "You told me on the phone that you were employed there for twenty-one years. A new chief financial officer was hired a year ago, and he hired a new controller five or six months ago. You also said that the controller hired someone else she previously worked with at another company to fill a job she newly created, and that person will replace you. Is all this right?"

"You've got it correct."

"How old are you, Michael?"

"Just turned fifty. In fact, there was a fiftieth-birthday breakfast for me two weeks before the so-called reorganization."

"Yes, you said that's how they positioned it to you—a reorganization in which they were cutting back to become more efficient. How old was your previous boss?"

"Fifty-nine."

"And the present CFO and controller? How old are they? Approximately."

"I'd say about late forties and early forties."

"The guy replacing you?"

"Mid to late thirties."

"Certainly sounds like they're lowering the ages. But is it intentional? We'd need more than that for an age-discrimination claim. You said on the phone that they sent you a revised contract that increased your severance pay and added a confidentiality clause."

"Yes." Michael reached across the desk and handed Vicarro copies of the first and second versions of the agreement.

"Thanks. I'll read through these for a few minutes."

Michael's mind went back seven days to when he was in Murphy's office being told that his employment was being terminated. Seven days ago, but it seemed longer since he had little else to think about. Until then, he'd had a list of issues to follow up on for the company, which he kept on a fourteen-inch yellow pad on his desk. Now the only issue was *with the company,* and finding a new job—at fifty and unemployed.

"Interesting," Vicarro finally said. "Seems that they might be afraid of you."

"Afraid of me?" Michael recalled Curtis's words.

"Or something you might do. Or say."

Michael waited for him to continue.

"What do you think that might be?"

"They're afraid I might sue them."

"Maybe. They doubled the amount of the severance pay being offered at the same time they inserted the confidentiality of information clause. They're worried you know something. Something not good … either about the company or about them."

"You're the second person who's said that. But I don't know what. I first assumed it was a *just-in-case* thing."

"They originally had the clause making it confidential about severance pay and the contract itself. They thought of that right out of the box. That one's so you, and maybe your former boss, if he was fired, and everyone else over fifty who's pushed out, can't tell anyone else all the details. If they could, it might show a pattern of age discrimination that could be used in a future age-discrimination suit. But your contract, and probably that of others, says that you must remain silent.

"Now this from the goodness of their heart, giving an additional half year's more pay, even before you try to negotiate, in exchange for muzzling you about anything and everything you know … well, seems like it might be for a specific reason. Who else thinks this has to do with things you know?"

"Uh, this guy, Curtis."

"Does he work for the company? He might have some specific reason for the thought."

"Nah, nah. He's a guy I know. Nothing to do with all this."

"Anyway, then be careful who you say what to. You never know who your friend Curtis might repeat things to."

Michael thought for the better part of a minute.

"When the meeting to fire me was over they insisted I leave the building without going back to say good-bye to friends. They said the reason was that I could take copies of company records from my computer. I was angry and said something like *how do you know I haven't already done that?* And I did go back to my office to say good-bye to people. They were very serious, but backed off when they saw how serious I was. I had nothing to lose. I mean, to be treated like garbage that's taken out the back entrance, not even allowed to say good-bye to people—I wouldn't have it."

"Was there a reaction to your parting sentence? Asking how they knew you hadn't already made copies of records."

"I don't know, actually. I turned around and walked out. But they did have the HR person follow me to my office to observe that I didn't use my computer."

Vicarro looked back down at the revised severance agreement. Michael stared at Vicarro, then past him when his mind returned to the end of the meeting a week earlier. *How do you know I haven't already made copies of records?* he heard himself saying before turning around and walking out of Murphy's office. *Their faces before I turned?*

* * *

White clouds blanketed the sky over Washington Square Park. Its daily visitors were in the locations for which they'd been cast. The college students mingled around and in the empty circular pool of the fountain that is never turned on. Local moms pushed their tots on swings in the playground. Dog lovers accompanied their furry pals to play dates at the doggie run. Chess hustlers were at their posts in the southwest corner waiting for people willing to pay to challenge them to a game. Scattered about, not far from the center of the park, were people who were homeless; each had his own story.

Curtis saw a man in a suit get out of a taxi, lean back in, and pull out a bright green giant-sized two-wheel shopping cart. The man crossed the street with the cart and entered the park. "That's Michael," he muttered with a chuckle. "Suit and tie, and a shopping cart. The man is funny."

Michael spotted Curtis and walked directly to him.

"How you doing, Curtis?"

"Good, Michael. Good. You come to the park to go shoppin' today?"

"No, wise guy. I picked up this shopping cart at Macy's for you."

"For me?"

"That's right. I figured it was time for you to stop dragging around that bag full of your stuff, and just pull it in the wagon. There's a tag on the handle that has your name written in."

"Hey, thanks."

"Put your bag in it to be sure it fits."

Curtis lifted his big bag up and swung it over the tall sides of the wagon.

"It fits."

"One other thing," Michael said. "I know that homeless people worry about their things being stolen. I don't want the ease of moving your stuff to make it easier for someone else to steal everything, and cart it away in the wagon. Here's a chain you can slip through the wheels when you're sleeping or not looking, and a lock for the chain."

"Man, you think of everything. You're a smart guy."

"Don't repeat that. People might laugh at you. I brought *two* sandwiches and drinks today. All the same, so there'll be no bickering about who gets what. Hope you like ham and American cheese on hero bread, and diet Coke."

"I ain't fussy. But yeah, I do like that. Thanks."

The package of food was unpacked and sorted out.

"You tell your family about your job situation?" Curtis asked, about to bite into his sandwich.

"Turns out I didn't have a chance … and this may be something for you to think about, Mr. Williams. My son found out when a friend from my office called to ask how I was doing. I wasn't home because I was taking the morning train into the city, like always."

"Pretending you're working."

"Yeah, like you pretending to your brothers that you're living in your old apartment."

Curtis ignored the dig. "And your son spilled the beans to your wife."

"No. He asked me about it when we were alone. Then I had to tell my wife and daughter. I didn't want to put my son in the position of lying or covering for me. You know, it was better to get it out. I don't know what I was thinking, keeping losing my job a secret from my family. You were right."

Curtis looked at Michael and laughed. "I know where ya goin'."

"There's something else you were right about."

"Me? Well, what do you know? What was that?"

"Remember you said to me something like *maybe my bosses got rid of me because I know something, and maybe I don't know yet what it is I know that makes them scared of me and want me out*?"

"Yup."

"Well, you might have hit the nail on the head. Exactly how much, I'm not certain. But there's something to it."

Curtis smiled with satisfaction, turned to face Michael, and waited.

"First, a week after getting fired they increase the severance pay offer from six months to twelve months. But they insist on adding a requirement to the agreement that I can never disclose any information about the company, the officers, and so on, that isn't already public to anyone in any way—not verbally, not in writing, nothing. They must have thought I'd jump to sign the contract and get the twelve months, but I was taking my time because I had twenty-one days."

"So there's more."

"You bet. Another week goes by and they increase the offer to two years severance pay."

"Oh, man. They're crappin' in their pants about somethin'."

"I'd say."

"How many more days you got to sign?"

"With the last increase, they didn't agree to start the clock running again so I've got fourteen days."

"Wait. Don't sign yet. Let 'em sweat. They're not doing you a favor, Michael. Remember that. "They're afraid 'o somethin'. You can always sign on the last day, or the day before. They screwed you, and now they're scared of you even more than they were when they fired you. Wait, man."

"Are you the house lawyer around here?"

"Nah. No education past high school. Wish I did. Your kids go to college?"

"My son just finished his first year in college. My daughter's a high school senior."

"Where does your son go?"

Michael felt awkward. "Columbia."

"Whew. Big-time school."

"And expensive. That worries me now. If you were able to have gone to college, what would you have liked to be?" Michael asked. "Ever think about it back then?"

Curtis leaned back on the park bench. "Long time ago," he answered with a shake of his head. "A billionaire," he answered, laughing. "Seriously, back then I might have said *teacher* if there was a real chance of going to college. Today, I can't even think of myself as doing anything but blue-collar work—if I ever get a chance to work again. Look at me."

"Do you have a driver's license? Michael asked.

"You mean get a job driving? Gotta have a special license for that."

"That's not where I was going. Do you have a driver's license that could be used as an ID?"

"Yeah. With my old address on it. Why you askin' that?"

* * *

Michael received a voicemail message from Elizabeth Green:

"Hello, Michael. I'm touching base with you to see if there are any questions you might have regarding your contract. Though you still have time to sign it, time has been moving by and I've been wondering if I can help respond to any issues you might be thinking about. You have my number, so don't hesitate to call."

No doubt that Murphy put her up to that call, Michael thought. *She couldn't give a crap about me.* Michael played the message again, and saved it. He sat back in his den chair and thought, tapping on the armrest until he popped up, walked over to the desk, and punched numbers into the phone.

"Good morning, Mr. Murphy's office."

"Good morning, Tracey. This is Michael Damsky. I'd like to speak to Dennis."

There were a couple of seconds of throat clearing. "I'm not sure if he's in his office."

"Can you please check?"

"Okay. Hold on … sorry, he said he's too busy to talk to you."

"If that's the case, tell him I'm too busy to consider the terms offered. Tell him that, Tracey. I'll stay on the line."

"Okay, I'll tell him.

Michael waited.

"He said he'll talk to you for just a couple of minutes. I'm transferring you now."

"What is it you want?" Murphy said, picking up the call.

"I want to meet with you … in person. Just the two of us."

"No. You're not allowed in the building."

"I don't give a damn about being in the building. It's probably better if it's somewhere else anyway. Better for both of us. Somewhere quiet and kind of private."

"Why better for me?"

"More comfortable for you to not be seen talking with me."

"And why would I want to meet with you? You're a former employee who's been offered a generous package."

"Yes, and that's why you might want to meet with me. I'm not certain that I'm going to sign the agreement. Not yet."

Dead silence for ten seconds.

"So Dennis, maybe you want to pick a quiet restaurant somewhere near your apartment in the East Seventies, and we meet for dinner within a couple of days. Time's a runnin'."

* * *

Michael hopped out of a yellow cab at the entrance to Washington Square Park after paying the driver for the ride and giving him an extra ten dollars to wait around. He scanned the park till he spotted Curtis.

"Hey, what's up, Michael?"

"Some things. You got any appointments here today?"

"What?"

"No appointments with agents, publishers, TV interviewers?"

"Check with my booking agent, man. She keeps track of that."

"I did. You're free. So come with me."

"Where?"

"There's a cab over there waiting for us."

"Where we goin'?"

"Paris. Just for dinner. Can't you leave this park? Come on."

"My bag."

"It'll go in the trunk. I already spoke to the driver."

"He'll let me in the cab?"

"Cut the crap, Curtis. Come on."

Fifteen minutes later the taxi pulled up in front of the Pennsylvania Hotel, across from Pennsylvania Station. The driver popped the trunk so Curtis could remove his stuff, and Michael paid the fare.

"Where now?" Curtis asked.

"Here. Inside the hotel."

"They won't like me coming in."

"Well, they'll have to accept it because I've already listed you as my roommate when I checked myself in for a week."

"What? You kiddin'?"

"I kid you about a lot of things. But I wouldn't kid you about this. Come on, just walk alongside me. And here's your own key card to the room. It's Room 1408. You got your driver's license for ID. Right?"

Michael and Curtis walked through the hotel lobby, Curtis pulling the big shopping cart filled with his belongings. Guests sitting in the lobby stared. A concierge approached Curtis to ask why he was in the hotel, and apologized after Curtis showed his room key and cited his room number. More odd looks were encountered as they waited along with other hotel guests for the elevator. Nobody chose to get in the same elevator car with them.

"Don't let that get to you," Michael said as they began to ride up to the fourteenth floor. "It's not about who you are. They don't know you."

"I've gotten used to that."

The two exited the elevator and Michael led the way to Room 1408, slipped the extra copy of the electronic key card in the door slot, and pushed the door open.

"Come on in," Michael said.

Curtis pulled his cart halfway into the room and stood still.

"Damn. Real beds."

"I'm not staying here, you know. I asked for twin beds instead of one king or queen because I was registering two names. You can have a chance to shower, take a bath if you like, get cleaned up."

"I really appreciate this, Michael. I don't know what to say. What's that stuff over there?" he asked, pointing to a large assortment of boxes and bags. "You said you're not staying here."

"Well, I figured it's time you had some new clothes, especially to wear when you apply for a job. There's four pair of pants, eight shirts, a dozen pair of shorts, and a dozen pair of socks."

Curtis looked at Michael with tears in his eyes. "I don't know how to thank you."

"Once you're on your feet, a day might come when you'll see a worthy person who can use some help."

"I hear you."

"That closet's stocked with food. Hope you like what's in there. Listen up. Wash your hair really good tonight. Tomorrow, you've got an appointment at two o'clock with a barber. Then you're going to open a bank account with a minimum deposit—so be sure you've got that driver's license on you. See you here around one."

* * *

Michael walked across East Seventy-Fourth Street in Manhattan that Tuesday evening. He knew he was getting closer when he reached Second Avenue, heading toward First. *Should be somewhere around the middle of the block.* He continued along Seventy-Fourth, soon reaching a row of below-street-level restaurants, each seeming relatively quiet for eight o'clock. But it was Tuesday night. *This is it. La Casa Antoinette. Corny name. Never liked French food, but I'm not really here to eat.*

Michael walked down the four steps from the street and entered the restaurant.

"May I help you, monsieur?" he was greeted by a maître d'.

"I'm meeting someone here."

"And the name of the person you're meeting?"

"Dennis Murphy."

"He is here. Allow me to take you to your table, monsieur."

Michael was escorted to the end of the front of the restaurant, and around a bend to a smaller room in which only one table in the far corner was occupied. Dennis Murphy sat at that table with a cocktail and a menu in front of him. The maître d' approached with Michael by his side.

"Monsieur Murphy, your guest has arrived."

"Thank you, Henri," Murphy replied with a nod, letting Henri know he should leave.

Michael immediately sat down opposite Murphy. "Do you have any suggestions, Dennis?"

"About what?"

"The menu. You're obviously a regular here. A majordomo. I don't know much about French food. And listen, we'll split the check fifty-fifty … unless you run up a big liquor tab. I understand you probably don't want to submit this to be reimbursed by the company—dinner with Michael Damsky, former employee."

"So why are we here? What's your problem?"

"My severance pay isn't enough."

A waiter walked into the room and Murphy waved him away.

"You've been given two years' severance pay. That's extremely generous."

"Not generous enough under the circumstances … *all* the circumstances."

Silence.

"What are you proposing?" Murphy finally asked.

"Five years' and three months' pay."

"What? That's extraordinary. It isn't done. And where do you get the five years and three months from?"

"That's twenty-one calendar quarters. One for each of the twenty-one years I've been a dedicated employee. Being a person who's taken the political risks of speaking up again and again to warn especially people like Kelly and you against taking the wrong course of action."

"Like what?"

"You know what, Dennis. Read all your emails from me if you've forgotten. If you've deleted them, I'll be glad to send you copies. I still have them. *All of them.*"

Murphy picked up his glass and sipped from it. The waiter entered the room again.

"Not yet! I'll let you know when we want something," Murphy told him.

"I have four copies of the contract with me," Michael stated. "Each one revised to reflect the amount of severance to equal five and one quarter times my annual pay. You can check the math."

"You have it with you. Very presumptuous."

"I wanted to make things easier. And quicker. We can execute all four copies right now if you agree, and get it over with. You can take your time to read them … all four copies. The only thing that's changed besides the dollar amount of severance pay is mentioned in the last paragraph—the part that states that the agreement is not effective until the money can be confirmed as transferred to my bank account. The bank name, my account and routing numbers are noted. The agreement is effective when the money reaches my account, but not before."

Murphy read the copies of the agreement that Michael placed before him—all four copies, to be certain they read the same.

"You've got a big pair of balls."

Michael nodded his head. "I finally learned through observation. There's one more thing I'm requiring."

Murphy stared at Michael.

"It's via a side agreement," Michael said, presenting another sheet of paper. "The company needs to pay my consultant who's helped me through this situation. This states that, as an additional inducement to sign my severance agreement, Great Brands agrees to pay consulting fees in the amount of twenty-five thousand dollars, on my behalf, directly to Curtis Williams by wire transfer to his bank account immediately before the wire transfer to my bank account. His bank, account number, and related routing number are stated. This also has to be signed."

"You're an idiot, Damsky."

"Maybe. If I am, I'm not the only idiot at this table. You don't have to make up your mind right now, Dennis. You can think about it. I'm in no hurry at the moment. I still have twelve days to accept or reject the offer that's on the table. Your time frame is your own. I suggested we get together now because I thought you might like to get it all resolved, and out of the way. I'm getting hungry. Let's look at the menu. Maybe you can give me a recommendation, or let the waiter come in the room and advise me."

"I don't want to eat with you. Okay, I get you. I'll sign the agreement."

"Good. We'll be done with it. We'll need both our signatures to be notarized," Michael said, taking his cell phone out of his pocket. "I'll call the notary public that I arranged to be on call only a few minutes from here."

* * *

New York Times Business Section, Page 3

Great Brands announced yesterday that its earnings for the three quarters ended March 31 is being reduced from the previously reported $3.20 per share to $2.68 per share. The company's public relations director, Steven Wilson, announced that the adjustment was the result of three items: (1) Interest costs in the amount of $52 million, and real estate taxes in the amount of $7 million, were erroneously recorded as an addition to the cost of a newly opened factory, but should have been recorded as current period expenses; (2) Failure of a new cost accounting system to match costs of units sold with sales revenues resulted in a $58 million understatement of costs of goods sold and an equal overstatement of inventory on hand; (3) Understatement of federal and state income tax costs by $17 million resulting from errors in various calculations. Further details of these issues are provided in a related article on page 16. All together, these issues resulted in an overstatement of pretax net income for the first three quarters by $117 million, and after tax income by $87 million—15 percent of the previously reported net income after taxes of $640 million for the first three quarters. It's been reported to the Times that the incorrectness of the previously reported information was first noted during the early stages of the audit being performed by Deloitte, Price & Young, the *company's outside CPA firm. The market value of the common stock of Great Brands dropped yesterday from $50.12 to 39.78. Calls to the office of President Jonathon Ashton, and Chief Financial Officer Dennis Murphy were not returned.*

* * *

Email

To: Dennis Murphy
From: Michael Damsky

I've read the article in today's *New York Times*. It mentions three specific categories of errors made that resulted in the net profits of Great Brands being overstated for the first three quarters.

If you have any difficulty understanding these issues, you might want to refer to emails I sent to you and Kelly on January 8, January 29, February 20, March 5, March 25, and April 18.

I plan to not discuss this matter with any other person or persons. Of course, you do understand that under fairly new SEC rules subpoenas trump confidentiality agreements.

All the best,
Your former employee,
Michael ☺☺☺

AFTER ALL THESE YEARS

Richard Colucci sat at his kitchen table fiddling with the announce-ment he'd received in the mail the day before. Cup of coffee in his left hand, he read it, read it again, and placed it down. It was time to shave, get dressed, then fetch his twelve-year-old grandson and drive him to school. His purpose in relocating to Ohio was to help his daughter, Andrea, with Timmy so she could perform her high-octane job at the hospital.

He looked into the bathroom mirror extra long after shaving—straight ahead, then to the right, wondering about the lighting in the room. Was it too harsh? Or maybe too kind? He confirmed that his hair was still thick and wavy, with only sprinkles of gray. Richard went into the bedroom and retrieved his high school yearbook from the shelf in his closet. He flipped the pages until he came to the section of graduates with last names beginning with the letter *C*, and stared at his photo. *Would people recognize me?* he wondered.

Back at the kitchen table, he picked up his keys and read the beginning of the announcement: "The Flushing High School Reunion Committee, Class of 1963, is excited to announce the reunion to celebrate the 50th anniversary of the class graduation…" The question regarding physical changes still weighing on his mind, he headed out the door of his condo apartment and walked toward his light blue Chevy Impala.

Richard pulled up in front of Andrea's house ten minutes later. She and Timmy were waiting in her car parked in the driveway. Timmy switched to Richard's car, and the two cars drove off in opposite directions.

"How you doing today?" Richard asked his grandson.

"Good."

"You did all your homework?"

"Of course, Grandpa."

"Just asking."

"Are you coming to my baseball game on Saturday?"

"Of course. Don't I always come to your games?"

"Just asking," Timmy said, looking at his grandfather with a smirk.

There was a minute of no conversation while music played from the car radio.

"What's this music, Grandpa? I mean what kind. I never hear it except when I'm in your car."

"The name of the group singing is The Temptations, and the type of music is called Motown."

"I never heard of that."

"It's not from now. It was popular forty and fifty years ago."

"How come you listen to it now?"

How come I listen to it now? Richard mused. "Because I still like it."

"Do you like the music that's popular now?"

"No ... maybe some of it."

"Who do you like?"

"Uh, Alicia Keys. She's good."

Timmy burst into laughter. "Grandpa, you're joking. She hasn't been popular for like two years."

"Then, of course, I was joking. I won't be going on that show where you can win a million dollars for knowing a lot of trivia, will I? Alright, here's one for you. What year did Roger Maris hit sixty-one home runs to break what was then the home run record for one season held by Babe Ruth?"

"That's not fair, Grandpa."

"Why's that not fair?"

"Because that's the past."

"I suppose it is... but don't they teach you about history in school? The Revolutionary War, Civil War, and World War II? That's the past."

"Yeah, they teach us about that stuff in history … and the Vietnam War."

"The Vietnam War?"

"That's in our history book, too."

Richard paused. *Vietnam is taught in history books.* "But not Roger Maris, I guess," he said to Timmy.

"The only baseball player in my history book is Jackie Robinson."

"Besides being the first black player in major league baseball, he was a very exciting player," Richard said, "dancing off the bases and threatening to steal the next base whenever he got on. I couldn't stand him."

"Really? Because he was black?"

"Of course not because he was black. You know better than that, Timmy. It had nothing to do with the color of his skin. It was because *Dodgers* was written across the front of his uniform. He was a Dodger. I was a Giant fan, and both the Giants and Dodgers played in New York back then. The two teams were big, big rivals. Dodger fans hated the Giants, and Giant fans hated the Dodgers—and Jackie Robinson was a Dodger. I loved Willie Mays, the Giants' centerfielder. He's a black guy, and I think the best all-around player, ever. I worshipped him when I was your age. You heard of Willie Mays, Timmy?"

"I don't think so."

Six hundred and sixty home runs—without steroids—and arguably the best fielding outfielder ever, countless clutch hits, catches, throws, and stolen bases, and a generation doesn't even know his name. He quietly pondered that until Timmy broke the silence.

"Grandpa, I forgot to tell you that Billy's dad said he would take us to the batting practice cage after school today, if that's okay with you. Is it? You'd have to pick me up there around five. Is that okay?"

"Yeah, that's fine."

Ten minutes later, Richard's blue Chevy Impala pulled up to the curb in front of the school. He ruffled Timmy's light brown hair with his big right hand, then reached over and hugged Timmy's right shoulder.

"See you later, Timmy. Have fun."

* * *

Richard was seated in his favorite booth at the Maplewood Diner, looking at the menu when the red-haired waitress approached.

"Hey, what's with the menu? Herb's probably already put up your omelet with a side of bacon and an English muffin. Here's your brew," she added, placing a cup of black coffee in front of him.

"Am I that predicable, Rosalie?"

"Sometimes you add mushrooms to the omelet."

"Or onions."

"No you don't. You don't like onions. You want something different today?"

"Maybe oatmeal."

"Oatmeal?" Rosalie repeated with a laugh, slapping her thigh. "I'm gonna sit outside all night tonight to watch for Haley's Comet. What's gotten into you?"

"I've been thinking that maybe I should eat more healthy sometimes... Not all the time."

"Okay. You really want oatmeal? Or maybe an omelet made with egg whites, only half a portion of cheese with mushrooms ... and a low fat yogurt."

Richard looked at Rosalie and grinned. "Yeah, I'll have that instead."

"Okay. Coming up."

* * *

Richard's suitcase was packed, and he'd already driven Timmy to school. He had procrastinated about whether to drive his car to the airport and leave it there for a few days, or call a taxi. The thought of leaving his car at the airport was unappealing.

"Hello, I'd like a taxi to pick me up at noon. I'm at 12 East Park Drive... The airport... American Airlines terminal.... Right... One person, one bag. How much will that be? ... Okay... My number is

555-672-1515… No, I'm not going to be sitting out on the porch in a rocking chair like an old man. Tell the driver to honk the horn and I'll come out. See you at noon."

There were other things to decide, like what to tell his old classmates and friends about the past fifty years —especially certain periods. He spoke about that with Andrea during the previous two evenings after Timmy was asleep.

"What would I say to them?" he'd asked her. "People I'd been close with."

"You don't, Dad. It's not an interview. Old friends aren't going to be exchanging résumés."

"Oh, I've heard from people that's what reunions can be like."

"What people?"

"People."

"Oh, this is so unlike you. Listen to yourself."

"Okay, but still. What do I say?"

"As much or as little as you want."

That settled it for that moment, but he would think about it.

Richard reviewed the morning mail while waiting for the taxi. It was the usual clutter of unrequested solicitations and advertisements, and also the month's end investment statements. *Might as well look through them while I'm waiting for the taxi,* he thought, though he was not expecting much of a change since the prior month because all his accounts were invested fairly conservatively. There was little change: $4.7 million in the Traditional IRA, and $2.1 million in the Roth IRA, all invested in long-term inflation-protected U.S. government bonds; $7.8 million in the 401(k) account, invested in sundry stock index funds such as the S&P 500; and $7.1 million in the taxable account, primarily invested in AA-rated medium-term tax-free municipal bonds. A slight uptick in value from the prior month. He filed the statements in his desk and filed the rest of the mail in the trash.

Noon on the dot, Richard heard the honk of a car outside and was on his way to the airport a few moments later. He waited on line at the airport security checkpoint along with hundreds of other passengers.

When his turn came, he took off his shoes and placed them in the gray plastic bin along with his keys, cell phone, coins, pens, and package of chewing gum wrapped in aluminum foil. He then took off his belt and watch, tossing them in the bin as well. Richard pushed both the bin and his suitcase onto the conveyer belt that would carry them through the scanning machine, then walked through the gate. An alarm screeched and a uniformed man immediately approached Richard.

"Please hold your arms high out to your sides, sir."

He calmly complied. The security guard moved a black wand up and down Richard's body, over and over again in certain spots where the wand wheezed loudly.

"Follow me over to the side, please," the guard requested.

Richard glanced to his right. "My bag is over there."

"Which one?"

"The light blue one, second from the left."

"The security guard looked over to one his colleagues. "Carl, would you get this man's light blue bag over there? Thanks."

"And my keys, phone, coins, and stuff next to it, please," Richard called out. He turned back to the first security guard. "I know why the alarm went off and your wand was beeping."

"Go ahead."

"It's the metal in my body. I have this issue every time I fly."

"You have a knee replacement? The wand is reacting at places in addition to your knee."

"Well, I've had a knee replacement. But there's also metal in my shoulder, my foot, and there's a metal plate in my head."

"Why is that?"

"I don't think it's necessary for me to get into why. That's not a security issue for you or the airline. I think you have those sophisticated machines at this airport—the ones that can scan the body and confirm what I've said. "

The guard nodded. "Follow me."

* * *

The passengers of Flight 1512 to New York's JFK Airport landed only half an hour late without incident. Richard retrieved his bag from the luggage bin overhead, and then helped a short older man do the same. When the passengers walked out of the plane and across the connecting ramp, many were greeted by relatives or hired drivers holding signs with names of people they were waiting to pick up. Richard followed the airport signs to the car rental area until he stood in front of an Avis Rent-A-Car representative.

"Hello, sir. How can I help you?" Do you have a car reserved?"

"Yeah, I do. The name's Richard Colucci."

"Okay, let's see," she said, entering key strokes in her computer. "That's for three days at forty-nine dollars and ninety-nine cents per day – to be dropped off back here at this airport location. Is that correct?"

"Yes, it is. It's for a Chevy Impala."

"Right… But I have to check if we actually have an Impala on the lot. It not, we might have to give you a Ford Taurus or a Buick LaCrosse. They're also full size cars."

"I reserved a Chevy Impala. I'm going to my fiftieth high school reunion, and I want to go in a Chevy Impala. I didn't book with Hertz or Budget because they said they couldn't give me an Impala. I could go over to their windows now to see what they've got."

"I hope you won't choose to do that, Mr. Colucci. Give me a moment to check what's in our lot and what's coming in." After looking through the available car inventory on her computer, the Avis representative picked up her phone. "Hello, Charlie. I'm reading on my computer that there was a Chevy Impala that was returned twenty minutes ago. How long till it would be cleaned up and checked out to be available for another customer?... Uh-huh… Yeah, I have a man with me who's reserved an Impala, and that's what he wants… It's a fire engine red convertible?" she said, looking purposefully at Richard who shrugged and smiled. "Forty minutes?" She looked at Richard again, and he nodded in a yes motion. "Okay, we'll hold that car for Mr. Colucci."

"Thank you," Richard said to the rep.

"You're welcome. I hope you enjoy the car. It's one of the few like it that we have in our inventory."

* * *

Richard chose to stay at the Sheraton Hotel just behind Main Street in Flushing. It was less than a mile from the school, and would permit him the option of visiting some of his old haunts on foot. He left the fire engine red Impala with the hotel parking valet at the garage entrance, was greeted "good day" by an Asian doorman as he entered the lobby, and proceeded to the front desk.

"Welcome to the Flushing Sheraton," said the strikingly beautiful Asian front desk clerk in perfect English. "I'm Jennifer. Are you checking in?"

"Yes. I have a reservation for three days. The name is Colucci… Richard Colucci."

She entered some information into the computer. "Here you are, sir. You'll be in room 1203. That's away from the elevators, as you requested. A queen bed for one hundred and sixty-nine per night before taxes, for a total of one hundred ninety-four dollars and twelve cents with sales and occupancy taxes. I'll need you to sign here," she said, handing Richard a print-out of the details. "Will you be paying with the American Express card used to hold this reservation?"

"Yes. You want to make an imprint of the card," Richard said, reaching into his wallet. "Here it is."

"I do need to. Thank you. Is this a trip for business or pleasure, Mr. Colucci?"

"Well, I'm hoping it's for pleasure. It's for my high school reunion."

"You went to high school around here?"

"Yes. Flushing High School."

"Really! Isn't that nice. Did you like living in Flushing when you were in high school?"

"I did. It was a good place for a kid to grow up, in my opinion. Though I didn't know it at the time. Hardworking lower middle-class families, and not many people with money enough to try to show off by buying fancy things. People were pretty much on an even level, and if kids wanted extra stuff, we worked a part-time job after school. Flushing was a very good place to grow up. Where did you grow up?"

"Hong Kong. I came to America fourteen years ago. My family still lives in Hong Kong, except for my brother and his family. They're in New Jersey."

"I'm guessing you learned to speak English in Hong Kong."

"You're right."

Two people walked into the hotel lobby, and up to the reception desk to check in.

"I'm sorry, but I must take care of these guests. It's been nice talking to you, Mr. Colucci. Let's hope your stay here at the Sheraton adds to the enjoyment of your reunion party. Here's your key card. Would you like assistance with your bag?"

"I'll be fine. It's on wheels."

* * *

Richard unpacked his suitcase, freshened up, and was ready to embark upon a late afternoon stroll down Main Street.

As he exited the elevator in the lobby, he got a friendly smile from the beautiful Asian woman who had checked him in and a nod from the doorman as he held the door open. Reaching the corner at Main Street, Richard noticed that the signs atop most stores were written in Chinese, and primarily Asian people were going in and out of the fruit and vegetable produce store on the corner—and all the other stores. He walked down one block and looked across the street. The bank on the corner was gone. Surely, landmark *Gloria Pizza* must still be there. He walked five stores down to confirm; it was a trinket shop. Already anticipating that it wouldn't be there, Richard walked farther down Main Street toward Northern Boulevard to see what would be residing at the site of John's Bargain Store, where he used to buy *78 rpm single records,* and, sure enough, it was a generic box store.

He began to wonder who else might be in town that night and staying nearby. Maybe he could have arranged to meet someone for dinner. Or would he have been too self-conscious to initiate the necessary contact? *Hi, this is Richard Colucci from your high school senior year math class. Remember me? ... Oh, that's okay. Well, Maybe I'll see you at the reunion. Sorry to bother you.*

Richard walked farther down to where Main Street ended at Northern Boulevard. *That didn't change,* he thought. *Nobody moved or renamed Northern Boulevard. But the old Nedicks store isn't on the corner.* The high school was only six blocks away, and he thought about continuing his walk right up to it. But he decided it would be better to go back to the hotel to get the rented Impala in case he wanted to take in more sites than the school.

Twenty minutes later, a left turn from Northern Boulevard took him onto Union Street, and then a right on Thirty-Fourth Road put him alongside the entrance he entered fifty years earlier. He parked the car, got out, and stared. *Looks the same,* he thought, *but smaller somehow. These kids walking by look smaller... everything looks smaller... but yet the same.*

Not long after, he stood in front of the apartment building he grew up in and looked up at the windows of his family's old apartment. *Wonder who lives there, now.* Could there possibly be any familiar faces passing through the lobby? Richard walked through the first door, and peered through the locked glass door towards the elevator and the mailboxes. Nobody was there.

He was strolling up the block toward the schoolyard where he and his pals used to play softball and basketball when his cell phone rang.

"Hello."

"Hello, is this Richard Colucci?"

"Yes. Who's calling?"

"It's Colonel Baisley."

"And Colonel, your code is what?"

"I'll call you when the cows come home. And your code?"

"Imagine all the people."

"This should be good news to you, Richard," the colonel said.

"Did *all* the cows come home?"

"Yes, they did."

"When?"

"The last one was positively confirmed home three days ago. I got word this morning. How have you been?"

"I'm good, I guess. Better now. Well, once this sinks in. Funny, I just arrived in New York today, where my life began. Maybe that's symbolic. Does this mean I don't have to have any secrets to keep anymore?"

"I don't know about your personal life."

"Good one. You know, I'm so accustomed to keeping my mouth shut, I don't know if I'm *able* to say anything."

"That's up to you now. I wanted to let you know the burden is off your shoulders. You know how to reach me if you need something. Good luck to you, my friend."

"And to you."

Hands raised, Richard leaned into the schoolyard fence and stared at the softball diamond, in his mind seeing friends of long ago at each position.

* * *

The hotel alarm clock began playing music in Richard's room at nine o'clock the next morning. He swung his arm over and hit the snooze button that he had located before turning out the light when he crawled into bed. Richard wished to fall back to sleep for the number of minutes the snooze would loan him, but his mind was activated wondering who would show up at the reunion.

Might *she* be there? Rebecca Hanley was his high school girlfriend, and they were crazy about each other. But her parents were not as enthusiastic about their relationship as they were, and made certain that Rebecca went to college three thousand miles away in California. The cost mattered little to them, so they didn't care about the lost scholarship opportunities at the northeastern schools. Being a family of financial means, they aimed for Rebecca to marry into a family of similar or greater wealth. The phone calls between Rebecca and Richard were frequent at the beginning, then fewer when final exams came around. Eventually, she was courted by many other boys. While a sophomore, a junior named Walter Howard won her over. Richard had fantasized that he and Rebecca would reunite, and was brokenhearted when he heard that she married shortly after graduation. He allowed himself to date other girls with the possibility of serious intent, and married Ellen. He and Ellen divorced when Andrea was three. Ellen died four years later in a car crash.

Richard hoped Rob Fisher would show up. They grew up around the corner from each other, Rob being the new kid in the neighborhood when he was nine. The smaller Rob was often the wisecracker, making Richard keel over laughing, sometimes at the most inopportune times. They played in the junior high school and high school bands together, Richard playing trumpet and Rob saxophone. Standing next to each other during a final rehearsal, Rob softly let loose with one of his witticisms while Richard prepared for a solo that he couldn't begin because he'd been doubled over in laughter. They were both very good musicians at their level and together joined up with a locally successful rock band. Richard secretly had fantasies of living the life of a successful rock musician. More pragmatic decisions caused him to take a different fork in the road.

Maybe Johnny Hanson, Richard's old infield partner, would be there. That would be a blast. They had had three years together on the high school baseball team, but they were pals before Richard was scooping Johnny's throws from third base out of the dirt at first base. "Would you try to get those throws up a few feet?" Richard would needle him. "I like to watch you dig 'em out," Johnny would lie with a grin. They were both good hitters, and the team nearly always won.

Off the field, they'd go cruising for girls together until Richard was smitten with Rebecca. Richard had fantasized about being a major league baseball player, but he figured he wasn't good enough to pursue that route so it didn't make sense.

Richard briefly studied the breakfast menu, and dialed room service.

"Good morning, Mr. Colucci. What can we get for you this morning?"

"Do you make a Swiss cheese omelet with egg whites?"

"We can do that for you."

"Good. Not too much cheese, and I'll have whole wheat toast rather than the bagel. And do you have low-fat apple yogurt?"

"Yes, we do. And would you like a small pot of coffee?"

"It's a deal."

"And when would like your breakfast delivered? The soonest is half an hour. It's now 9:12."

"I'd like it at 9:54."

A few seconds of silence.

"Ten o'clock will be fine. It'll give me time to shower."

* * *

Richard called the garage valet to ask that his car be brought to the front of the hotel, then left his room. Jennifer, the beautiful check-in lady, called to him when he walked out of the elevator into the lobby, dressed in a dark blue suit, pink shirt, red and blue tie.

"Good morning, Mr. Colucci."

"Good morning, Jennifer."

"You're looking very sharp. Must be going somewhere special with your lady friend."

"I'm dressed for the reunion. I don't have a lady friend," he answered, stopping for a moment.

"I bet you do back home," she said with a smirk in a low voice drawing Richard closer to the desk.

"No, not anywhere."

"You should have someone."

Richard felt awkward.

"Do you?" he replied, deciding to deflect her comment.

"Nooo."

"Well there you go. I'm sure *you* don't really *need* anyone. If you did, you'd have someone."

She shrugged. "Is the reunion at the high school?"

"No, it's at Verdi's restaurant in Whitestone."

"Sir," the doorman called. "Did you ask for your car to be brought up from the garage?"

"Yes, I did."

"I think it's here. A red convertible."

"I can explain that."

"Explain?"

"Never mind. It's my car. Thanks for letting me know."

He looked over at Jennifer. "I better get going. Nice speaking with you."

"The same. Have a good time at your reunion, Mr. Colucci. I hope you enjoy Verdi's. Maybe I'll see you when you get back. Or tomorrow."

Hmm. Wonder what that was about, Richard thought. *Gorgeous young woman chatting me up. Maybe I remind her of her father. Do I look Chinese?*

As Richard entered the car, he reached in his pocket to turn on his cell phone since he could no longer be reached at the hotel. "Oh crap," he mumbled. He'd left the phone on the entire previous day and night, and the battery was down to one bar. *Better preserve the battery for a time I really the need the phone,* he thought, and shut it off.

* * *

The red convertible rolled down Linden Place on the way to the Whitestone Parkway to head to Verdi's. Yep, Whitestone Bowling Lanes was still standing on the corner to the left as a testament to the 1960s. *Something's remained,* he thought. Fifteen minutes later,

Richard pulled up in front of Verdi's, then parked two blocks away around the corner. He sat in the car for five minutes prepping himself.

Richard walked to the restaurant, entering through the glass doors at the front. He was directed to a desk to pick up an identification tag hanging on a string to put around his neck. The tag had his high school yearbook photo and name, and it hung down to the middle of his chest. *There's food on a buffet table. Nah, let's go looking for friends. Just grab a soda first.*

Richard looked for long lost friends of his youth, but all he saw the first ten minutes were unfamiliar-looking old people. He walked toward the tables where people were seated and eating, and then he stepped between the tables with the hope of seeing more people closer up in the only moderately lit party room. Nobody yet. He started to feel self-conscious about peering at one group of people after another, their faces in their plates or talking to a person at their side or opposite them. *Will somebody please look up and call my name? Here's my ID tag. Remember this face from fifty years ago? I can't see your ID tags.*

* * *

It was Saturday, and fifty-year-old Jack Baisley, Director of CIA Clandestine Operations, was dressed in civilian clothes. He looked up when he heard a tap-tap at his door.

"Come in, John. I was just finishing up reading a report."

The man, in his late thirties, entered. "Do you have time, sir?"

"Time for what? You look serious. The expression on your face."

"It's a serious matter."

"I'll make time. Have a seat. Tell me about the serious matter."

"Everybody truly believed that all of them were accounted for, sir."

"All of who?"

"The Paschke family. The avengers."

"From what you're telling me, they're not."

"Well, we think they are accounted for now ... but they're not all dead, as we had believed twenty-four hours ago."

The colonel breathed in and then exhaled his frustration and concern. His left fist fell down on the desk.

"And what leads you, or others, to believe that now?"

"Communications. Current communications that are later than the confirmed death of Bojan."

"What kind of communications? Internet? Phone? What?"

"Both Internet and phone. They've been triple confirmed, sir. They're from Canada."

"What do these communications discuss and from what geographical location do they originate? Is there something afoot?"

"Revenge actions are going to take place very soon. Against somebody who has worked with us. The goal is to finish what they did to him fifteen years ago or something like that. The originating source is traced to Toronto, and the receiving source is in New York City."

The colonel stood up from his chair, turned around, and then turned back to John. "Are you certain about New York City?"

"Yes. As I said, all this is triple confirmed. And so far as we can tell, only two people are involved: the sender and the receiver of the communication—one of them a surviving family member. A son."

"Where in New York? I need to know exactly where in New York. Not that a person can't move around to a totally different part of the city within half an hour. But where?"

"I'll find that out."

"We have a man visiting New York. Got there yesterday, and I told him just yesterday that the last one was dead. You know what that meant to him?" the colonel asked.

"What, sir?"

Baisley leaned forward. "That he no longer had to look over his shoulder like he's had to for the past fifteen years after he stuck his neck out for his country. That's what. In his high-level business position that had taken him across Europe and northern Africa he was our courier, taking risks with all kinds of people and playing a key role in helping us destroy nearly all of the Paschke network. *Nearly* all. But not all, as you know."

"So they knew it? His role?"

"They knew it alright. A band of a dozen of them kidnapped him and held him hostage as a bargaining chip to get safe passage for themselves out of Banja Luka, and for another twenty-two out of Sarajevo and Ostrava. While they had him, they brutalized him, beating him to the point where he needed a metal plate placed in his head after he was finally freed—without ever turning over any of the information they were trying to beat out of him. His foot and shoulder were mangled so badly that they also required extensive reconstruction, including plenty of hardware. That wasn't necessary to do to a hostage. They did it because they hated him for his role."

"How come they didn't get him by now?"

"His phone has been unlisted, though he has Internet contact. Of course, that shouldn't stop them. At first, we gave him an assumed identity. But after five years, all but six of them were accounted for as killed, and he wanted to quietly assume his own identity again. Most likely, it's because they've always been on the run themselves, for the most part. Bring me the transcripts of all the communications you've told me about. I mean every detail. I'm concerned that this activity is concentrated where you said. Get to it right now. I want to give our guy a call."

Baisley checked his files for Richard's phone number, picked up his phone and dialed. The call went directly to voicemail without ringing. *Damn. Sounds like he has the phone shut off,* the colonel thought. Baisley considered leaving a message for Richard to hear when he turned the phone on, but thought it better to try again later.

* * *

Richard stood by himself in the middle of the room, ginger ale in hand, eyes roaming the room. A restaurant worker walked toward him and offered a tray of hors d'oeuvres.

"Fried shrimp, sir?" he asked, looking downward toward Richard's chest.

"Thank you, but I'll pass on fried."

The worker lifted his gaze up to Richard's face, nodded, and walked on to other people.

Richard then saw what he thought to be a familiar face fifty feet away and smiled. The other guy pantomimed taking two steps forward, picking up a ball, and throwing it overhand in one motion. Richard moved his left leg forward, scooped the invisible ball out of the dirt, and made an emphatic out call with his right hand. The two sixty-seven-year-old men scooted toward each other like kids and embraced.

"I was hoping you'd be here, Johnny," Richard exclaimed, "but I was also hoping your throw would be higher these days."

"Ah, you son of a gun. I always liked to keep you on your toes. If I have to pick the ball up from the dirt, you should, too. You look great, Rich."

"Really?"

"Yeah."

"You're looking fantastic yourself. I think I felt some impressive muscles when I hugged you just now. You're feeling strong."

"Me? You almost squeezed me in half. You're still like a bear."

"You know, I don't know what I remember you for most—that night with the twin sisters parked in your car in Cunningham Park, or the game in which you stole home twice," Richard said, his right arm swung around his old pal as the two laughed like teenagers.

"Fifty years, my old friend. Are you good?"

"Yeah. Yeah, I am. How about you?"

Richard and Johnny made sure to first exchange contact information, then shared some of the highlights of the previous five decades—not including Richard's experiences relating to, and resulting from, his assistance to the CIA.

* * *

Baisley again keyed in Richard's phone number, and again immediately heard the voicemail greeting.

"Damn it!" Baisley smacked his desk. He walked outside his office and stood in the doorway. "Alison, I need you to search for the phone number of anybody living near Columbus, Ohio with the surname of Colucci."

She looked up at him. "Would you like Smith as well?"

"This isn't a humorous situation. Tell Martinson that we need to search the email message traffic on Richard Colucci residing in that area so that we might find a contact who could help us locate his exact current whereabouts ... and I need to know his credit card activity for the past three days. Not only charges, but holds as well."

"Will that require a warrant?"

"No, it will not. It's a national security issue, and it's to be done under my authority. The results are to be shared with John and with me, wherever I might be."

"Wherever you might be?"

"Yes. Tell Tessler to arrange an immediate flight for me to New York... and a car waiting for me with two agents."

* * *

Richard stepped over to the buffet table for the first time of the afternoon. The chicken teriyaki had gotten dried out by then. Ribs? He thought he should stick with something easy to eat with one hand while standing. Genoa salami and cheese? Nah. He reached for half a shrimp salad sandwich, and felt a hand on his left shoulder.

"You're Richie Colucci or you're his twin brother," a voice said.

He turned, stood erect, and dropped his plate. "Rob! Oh man." Richard hugged the mid-sized man and nearly lifted him off the ground. You *are* here! I've been looking around for you."

"Look no further. You're looking great, big buddy."

"Still a chronic liar."

"Truly."

"Thanks. Do you still play music?"

"I do. I'm in a wedding band on weekends," Rob answered. "Not exactly like when we used to rock the house. Those were the days, man. But I get to play, make a few coins to throw around. What about you, Richie? Are those magic lips blowing those sweet sounds from a trumpet?"

"Actually, I haven't played since I was about twenty-seven. Life got busy and complicated. Still have it though. Sitting in the back of my closet along with my baseball glove. My baseball cards would probably be tucked away with 'em if my mother hadn't thrown them out," Richard added with a laugh.

"Your mother, too? Maybe we should get the old band together."

Richard raised an eyebrow. "You sure everybody's still walking around?"

"Of course. We people of the sixties are indestructible. Remember?"

"I forgot. How's your sister?"

"You mean the little brat who always wanted to tag after us from the time she was eight and we were ten?"

"Yeah, that brat."

"She's good. Retired from teaching two years ago. Got two sons, two daughters and nine grandkids. Me, I got two daughters, a son, and seven grandkids. I tell you, I need the wedding gigs for Hanukkah and birthday gifts," Rob added. "How many Christmas gifts on your list?"

"Just two. My daughter and grandson. She's unattached, like me."

"Did something happen, Richie?"

"You mean to my wife?"

"Yeah."

"Actually, yes. But it was many years ago that she was killed in a car accident. That was a few years after we were divorced."

"Gee, sorry to hear all that. Do you have a girlfriend?"

"No. I've dated ... still do sometimes. No girlfriend."

"Do you know that *she's* here?"

"She?"

"I mean Rebecca. I don't know how you feel about that, one way or the other. Or maybe you just don't give a crap after all these years.

But if you haven't met up with her yet, I thought I'd put you on notice that you might."

"To be honest, I thought about whether I might meet her here. Not like I was eager to, like seeing you or Johnny Hanson, but wondering *if* I would, and what it would feel like."

"So you know, she's also single now. Divorced twice. She came over to me earlier, and we spoke. She's sitting at the table in the corner, three seats from the end. The one with the very obvious jet-black dye job. She's wearing a silver blouse and silver earrings. Don't stare and be so obvious, Richie. You'll embarrass us both. She'll know we're gossiping about her."

"I'm not gossiping. I haven't said anything about her."

"Look at the doorway. Okay?"

"Okay. I don't think I'm gonna go over to her—at least not now. If she walks over to me, or we bump into each other, alright. But I'm not marching over to her table, leaning three seats over and saying, *Hey, Rebecca, what's new?*"

"Gotcha."

"There is something in particular I want to say to you, Rob."

"And what's that?"

"Remember one day when were kids, we were playing in my room and I was swinging a bat like a golf club all over the place?"

"Which particular time do you mean?" Rob asked with a smirk.

"The time I swung and broke a leg of my bed."

Rob heaved with laughter. "Yeah, I remember the three-hundred-yard swing."

"Well, I've always remembered how you covered up for me, taking the blame for it, knowing that my mother would nearly kill me if she knew I did it."

"She only made me go home."

"Yeah, she did," Richard said, nodding his head, moisture welling in his eyes. "I never forgot that, Rob." He placed a hand on his childhood buddy's shoulder. "You were always a great friend."

"Thanks. You were, too, Richie. But I made up for it by making you crack up in band rehearsal."

"Yes, you did. I take it all back."

"How long did that '58 Chevy Impala last you?"

"Till two years after I graduated college. That would be 1969. She was a beauty, heh? White convertible, long sexy white fins."

"You describe it like a woman," Rob said with a laugh.

"Yes, and she was five years old, already middle-aged, when I got her."

"I remember the rides with the rock band to get to our gigs. Vroom vroom."

"Oh, yeah. Listen, I want you and Johnny to walk out of here with me when the party is over. Promise me. We'll all get a kick out of it."

"Okay, I promise."

"What are you promising?" a bearded man to Rob's right asked.

Richard and Rob both looked at him with a question mark on their faces. They glanced at the name tag hanging down on his chest but failed to see it well enough in the dimly lit room to guess the name of the secret friend.

"Sing a few bars for me," Richard said to him.

"Okay … Mr. Colucci, *The Catcher in the Rye* does not have anything to do with baseball. And, listen closely. *The Great Gatsby* is not, and never was, centerfielder for the Giants. Mr. Fisher, can you help your friend, Mr. Colucci, get that straight? He thinks he can get through senior year English on an athletic scholarship."

Richard and Rob laughed and smacked their thighs.

"Mark Macy, is that you behind that bush of hair? Or is Mr. Greeley still alive?" Richard asked.

"Macy," Rob exclaimed, wrapping his arm around Mark's shoulder, "if I knew you would be here … I wouldna come."

"Me, too. How the hell are you guys? Where are you living? Whatta ya been doing? You working? Hey, do you guys still have your baseball cards from the '50s and '60s?"

The three pals continued catching up for twenty minutes until Rob and Mark peeled off to say hello to other old friends. As Richard stood alone, the restaurant worker who had earlier offered him fried shrimp approached him holding a tray with a single tap-drawn beer with a big head atop it.

"Sir, would you like a beer?"

"No thank you."

"Are you sure? Fresh from the tap?"

"I'll be driving when I leave here. I make a point to never drink alcoholic beverages when I'm going to drive."

The restaurant employee nodded, smiled and walked away."

* * *

Rebecca chatted in a circle of people next to a group that included Richard. She gradually inched her way around her circle until her back was opposite Richard's. Her elbow bumped his and they both turned around.

"There you are, Richard. Good to see you. It's me, Rebecca," she added, avoiding any embarrassing questions of identity.

"Hi Rebecca. Nice to see you, too. "Why don't we go over to the side and talk? Come," she directed, turning and walking over to a table left unoccupied by attendees who had left early. With no polite choice, he followed and sat down opposite Rebecca.

"So, tell me where you live."

"Columbus. About an hour from of Chicago."

"With who?"

"With myself. I live near my daughter because—"

"I suppose it could be good to live nearby family. You might need them."

"Actually, I moved nearby so I could help her with my grandson. He's twelve, and she's a single mom—divorced. It's good for me, too. I get to spend a lot of cool time with Timmy. Probably more and better time than I got to spend with my daughter when she was twelve."

"Divorce. Been there twice."

"Sorry."

"But I've come out good both times. I'm loaded. I have whatever I want."

Richard replied with a faint smile.

"Remember when were in high school?" Rebecca asked.

"Of course. That's why we're all here today. To remember and reminisce."

"You were really crazy about me," Rebecca said.

Richard's feet shifted under the table.

"You always made me feel so good. Better than anybody ever did."

Richard's pointer finger tapped lightly on the table three times.

"I don't know what you're trying to convey. Is this a fifty-year belated thank you? Or ..."

"Oh, no. Not that. I'm just remembering. You *were* crazy about me, right?"

Richard turned slightly, his eyes catching those of Johnny Hanson, and he placed his hands together in prayer position under his lips. He then turned his attention back to Rebecca before five seconds elapsed.

"Fifty years ago. That's a long time. Heh?" he said to Rebecca.

"Hey, you two. Sorry to interrupt," Johnny Hanson said, standing over the table. "Some of the baseball guys want to get a dugout talk together and I was designated to go find our first baseman. Hope you don't mind, uh," he looked down at her ID tag, "Rebecca."

"No, it's okay. If his team needs him."

"Good to see you, Rebecca," Richard said as he got up and followed Johnny away from the table.

A tall, gray-haired man wearing a blue blazer and an open-collar blue shirt walked into the restaurant and looked around. Stopping at the table with the yet unclaimed ID tags, he picked one and strung it around his neck. The newcomer nodded and smiled at people as he walked about, coming to another stop at the buffet table and snagging an hors d' oeuvre with his bare hand. He picked up a plate and tossed on a half dozen pieces of finger food, grabbed a napkin, and melted into the crowd.

Johnny carried five tap beers over to a circle of men and women that included Richard and Rob.

"These are all I could carry for whoever wants," he said. "They're on me."

"What a sport," someone said. "The drinks are included in what we paid the restaurant."

"I hauled them over."

"How do you do that?" Angelo asked. Carry five tap beers."

"He's got big hands," Rob pointed out.

"Matches his head," Richard observed.

"Hey!"

Five minutes of further banter and the group splintered in several directions.

The gray-haired guy in the blue blazer walked over to Richard and Rob, carefully observing Richard's face. Their eyes met.

"Hi," said Richard as polite acknowledgement.

"Hi. You're Richard Colucci. Right?"

"Yeah. This is Rob Fisher."

"Norm Feldman," the new attendee replied, shaking both their hands.

Rob looked at him. "Were we in any classes together?"

"Not that I recall, Rob."

"You recognized Richie pretty easily. You two hang out?"

"Do you remember Mr. Gray's English class?" he asked, turning to Richard. And French with Mademoiselle Ouizelle. She was not something to forget. Or seeing a young Mr. Colucci on the dance floor at Springfield Gardens."

"Of course. Of course," Richard bluffed, feeling guilty about having to fake remembrance and recognition.

Rob was looking at the ID tag hanging from Norm's neck, including the photo from the 1963 yearbook.

"You know, actually, I think I'm remembering you now," Rob said. "You were in the glee club, Right?"

"Yeah. Right."

"I remember you'd be in the front row every time the glee club performed. You sure got much taller since graduating high school — like at least six inches?"

"I don't think that much. So how are you?" Norm asked, turning to Richard.

"Good. I'm retired now. How about yourself?"

"Still working. In a way, I'm kind of on duty even now. But I like my job. You know before we go any further and get separated, let's exchange phone numbers," Norm said, taking out his cell phone so he could enter Richard's number.

"My cell phone is off because I have only one bar remaining," Richard explained. "Maybe I can write down your number on a napkin."

Norm stared directly at Richard. "No, I think you should turn on your cell phone, Richard."

"What?"

"I said that I think you should turn on your cell phone. You can enter my phone number without worrying about losing a paper napkin. And you might see if you received any urgent messages that you're not aware of because your phone has been off."

"Are you trying to tell me something I don't know? Are you Norm Feldman?"

"Richard, I think you might have had your phone off for too long."

"And why would you think that after not seeing me for fifty years?"

The tall gray-haired man looked straight into Richard's eyes. "Because a calf has not yet come home."

* * *

The waiter devoted to Richard approached him once again while he was huddled with Johnny, Rob, and several others.

"What can I get for you to drink, sir?"

"Um, can I ask a favor of you?"

"Certainly."

"Can you bring me a Coke in a paper cup with a lid on it? You know, like a takeout coffee cup. I won't have to worry about spilling when people bump into me, or 'cause I'm balancing food in the other hand ... and besides, some of the glasses in this place don't look so clean to me."

"Certainly, sir. I can do that." The waiter looked at the others.

"They don't want anything," Richard said. "They've had enough to drink. Thanks."

The waiter went off to fill Richard's request.

"Practical jokes were always my department," Rob said. "What's up with the paper cup and lid?"

"Rich, are you gonna spill out the Coke and fill the cup up with food from the buffet to take back to your hotel room?" Johnny kidded.

"I'm not going to drink the soda," Richard answered. "That's for sure. And I'm not going to spill it out either."

"You're saving it," Mark said.

"If I can."

"That's strange, Richie," Rob said. "Are you okay?"

"Was it seeing Rebecca?" Johnny asked. Did that throw you off?"

"No, no," Richard assured them with light laughter. "Nothing to do with her. There's stuff I've lived through …and *with*. I'd been advised very recently that it's over now, but that doesn't actually seem to be the case. Anyway, I've trained myself to react to certain stimuli."

"Like a laboratory rat?" Mark joked.

"Cut it out," Johnny said. "Rich is telling us something serious. Is there something we can do to help, Rich?"

"For the immediate moment, there are two things. Keep an eye on the door and that waiter after he brings me the Coke in the paper cup with the lid. If he starts out the front door before the party is over, let me know. Especially if he leaves very soon after bringing the Coke."

"The second thing?" Rob asked.

"I'd appreciate it if one of you guys would hold onto the paper cup without spilling the contents, and definitely not allow anybody to drink from it."

"I feel like I'm part of a mystery novel," Mark said.

Rob made a face at him. "After ten, fifteen minutes, I'll take the cup of Coke to my car," Rob said.

Norm listened to the conversation, faded back, and keyed a text message into his phone.

The waiter returned in a few minutes with the Coke in a coffee cup with a lid, as requested, for Richard. Norm had his cell phone ready to take a photo of Richard and the others.

"Hold still, and look at me, guys."

The waiter held back.

"You, too," he said to the waiter. "You're part of the party. Step in with the guys and smile with them. Got it. One more time. Okay. Thanks, guys."

Norm fiddled with the keypad of his cell phone, the waiter handed the coffee cup filled with Coke to Richard, and Richard passed it to Rob after the waiter left.

* * *

The waiter stepped out the back door of the restaurant fifteen minutes after giving the Coke to Richard. He walked slowly for thirty feet as though taking a break and getting some air.

Another twenty feet and he slipped the waiter jacket off, and began walking more quickly. He passed the back lot of the restaurant, turned right onto the street, walked one block and got behind the wheel of his car.

A burly man who had been walking behind him tapped on his window and showed him a badge.

"Where you going, pal? The party's still at its peak. Keep your hands where I can see them."

Another man, more average in build, walked up to the other side of the car and flashed his badge, too.

"FBI. Get out of the car, please. Hands where they can be seen. No sudden movements."

"What did I do?"

"You left the party. Get out, please."

The waiter seemed nervous as he got out of the car.

The first FBI man checked the photo transmitted to his cell phone. "I'd say this is him. Isn't this you, pal?"

No comment.

Norm came upon the scene. "That's the guy. Where'd you go, buddy? A short while ago you were a waiter at the reunion party in Verdi's restaurant. You just walk out and leave them shorthanded? What's up with that? Don't you wanna get paid for the day?"

"I didn't feel well. I had to leave."

"What's making you not feel well? Besides us? Being picked up by the FBI often makes people not feel well. But what about before?"

"I feel like fever?"

"Yeah? You seemed pretty upbeat when you were serving the soda to one of the guests. What was in it?"

"In what?"

"The Coke in the coffee cup."

"Coke."

"What else?"

"Just Coke. I'm sick. I want to go."

"We'll take your temperature at headquarters. Cuff him," *Norm* said to the other two. I'll go back inside to tell our subject what's happened out here, get the Coke sample, and then we'll bring this guy in and report to our CIA liaisons."

* * *

Richard, Rob and Johnny passed through the thinning crowd fifteen minutes after the official closing time of the party, exited through the big brown double doors onto Fifteenth Avenue, and followed Richard's lead with a right turn.

"How far are we going?" Johnny asked Richard.

"You tired?"

"Just curious. I could go eighteen innings," Johnny answered, grinning.

"One block up, then a block and a half to the right. Hey, thanks for remembering the *come save me* sign when I was sitting with Rebecca."

"What's he talking about?" Rob asked.

"He was trapped with her and needed to be rescued. He gave me the same signal—hands in praying position—like we used back when we were seventeen, eighteen, and one of us needed the other one to break up a twosome we wanted out of."

"It was that uncomfortable?" Rob asked.

"Not for the reasons you're thinking," Richard answered. "After many years, some people aren't the same as they were way back. Inside or out. We all change. Some for better, some for worse. And *some* merely become an exaggerated version of what they always were—the traits that long ago went barely noticed ballooning into caricature proportions," Richard said as they reached the next street corner. "We turn right here."

The three amigos walked silently for the next half block, Rob and Johnny taking in Richard's comment.

"So, you guys see Ellen Beecher? I'd say she looked damned good," Richard declared to shake the other two out of the mood he'd just created.

"Yeah, she even looked hot," Johnny agreed.

"I thought I noticed you staring at her," Rob said. "Jumping grand-mas now, huh?"

"Really, my reputation was always too large."

"I bet your car is coming up. Right?" Rob asked.

"Yup."

"I bet that's it five cars down."

Richard laughed.

"Unbelievable!" Johnny shouted.

"You're kidding us," Rob squealed. "An Impala! A red convertible Impala, no less!"

"Guys," Richard said, holding both his hands out, palms up, "would I come back to high school driving anything else? Would I?"

Johnny and Rob laughed, hitting each other on the shoulders, and then smacking Richard on the back.

"You're too much, man." Johnny declared.

"What kind of car do you drive at home?" Rob asked.

Richard paused. "The truth?"

"No, make something up. Of course, the truth."

"An Impala."

"Geez," Johnny said, "So it's like you never got out of high school."

"Punk."

Rob laughed at the two of them. "Okay, let's go see your babemobile."

"I guess it is. Come on."

"Hmm, hmm, hmm." Johnny said, shaking his right hand up and down next to his body as he circled round the red convertible. "Serious business, young man."

"How many phone numbers did you get last night," Rob asked Richard.

"I'm not sharing; get your own numbers. I knew you guys would get a kick out of this."

"So how about a spin like old times?" Johnny said to Richard who was already standing near the driver's door.

"Okay. We can cruise over to the senior citizens center and check out any new stuff that's hanging around," he answered, pulling the car keys out of his pocket. He then stood still.

"Open the door, Rich."

"Come on, Richie. Let's go cruising Flushing in an Impala that goes more than a mile without breaking down."

Richard was frozen, staring at the driver's door. Finally, he looked inside the car at the steering wheel and the floor, then looked toward the front wheel of the car.

"Rich, why aren't you opening the door?"

"Cause it *is open*. On *my* side it's already open."

"Whataya mean?" Johnny asked. "You didn't lock it when you parked before?"

"No, that's not what I mean at all. I locked it. I'm always careful to lock my car when I park."

"So what are you saying?" Rob asked, walking around the car to Richard.

"Someone's been in this car. To do what, I don't know for certain."

"This is sounding creepy, Rich."

"I'm going to walk at an even pace toward the store on the corner. You guys do the same. Start now and I'll catch up with you. Go."

Rob and Johnny did as Richard requested, and he felt a sense of relief after they, and then he, were a hundred feet from the car. They slowed a bit, and the three walked in unison.

"You think your car was rigged with a bomb. Right?" Rob asked.

"That's right."

"Are you a spy, Rich?" Johnny asked.

"I once was."

"For us, right?"

Richard looked at Johnny with a scrunched face. "Of course for us. I want to talk to that guy selling hot dogs on the corner. Maybe you guys should keep walking."

"Nah. And leave you uncovered?" Rob answered.

"Miss a real live spy drama? I've never been part of a spy ring before," Johnny said.

They walked the short distance to the hot dog stand with a Sabrett umbrella over it. A short Hispanic man smiled at them.

"Hot dogs? Sausage? You want soda?"

"You have Cokes?" Richard asked.

"Yes. One dollar each."

"We'll take three," he said, reaching in his pocket and taking out three one-dollar bills.

The vendor pulled out three wet cans of Coke, dried them off with a paper towel, and handed them over with three straws.

"Thank you. How long have you been out here on at this stand today?"

"Since eleven o'clock."

"How late will you stay out?"

"Bout eight o'clock."

"You mind if I ask you a question?"

"What's your question?"

"Can you see that red convertible car on the other side of the street a block away?"

The vendor smiled. Si. Yes. So red. I see it."

"Did you notice anybody going in or out of that car, or underneath it like to fix something, in the last three or four hours?"

The small man looked at Richard. "Listen, I tell you I don't want no trouble. Are you the police?"

"No, I'm not the police."

"So why you ask if anybody go in, go out, go under that red car?"

"Because it's my car. And if it were your car, and I saw someone go in, go out or go under your car when you weren't there I would tell you."

The hotdog vendor stood quietly, looking down at the sidewalk. Finally, he responded. "Yes, I saw a man go in that car. Two, maybe three hours ago."

"Did you notice how he got in, and how long he stayed in the car?"

"He stand by the door maybe three, four minutes. Then he open it. He didn't stay in the car long. Couple minutes."

"I see. What made you notice and remember what happened in five or six minutes?"

"The man was very tall. Very, very tall."

"Did you see where he went after getting out of my car?"

"Something missing in your car, you call police."

"Oh, I plan on calling the police. But did you see where the very, very tall man went?"

"I don't want no trouble."

"I'm already in trouble. Are you illegal?"

No reply.

"I understand. Can you just tell me if the very tall man is gone, or if he's still on this street?"

"Still on the street," the vendor answered with a nod, and then looked down again.

"Okay, that helps some. It tells me the bomb he planted in my car will be set off after he sees me get in the car. At least that's his plan."

The small man gasped, turned, and walked several steps away.

"Shouldn't you ask him where the guy is?" Rob asked Richard.

"He's too scared to tell me. Besides, how many places can a *very, very, tall man* be on the block without being seen?"

"Maybe he's in the store on the corner," Johnny said.

The three turned and stared at the coffee shop on the other corner, each wondering if they should be walking toward or away from it. Hesitation and silence.

"Colucci!" shouted a voice from half a block away. "Richard Colucci!" the voice immediately echoed.

"Get down!" Richard yelled, pushing Johnny to the ground and throwing himself on top of Rob.

Three men dressed in casual clothes trotted toward them.

"Colucci, are you okay?" one called out.

Richard looked up as the three strangers were fifteen feet from him. "What do you want?"

"You are Richard Colucci. Right?"

Johnny had gotten up from the ground and Rob was crawling out from underneath Richard.

"Who's looking for Richard Colucci?"

"Me. Richard, can you *imagine all the people?*"

"Christ, it's you. You just gave me such a scare … and my friends," he added, getting up from the ground. "It's okay guys," he said, turning to Johnny and Rob. This is the sheriff's posse.

"How did you find me, Baisley?"

"That's what we do. Remember? You used your credit cards for your flight, your rental car, and your hotel where you mentioned why you were in town and the restaurant where your reunion would be. Oh, and be sure to let Jennifer know you're okay."

"Jennifer? At my hotel?"

"Yes. The woman at the front desk. She seemed very concerned when we insisted on information because you could be in danger."

"Really?"

"That's the truth. And you are in danger."

"I know that. I'm pretty certain my rental car has been rigged with a bomb."

"Why do you say that?"

Richard explained to Baisley about the front door being open, and what the hotdog vendor told him about the very, very tall man. Baisley and his two colleagues crossed the street to talk to the hot dog vendor. Richard began to cross the street, too, leaving Rob and Johnny behind, when a dark green car pulled out of a parking spot on the corner a block away. Suddenly, it revved into high speed, racing directly at Richard.

Richard froze in the middle of the road, and then turned back to the corner he'd just left. The green car was aiming right at him. Four gun shots rang out! Six more! The car careened into the cars parked along the curb and spun around. Baisley and the two agents approached slowly along both sides with guns drawn. One dropped to the sidewalk and crawled along behind parked cars until he could get a view of the front seat of the green car. He waved to Baisley and the other agent.

"There's a lot of blood in there."

The second agent crept along the passenger side of the car, popped up, and trained his gun on the bloody man behind the wheel.

"Don't move or I'll blow your head off."

Baisley and the first agent moved in, their guns aimed at the driver too.

Richard walked over to the car.

"This isn't civilian work," Baisley said, looking at Richard.

"You're telling *me* what isn't civilian work? I want to get a look at this piece of garbage."

Baisley nodded.

"I'm betting he's very, very tall."

"Actually, he is," the first agent said. "I understand if you want to have a go at him. But that's not how it's done."

"No. I just want to see him dead. Or even better, dying. Is he alive?"

"His eyes are moving," the agent said, already in the car to be sure the very, very tall man couldn't grab a gun. "He's breathing … shallow."

Richard leaned in a window. "Was it worth it?" he addressed the severely wounded man. "Was all your hate worth it?"

"Because of you … my father is dead," the man managed to say with struggling breath.

"Your father is dead because he devoted his life to hate. And I have paid your father's price by being beaten while tied up. My head broken, my shoulder and foot broken. Beaten up by a gang of cowards. Who should be doing the avenging? You could have lived your life, but hate and revenge were more important… And now, you are *dying*. I see it. I've seen enough." Richard turned and walked away.

IN THE END

Michael Riley felt stricken when he read that John Rickets had just passed away. The fond memories of shared experiences during their teens and early twenties were still vivid despite not having seen each other for forty years, or being in touch for thirty years—around the time that Michael's career took him to London. Long distance phone calls were expensive in the 1980s and emails didn't exist.

Michael was en route home to Chicago and took a stopover in New York for a few days to take in Broadway shows and revisit the scenes of teenage debauchery. News of John's death was not consistent with the purpose of his stop.

The newspaper said that a wake would be held at Anthony's Funeral Home in Brooklyn later that evening, and Michael called information for the phone number.

"Good afternoon, Anthony's Funeral Home," a male voice answered in a subdued tone.

"Hello. It's my understanding that there's a wake this evening for John Rickets."

"Yes. At six o'clock."

"Can you tell me exactly where Anthony's Funeral Home is located?"

"We're next to Cacciatore's down on Sullivan Street, across from the medical center—2710 Sullivan Street."

"Thank you."

* * *

Michael stepped out of a yellow taxi in front of Anthony's Funeral Home at ten minutes before six o'clock, and walked through the big brown front door into the lobby. There were three obvious mourners walking into a room to the right and he followed. He was surprised by the number of people already in the large room filled with seats. The coffin was at the front of the room. *Is it open?* he wondered as he made his way to the front of the room, recognizing no one. It was open. *Doesn't look like him. Well, it's been many years,* Michael thought. He stood quietly with his memories and private thoughts, said a prayer, and then turned around.

He didn't know how to introduce himself to John's family. Actually, he didn't know who among the mourners were family and who were friends. An attempt to reach a woman appearing to be John's age was impeded by two others consoling her. *That must be John's wife.* He drew back five or six steps.

"You'd think this guy was a freakin' saint the way they're talking about him now," Michael heard a male voice behind him say. "Dead, he's a saint. Alive, he was a crook."

"Shhh. Stop," a female voice whispered, loud enough for Michael to hear.

He waited an appropriate period of time to turn around, and saw a man with gray hair around the sides of his otherwise bald head and a scowl on his face. The guy looked at him.

"Who're you?" the guy asked, the lady no longer at his side.

"I'm Michael Riley. I was a friend of John's back in school. Hadn't actually seen him in forty years. Been out of touch a long time. And you?"

"Dave, his brother-in-law. He robbed me blind for years. I'm here 'cause it's still family."

"He robbed you?"

"Right. I let him into my business because he was out of work for two years. Figured I could trust him, being my wife's brother-in-law, you know. Well, after seven years, I discovered he was embezzling from the business. The low-life bastard."

"I'm really surprised. That's not like the John I knew."

"You just said you knew him forty years ago."

"I assume that caused problems in the family."

"I didn't go to the police. Didn't let his wife and kids know, either—for my wife's sake. For the sake of the relationship of the sisters."

"That was nice of you."

"I just told him to drop dead." Dave shook his head and sighed. "Now he can rest in peace."

"Let's hope so."

Michael was shocked by the information he'd just learned. He parted from Dave to make another attempt to approach John's wife but was thwarted once again due to a bevy of people surrounding her. He considered what he would say when he reached the widow: Hi, I'm Michael, John's friend from school whom he hadn't spoken to for thirty years, and probably never mentioned. I'm really sorry to hear about him. Please accept my condolences. *Clumsy to interrupt intimate comforting with that explanation.*

He hoped he might meet other family members or close friends, and approached a fiftyish man. Maybe he'd be a nephew or younger cousin.

"Hi, I'm Michael Riley, a friend of John's back in school."

"Hi."

"Are you related to John?"

"No. My wife is fond of his wife. She's good people. We're neighbors."

"They say good fences make good neighbors—something like that. Is it true?"

"Could be. Frankly, John never knew from stuff like that. He let his damn dog pee, and worse than that, on my lawn. And did he give a crap?"

"Doesn't sound good."

"You bet. And he cheated at poker. At least back when we still let him join our weekly game."

"He was caught blatantly cheating?"

"I don't know exactly how he did it, but nobody wins that often. Not as often as him."

Michael stepped away from the neighbor with the offended lawn, and looked over at John's wife. Still occupied.

"I'd like to be able to pay my respects to John's wife," he said to the mid-thirties woman he nearly walked into, "but she's always surrounded by people expressing sympathies. Understandably."

"She's my mother. I'm John's daughter, Jessica."

"Oh. Then please allow me to express my sincere regrets to you. Your father and I were friends from our teens and twenties. I'm so sorry about your loss."

"Thank you. What was my father like back then?"

"A great guy. A great friend."

"I know some people didn't think of him that way."

"Then they didn't know him very well. He was loyal, honest, looked out for other people."

"Like in what ways?"

"Well, I never would have passed high school chemistry if it weren't for him. He tutored me over and over so I could pass the final exam. And when my father and I were repairing the shed in our backyard, who spent the whole afternoon helping us? John. And he was the guy who'd most likely stand up to the neighborhood bully in defense of someone else."

"Really? All those things are true?"

"Yeah."

"That's nice to know. We weren't close. I didn't finish college. Got pregnant when I wasn't married. I think I was a disappointment to him," she said, glancing at the floor.

"Is that what you think? Really? That's not the way I heard it. I always heard, *Jessica this, and Jessica that*," Michael made believe. "*And you should see that gorgeous kid. So smart,* he'd tell me. Sorry, I forget your kid's name."

"Jason. He's twelve. A good boy. And very smart."

"I know. I know. And I've been told that you're a very good mother. You should be proud. Like your father was."

"Oh, thank you so much for sharing all that with me. It makes me feel so much better. I really didn't know."

"I guess sometimes what people feel isn't always communicated between them as clearly as it is with other people. I'm glad you now know."

Jessica grabbed both of Michael's hands. "Thank you."

Michael watched her walk across the room to a preadolescent boy.

An attractive woman in a green dress entered the room and went directly to the casket. She stared into it for several minutes, crossed herself, turned and walked past the throng of people without stopping to speak with anyone. She took a seat near the back of the room—one empty seat between her and Michael—and stared straight ahead for a few minutes, motionless. She turned to the side in Michael's direction. He acknowledged her presence with an exaggerated nod. She forced a smile.

"Are you okay?" he asked, leaning toward her.

"I will be. It's sad … very sad."

"Yes, it is."

Michael saw tears roll down her cheek and fumbled in his pocket for a tissue.

"Here, take this. I'm sorry it's a little rumpled up."

"Thank you."

Michael looked about, noting that nobody was on the way over to comfort the distraught woman.

"Were you close?" he asked.

She didn't respond to Michael's question. "How did *you* know him?"

"Oh, we were great pals from about fifteen to twenty-five. Thick as blood. But you know, it's only by accident that I'm here. I read about my old friend's passing in the newspaper while I happened to be in New York on a three-day stopover on my way home to Chicago."

The woman turned to Michael, giving him total attention. "Nobody contacted you?"

"No. I wouldn't have expected them to. You see, I moved to London forty years ago, and our communication petered out ten years later. Lousy, how that goes. But the feeling of a bond remained."

"That's why you came."

"Yes, I had to say good-bye. We hadn't before …"

"Then you don't know anybody in John's family, or any of his friends?"

"No," Michael answered with a shake of his head. "I got to meet his daughter for the first time a few minutes ago. Are you a relative, friend, or co-worker?"

"I'm John's lover."

Michael paused, wondering how to volley that ball.

"John must have remained quite a guy," he said, immediately regretting his choice of words. "I mean you being very attractive, and rather young it seems to me."

"John was very warm and affectionate. Very loving. I felt aglow when I was with him. I'll miss him so much. You're the only person I've shared my sorrow with. You won't tell anybody? I don't want to spoil things with his family and friends, and cause them further pain. You said you hadn't been in touch for thirty years, so I thought, well …" She began to cry.

Michael took her hand, and reached in his pocket for another crumpled tissue. In low voices, they shared stories about John for twenty minutes. She thanked Michael for helping her get through being there, got up and walked to the door.

People turned their heads toward a man making his way through the center of the room. He was a priest, and was approaching the front where John was laid in the casket.

"The priest is going to speak," a lady behind Michael said. "Is he from John and Beverly's church?"

"I don't know," a male voice replied.

The priest walked over to the widow, and they spoke for a few moments. He returned to the front of the room near the casket and prepared to speak.

"Family and friends of John Visconti …"

John Visconti, Visconti, Visconti, echoed in Michael's ears. *And what about the family and friends of John Rickets?*

"Is Visconti spelled with an e or an i at the end?" Michael asked the guy next to him.

87

"An i," he muttered, and turned away.

Michael's eyes scanned the room with no purpose. *No Rickets here? Where's John Rickets?*

Michael was in the middle of the room when the priest began, and wanted leave right away— within seconds. He inched backward and sideward toward the door, not meaning to bump into those people. Finally, he was at the exit and stepped out into the lobby where he stood dazed.

A woman walked over to him. "Are you here for John Rickets' wake?"

"I thought I was."

"I'm his daughter, Carrie. And you are?"

"Michael Riley. I was a friend of your father in our teens and twenties."

"You know, you look like you're related to a young man posing in an old photo that my father always kept on his shelf. It was of him and an old school buddy he called Mike. That must be you."

"It probably is."

She put her arm through his. "Come with me, Mike," she said, leading him to the room at the left. "Meet my father's family. Everybody'd probably like to meet the guy in the photo."

SECTION II

MITCHELL GRAYE STORIES

A NEW YEAR

The ball dropped in Times Square three hours earlier, ushering in 1986. My upstairs neighbors' drunken party guests had finally left and quiet blanketed the air—until the red phone on the living room table rang. It was the extra phone installed with the phone number used for the financial consulting and accounting business that I began by default. What does an unemployed white-collar professional do, if not become a consultant?

I stared at the phone as it rang a second and third time. *Who would be calling at three o'clock in the morning on New Year's Day?* My family would have called on my old tan phone if they needed to reach me. *Okay, pick it up already.*

"Hello."

"Hello, Dr. Harrison. It's Amala. I'm sorry to call you at this hour, but I'm in a really bad way."

"Amala, I'm really sorry to tell you this, but you must have dialed the wrong number. This isn't the doctor you're trying to reach," I said.

"Oh, no. Are you a doctor?"

"No. No, I'm not."

"Is this 555-4201?"

"Yeah, it is. But there's no Dr. Harrison here."

"I must have written his emergency number down wrong." She stopped talking, and began to cry. "I'm going to kill myself. It's just going to happen then," she continued, sobbing. "I'm sorry to disturb you, sir. Good night."

"Whoa, whoa! Wait a minute! Hold on a second. What do you mean when you say you're gonna kill yourself? Is it a way of expressing your frustration? Like in *I'm going to kill that guy*? Or do you literally mean that you plan to kill yourself?"

"Dr. Harrison is my psychiatrist. I was trying to reach him because I'm in a really bad way. I can't go on. I just can't go on."

"So you really meant it when you said you were going to kill yourself."

I heard muffled sobbing.

"Yes."

"I don't think you should hang up yet. Okay?"

"It's hopeless. I don't have a chance. The walls are all closing in on me."

"Which walls?" I asked, trying to keep her talking. "Which walls are closing in on you?"

"All of them."

"I've found that if people take things one at a time, they're not as overwhelming. Tell me about wall number one." I picked up the red phone from the table and put it on the floor so that the phone cord could reach me as I lay down on the couch.

"My parents are wall number one. They want me to marry an Indian man. Even when I was in high school, they'd go crazy if I dated a white guy. And there weren't many Indian guys in my school."

"How old are you now?"

"Thirty-two."

"I take it that you're not married."

"No, not yet."

There was silence from us both as I waited for her to expand on that remark, and wondered why she didn't.

"Amala, is that wall number two?"

She broke into thirty seconds of wailing. I heard her phone drop on something hard, like a table or floor. *What do I do? What can I do?* I thought. *Pick up the phone. Pick it up,* I urged in my mind, straightening up on the couch.

Finally, "I'm sorry. That *is* wall number two."

"You're not *yet* married—meaning you will be?"

"Yes. I'm engaged to be married to a nice man in six months."

I needed to think. My total experience in psychotherapy was six years earlier when I was a member of a therapy group. What would our psychologist leader have done next? How would I have addressed a member of that group if he or she were on the other end of the phone?

"And getting married to a nice man is wall number two. Why is that the case?"

"It's hard to explain."

"You describe the man you're going to marry as *nice*. As a man, hearing that as the only description of him sends a cold shiver down my spine. He's *nice*. You didn't say he's wonderful, fantastic, handsome, brilliant. He's a *nice man* – not sounding enthusiastic or romantic – like *yeah, he's okay.*"

"Oh, it's terrible," she said, "You're right. And it's not fair to Kumar. That's his name. I think Kumar doesn't know the difference. He thinks like my parents."

Parents, the magic word. Good parents, bad parents, absent parents, no parents—memories of my former group partners' histories were flooding my mind.

"I can't live like this. It's so bad. So, so bad. I can't. Driving over a bridge, or pills."

"Listen to me. You try to drive over a bridge, you'll end up doing it wrong and hurting other people. You hear me? You want to hurt other people?"

"No, no. Then pills."

"You'll do it wrong, and wind up living in a vegetative state, or hearing people around you talk and being unable to respond to them. Do you want that?"

"No."

"Now, let's get back to why your parents and fiancé think the same. Okay?"

"They're old country. We're Indian. My parents' marriage was prearranged, and they came to this country when they were mid-thirties, and I was five. My fiancé is forty-five, and was thirty years old when he came here."

"And so, they're still attached to the ways of doing things in the old country, so to speak." I said.

"In so many ways. They're willing to accept the American way of making money, and lots of it. But everything else should be done to establish and maintain a little India right here in America."

"That's probably true of many first generation Americans," I said, "if you mean living in neighborhoods where their group has clustered, teaching the motherland language to their children, and continuing to follow their customs."

"Well, how about insisting that their daughter marry an Indian man? And only a man from the specific region of India they emigrated from? Is that merely following customs of the country or is that making their daughter's life downright freaking miserable? Tell me!"

I was now in uncharted waters. Never heard this one before. Where does a woman find eligible men from the specific region of India from which her parents emigrated? Mail-order grooms? That's a sarcastic question. How many of them live in her area, and how would they comfortably meet? I needed to suppress and hide the anger that I felt about such an absurd circumstance, so that I could continue to talk her down from the ledge.

"Your parents' expectations are not reasonable," I said. "Not here in America where you've grown up. You don't need me to tell you that. It seems right to them because of how and where they grew up."

"And I will dishonor them in the eyes of the Indian community. The four hundred people they hardly know who will be invited to the wedding. They'll really be dishonored when I kill myself."

"You wouldn't kill yourself to get even with your parents," I said. "Would you?"

"No."

"Good. Now, getting back to the fact that you and your parents grew up in different cultures, with different expectations, why, in your adulthood, are you still living life according to your parents and the world they left behind, rather than the world to which they brought you?"

"Guilt. And dependence."

"Dependence?"

"Yeah. Yeah," she repeated, exhaling all the air from her lungs. "I work in the family business."

I felt an emotion not unlike what I might feel while watching a character in a movie being crushed between walls moving closer and closer together. Ironic that Amala and I had begun by speaking about walls number one and two.

"The family business."

"I don't want to get into what kind of family business. It doesn't matter."

"If you say it doesn't. Do you believe you could earn a living on your own?"

"Not what I earn working for my father. My parents convinced me that I didn't need to go to college. It was a waste of money to pay tuition for a girl who could make a good salary working for her father, and then get married. So, no, I wouldn't be able to pay for my apartment, my car, insurance, and eat if I worked somewhere else."

"You feel tied up." I offered.

"No kidding."

I felt the sarcasm like scratching on a blackboard.

"Have you actually limited your dating to the target group specified by your parents?"

"No."

"Your parents—did they found out?"

"My father saw me coming out of Eric's house; we were holding hands and exchanging looks. He spotted my car outside while he was driving by, and waited for I don't know how long for me to appear. I'm sure his blood pressure went over two hundred when he came up to us in a rage, and saw Eric's light skin, blue eyes, and blond hair."

I visualized the scene like a movie, and leaned forward on the couch.

"Screaming and screaming," she continued. "What are you doing with that man? You were inside that house! Who chaperoned you in the white man's house? Nobody! Right, you whore? You're a disgrace to me. To your mother. You're not my daughter.

"Eric is more than six feet tall. He took several steps toward my father, looked him in the eye, and threatened him: 'If you don't shut your damn mouth, I'm gonna beat your goddamn head into a pulp. You hear me Mr. Asshole?'"

"Was there a fight?" I asked.

"Almost. My father stepped forward, screaming, and I stepped in front of Eric. 'Dad, this is Eric. Now that you've found us together, you know. I love him, and he loves me. We've loved each other for more than a year, and if you have love in your heart for me, and care about my happiness, you will accept Eric and be happy for me.'"

"He didn't," I said, "or we wouldn't be talking now."

"So true, doctor."

Was she being snide with me? I thought *yes.* In a different situation, I might have gotten my hackles up and said something that would push the other person back a step. But I decided that it was just as well that Amala was pushing at someone other than herself.

"*Mitch,*" I gently corrected her. "That's my name," is all I said about it. "*So* that was the end of Eric? Just like that? And you're engaged to the nice Indian man?"

"That scene was four years ago. Eric and I continued to see each other secretly on a regular basis for eight months."

"Wasn't your father watching you?"

"Yes. But there were ways. A couple times, Eric posed as a repair guy, wearing a hat—he came to my place and never left. Different kinds of schemes. After a while, he didn't want to put up with it anymore. He said *choose—your father's crazy rules or our love.* I wanted to choose Eric, but I was too weak. Ridiculous. Right?"

"Not for me to judge. I didn't grow up in your shoes. But is it objectively logical? No, it's not. And you can't blame Eric for refusing to live his life like that indefinitely."

She didn't respond, and I knew I needed to keep her engaged.

"When did you meet Kumar?" I asked.

"A year ago. We were introduced by a friend of my aunt. He asked me to marry him seven months ago. My father had been yelling at me that I was going to become an old cow, too old to give milk. My mother was saying that soon, no bulls would come near me."

I breathed deeply, and shook my head. "You said yes to Kumar's marriage proposal." I didn't wait for unnecessary confirmation. "Did he ask your father's permission?"

"Of course. Before he asked me."

Why didn't this woman just run away from these people who call themselves family? She's here in the United States, not in the middle of a jungle, India or any other country. Why kill herself instead of starting a new life? I answered my own question. She's conditioned to doubt that she can survive without depending on them.

I unwound my extended phone cord, walked to the cabinet on the other side of the room, and retrieved the bar of dark chocolate that I needed by that time.

"How did you feel about that? Kumar asking your father first?"

"It's the traditional way."

"But how did you feel about it? You felt something about it, or you wouldn't have made comment that Kumar asked your father's permission to marry before he asked you."

"Okay, it was annoying. It's like my parents are in charge of my marriage, too. Aren't all the prior limitations enough? Do they and my husband have to strike a deal before I participate in the decision?"

"You're now sounding so Western," I said with intentional irony.

"I've been living here for twenty-seven years. It might not be as bad if I didn't know better."

"Right. So let me ask you: since you do know better, could you have long ago managed to get a job to support yourself, even if not in the same manner you're accustomed to? People with high school degrees do get jobs."

"Yes, they do. But not for fifteen hundred per week."

I paused for a breath and then said, "Okay."

"What are you thinking?" she asked.

"Just wondering if you've saved much money."

"A bit. I probably could've saved more. It's terrible. I'm hopeless. You can't imagine. Dr. Walker told me I should use some of my income to attend college classes in the evening."

"Dr. Walker?"

"He's my other psychiatrist."

"You have *two* psychiatrists?"

"Yes, I have two."

"At the same time?" I felt my shoulders sag.

"Uh-huh."

"Do the two of them know about each other?"

"No. I've been too embarrassed to tell them. It's like I'd be insulting both of them, so I keep it to myself."

I stroked the back of my head with my free hand.

"Amala, they should know about each other because … well, I don't know anything about psychiatry, but they could be utilizing two different types of therapy—or even have two different opinions of your diagnosis."

"You could be right. But that's not the worst of things."

I sat up and leaned forward. *"What's worse?"*

"What Dr. Cooper told me."

"And Dr. Cooper is your … *what?* … Not a third psychiatrist."

"My ob-gyn."

"Okay, I'm in. What did your ob-gyn say?" I asked, and took a deep breath.

"I'm pregnant," she blurted out, crying, while I struggled to find an appropriate response. "Okay, I'm back," she advised, as I gathered my thoughts.

"What month are you in?"

"Beginning the third month."

"Have you told Kumar?"

"No, I haven't. He's been away on business in India."

"How long? How long has he been away in India?"

"Three months," she sobbed.

"Are you telling me that it isn't Kumar's baby?"

Heavy crying was her only reply.

Tread lightly, I thought. "Your situation is upsetting. I understand. May I ask when the last time you've seen Eric was?"

"Yesterday. We've never really stopped seeing each other for more than two months at any time."

"And during the time you've known Kumar?"

"Not as often, of course. He's told me over and over that, once I'm married, he won't see me anymore."

Again, I didn't know what to say right in that moment. I needed to process.

"The baby is definitely Eric's. Right?"

"Yeah."

"Does he know? Does Eric know you're pregnant … with his child?"

"Not yet."

"Have you been considering an abortion?"

"No, I couldn't."

"Religious convictions?"

"No. I'm Hindu, not Catholic. It's a personal reluctance."

"And Eric, what would he think? I mean about an abortion. He doesn't know you're pregnant … but guess."

She didn't answer.

"If you have the baby, will Eric want to marry you? Now. I mean right now—after you tell Kumar."

"We love each other."

"I know you do. You've told me that before. You and Eric have a very intense love for each other. So you and he getting married, having the baby, and becoming a family of three *is* a choice."

"Yeah."

"There are only three other choices: One, have an abortion. Two, marry Kumar, knowing there is the risk that the baby could be white. Three, run off on your own, just you and the baby, and start your own new life, supporting yourself and your baby. Or, as I first said, marry Eric."

"Or kill myself. Kill myself! That's an option," she insisted, crying again.

"No, no, it's not!" I yelled into the phone. "That's not an option at all. This is where our conversation began earlier, and it's not an option. Listen to me. You just told me you wouldn't even consider an abortion. And what I got from that was you wouldn't prevent the baby from being born and having a chance at life. So listen up! If you kill yourself … if you kill yourself, what the hell is the end result for the baby you're carrying inside you? Huh? Can you answer that for me?"

She cried for a while, but I was just glad she didn't hang up.

"Amala, are you there?"

"Yes."

"Tell me some things about Eric. What does he do for a living?" I asked, deeply hoping that he wasn't tied to a particular local business—especially hoping he didn't work for his dad.

"He programs computer software."

"That's good," I said. "He could pick up and start over in another city, if necessary. How do his parents feel about you? Especially about you being an Indian Hindu?"

"I don't know. I never asked him."

"How has it felt being in their company?"

"I've never met them," she said. "I've never met Eric's parents."

"How come? You and he were in love for three years before Kumar came into the picture."

"Eric said it wouldn't be a good idea to put his parents in danger of my father's fury if he were following me at any time we met."

"But … that would be … forever." And again, "That would be forever. Even if you didn't meet Kumar, could you have gone on forever seeing Eric, never marrying him because you could never meet his parents for that reason?"

The phone was silent.

"Are you still there?"

"Yes?"

"Eric's friends—what are they like?"

"You're going to berate me."

"Why would I do that?"

"I never met any of his friends."

"Because?"

"His longtime friends have relocated to different cities, and he's worked very long hours since he began his current job five years ago, so he hasn't made new friends."

"I see. But I guess he's become friendly with the boyfriends of your friends when you've gone out together."

"We can't do that. We can't go out together. Eric is right that it could get back to my father."

"All your friends are Indian Hindus and know your father?"

"Not all of them."

"Are you *certain* his name is *Eric*? No kidding. Have you ever heard anyone else address him as *Eric*? Or as *anything*?"

"Well, no."

Just then I heard what sounded like an empty liquor bottle rolling above my head, across the uncarpeted floor in the apartment upstairs. One of them must have been stumbling about. And that's what Amala had been doing—*stumbling about, intoxicated with the romantic view of her and Eric's long-term affair, both of them serving her high doses of an elixir, and she not even knowing what was in the bottle.* The scorning of parents, who berate her for anything she might do that doesn't conform to meeting their own needs, created fear instead of clarity.

Dr. Harrison and Dr. Walker, where have you been? Have you heard what I heard? Is it possible to tell a stranger on the phone even more than a psychiatrist? But, then again, she didn't even tell them about each other."

By seven-thirty that morning, Amala's voice began drifting off, and I heard her yawn every few minutes.

"I'm tired. I think I'm going to go to sleep, Mitch."

I was satisfied that she was too tired to kill herself right then. "Okay ... I'll speak to you *next* New Year's? *Right?* Say, half hour after the ball drops."

* * *

It was a comfortable, sunny afternoon in late September. I decided to take my paperwork with me to one of my town's parks. When writing, I'd sit at one of the wooden picnic tables, but the chairs with metal armrests and multicolored plastic backs and seat slats were perfect when I needed to read. Kids were running around the playground at the other end, and young mothers of infants strolled or sat with their babies at wooden benches, chatting with one another and enjoying the perfect day.

I occasionally took a break from my business papers, and took time to observe the people in the park. I'd become a habitual *people watcher* since the onset of my interest in writing fiction. Real people – their appearance, speech patterns, manner of moving, and the stories I overheard them telling – would someday serve as raw clay to create characters in stories I would write some day. The back pages of my pad were used for notes written during a minute here and there for possible characters. Then back to business.

I readied myself to leave after a few hours, having had enough of business papers for the time being, and walked over to the playground. I watched two five-year-olds on swings with smiley, innocent faces, until my own face mirrored theirs. After walking a few paces, my attention turned to several three and four-year-olds playing in the sandbox, shoveling, and building "pies" from upside-down pails filled with sand. All of it so uncomplicated … but maybe not to them. I no longer remembered. I tried, but couldn't.

I strolled in the direction of the big trees in the corner of the park, and was about to pass three women with baby carriages.

"Amala, I'll call you tomorrow," one woman said, getting up from the wooden bench they shared. "We can talk then about what I should bring for lunch the next day. Bala, are you coming or staying?"

"I'm leaving, too. So beautiful here today that I hate to leave. But I told my mother I'd stop by. Amala, good to see you."

"Same. Bye, you two."

I walked closer after the two women left. The one the others called Amala rolled back the cover of the light brown carriage, and adjusted her baby's shirt, stopping to coo at the infant.

"Beautiful baby," I said to her.

"Oh, thank you," she responded, looking up at me.

"What's its name?"

She looked at me for a few seconds. "Ravi."

"A boy."

"Yes," she said.

I noted with a sense of relief that the baby boy named Ravi was not white.

"Would you mind if I sat down on this bench?"

"I don't own it," she answered with a laugh.

"Well, I ask in case you wanted to be alone."

"Sit. I don't mind sharing the bench."

"How old is young Ravi?" I asked.

"He's two months."

"Really cute. He seems very alert. How's the sleeping going? Are *you* getting much?"

"It's getting better," she said, showing her white teeth. "Are you from around here? There's something familiar about you."

"Oh, that's because I'm one of those guys who looks like a thousand other guys. I live a couple miles from here. Who picked the name *Ravi*? You or your husband?"

"I mostly wanted it. My father argued we should name him Haaroon. But my husband—he said it's Amala's wish to name him Ravi. So it will be. I won't have anyone bossing her." She beamed as she said it. Amala looked at me closely. "It's not the way you look. The way you talk sounds familiar."

"Yeah, very New York. And his name? Your husband."

"Kumar," she replied with a lilt in her voice and a broad smile.

"From the way you say his name and the look on your face, I think your husband is a good man."

"He's a *very* good man."

"That's nice to hear," I said. "That's very nice."

Amala breathed in lightly and let out a contented sigh as she exhaled.

What relief I felt to know that she made it through the dark hours back on January 1, and survived the ensuing months. I'd wondered ever since.

And what an emotional rush I felt seeing her with the baby and hearing how happy she was married to Kumar who turned out to be a genuinely loving husband. And then … then I didn't know what else to say.

"Is this park a favorite spot for you and your friends?"

"One of them. As long as the weather stays nice. We'll have to start finding a coffee shop that allows big carriages when it gets colder. Or start dirtying our own homes," she said.

"Just use paper plates. And don't let them in your living room. Shoes—they leave 'em at your door."

She let out a round of several laughs.

"Well, I should be picking up my business papers and getting back to my office to return some calls," I said as I started to get up. "It's been very nice chatting with you. Hope you keep getting more and more sleep."

"Nice talking to you, too."

I walked twenty feet toward the chair on which I'd left my papers earlier.

"Wait a minute," I heard Amala call out. "Just a minute," she called again, wheeling the carriage in my direction.

I turned and waited for her.

She stopped a couple feet away, looked down, then straight at my eyes.

"Thank you, Mitch. Thanks so much for what you did for me."

"Oh," I began, not knowing what to say. I'd tried to avoid any indication of recognition so that she wouldn't feel uncomfortable. And now she was the one laying it out in the open. "You're very welcome, Amala. I'm really glad that everything has turned out so well."

"There's one thing I didn't tell you the truth about."

Uh-oh, I thought. "What's that?"

"My baby's name. It's not Ravi."

"Hmm. Okay."

"I hope you don't mind. His name is Mitchell."

* * *

Amala calls me every January 1, sometimes as early as 12:30 a.m., to first let me know she is fine and then wish me a happy new year. I recently attended the Columbia University graduation of my honorary godson, Mitchell Sengupta.

SPEAK NO EVIL

She sat there at the same chrome-top table where I'd seen her so many times before: long gray hair, thick red lipstick, and holding an orange cosmetic bag in her hand. I seated myself at the opposite table. I'd often chosen this White Castle hamburger restaurant in the Bayside section of New York City to chill for two or three hours, eating lunch and writing stories. Though not always a quiet place to concentrate, nobody ever asked patrons to leave because they'd been there too long. Not me, and not even "Mildred" (as I had dubbed the lady opposite me) whom I'd never seen eating anything. I knew it wouldn't be long before she would begin her routine. For now, I would work without distraction on a story-in-progress.

I glanced up from my pad only now and then to find Mildred looking ahead at nothing in particular. Inevitably, she began her ritual. Mildred opened her orange cosmetic bag, removed a lipstick case and placed it on the table. She placed a second lipstick next to it. A third, fourth, fifth, until there was a row of nearly twenty lipsticks. She sat back, looked at them, then examined her face in a hand mirror for a full minute. One by one, Mildred placed each lipstick container back in the cosmetic bag. Only the mirror remained in her hand as she resumed staring straight ahead.

I thought it ironic that I was sitting there, trying to invent characters and stories, while this woman who sits at a table every Sunday afternoon (and maybe on other days too) surely had a complex story that nearly nobody knew or cared about. I had tried to get her attention on several previous occasions, but to no avail. I'd never seen her arrive or leave White Castle, or even get up to go to the ladies room.

It was time for me to get back to the story I was writing, but I first got on line to order five White Castle burgers and a drink. No, they're not full-size hamburgers. WC burgers are thin squares of chopped meat, cooked side by side on a grill that is covered in onions and oil. The bottoms of the little buns are placed on top of the grilling meat squares, and suck up the grease cooking out of the burger. Yes, it is definitely an acquired taste. Me, I acquired it as an eight-year-old in The Bronx.

My number was called ten minutes later, and I took my five WCs on two plates, and a soda, back to my table, nearly tripping over two small kids running past me. Mildred was at it again. She'd already lined up seven or eight lipsticks and continued until her cosmetic bag was empty. Once again, she stared at them for the usual time period, and opened her mirror.

"Hey, lady," said a ten-year-old girl standing in front of her table, "you're crazy."

Mildred showed no reaction, as though she neither heard nor saw the girl.

"You're nuts, lady."

I got up from my seat, walked to the girl, grabbed her arm, and pulled her fifteen feet away.

"You're ugly, and a very nasty kid," I told her. She started to cry, and then her mother came over.

"This man pulled me over here and said I was ugly," the girl said, sobbing.

The one-hundred-pound woman in front of me morphed into a rhinoceros.

"What kind of nasty excuse for a human being are you?" she asked, a finger waving in my face. "Saying something hurtful like that to a young girl—a *pretty* young girl. And keep your hands off her! I'm gonna call a cop. That's what I'm gonna do."

The girl stopped crying, and looked at me defiantly.

"Well, I think your daughter's behavior is ugly," I said, "and you should teach her better. She was taunting the lady sitting at that table next to the window, telling her that she's crazy. I thought that was uncalled for and downright mean. So I assisted your *pretty* daughter in removing herself from the area near the lady's table."

"What do you care about that old freak? Mind your own business!"

Stunned, I couldn't look at this woman. "Well," I began, turning to the kid, "I guess it's not entirely your fault." I did an about-face, and walked back to my table, manuscript, and WC burgers. Before I sat down, the girl's mother had rushed between my table and Mildred's.

"She's not eating anything. She shouldn't even be here."

The younger brat was shortly by her side.

"No, you're mistaken. Before your daughter created a scene with her obnoxious nastiness—clearly either a genetic factor or behavior learned from her mother—I was about to bring this lady the two White Castle burgers for which she gave me money to buy for her." I placed the plate with two WCs on Mildred's table. "Gosh, I just realized that I forgot to buy her a drink. Maybe you'd be kind enough to do that," I said with a smile.

Mama's body appeared to rise into combat posture, her expression hostile, nostrils flared.

"Let's go, Mom."

Finally, they were off.

As I eased back into my seat, I wondered if they would be back with the kid's father, uncle, and older male cousins, comprising the New York Giants' front line. At last, I took a first bite.

"Thank you," I heard a voice say.

I looked up.

"Thank you," Mildred said again.

Holy crap! She spoke—for the first time I'd ever heard. And she apparently knew what had gone on.

"You're welcome. You're very welcome."

She pointed to the two WC burgers on the paper plate in front of her. "For me?"

"Yes, they're for you."

She tilted her head and smiled.

"Would you like to have something to drink?"

Mildred looked at me questioningly.

"A cup of coffee or tea? Soda?" I asked.

She half turned her head, and waved her hand on the table. I took that to mean *no.*

I took a sip of my Diet Coke and then saw Mildred pointing at my table. She reached her arm higher and farther forward, pointer finger aimed at my papers, and raised her eyebrows.

"These papers? You're asking me about these papers?"

Mildred's red lips parted in another smile.

"Curious lady, aren't you? I'm a writer. These are manuscripts. They're stories I've written, or I'm writing now. I mean some are completed, but need fixing up, and others aren't finished yet." I paused and looked at her face. I now knew that she understood; at least in some way. "Or let's say that I write, but I'm actually not a writer. Not really. Not yet anyway. Nobody ever paid me to write anything, and nothing I've written is published anywhere," I said. I took a healthy bite into WC burger number one, cutting into the stingy thin slice of pickle, its taste mixing with onions, bread, and a skinny piece of meat. Loved it – and I needed the comfort it gave me after admitting that I wasn't a real writer.

Mildred looked at me for a few seconds, and again smiled. It was that pause—a pause to think and absorb, that made me realize that she was not only hearing, but also understanding all that I had said. And, all that the girl had said. She made a motion with her hand as though writing with an invisible pen, and nodded her head. I tilted my head toward her, and then returned to my work and WC burgers.

I'd witnessed painters in Paris, New Orleans, Greenwich Village, and at various outdoor fairs being watched by people as they performed their artistry on canvas. But I'd never known of a writer, performing his craft on a lined pad, to be a source of intense observation—not prior to Mildred's watching me. Though looking at my pad, I could raise my eyes and see that the contents of Mildred's cosmetic bag were not lined up on her table even once during the ensuing half hour. Perhaps she was not a fan of the WC burger meat, but I noticed her copying my action of biting off, and savoring, the grease-and-onion-moistened bun bottoms—an act fitting a culinary barbarian such as me, but not one I'd expect Mildred to mimic.

I'd not recalled previously being *on stage,* the subject of such focused attention. I had taken a couple of acting classes to assist in learning more about the art of characterization for writing, and to be around a group of people generally more extroverted than writers who are content to sit for hours staring at a pad. Incidentally, other than during improvisations, I was a terrible actor, so worried about my lines that I was robotic. Besides, I didn't feel like myself acting out memorized lines written by someone else. That's the exercise of acting – pretending to be someone else. Writing the lines—that feels more natural for me. I'd now begun to wonder what lines I would write for Mildred, but I didn't know her story. I could invent them in my mind, as I'd done in response to people I'd seen on a train, or in a restaurant or bar. But for Mildred there would be so little dialogue. Could it work? Hmm. Back to my manuscript.

Mildred's eyes were still fixed on me fifteen minutes later. I dropped my pen and she adjusted her stare.

I got it, I thought. She's an old-time movie star, going back to the days of Cary Grant. Always viewing her hair and makeup, checking to see that her lipsticks are all in place. The way she sits. Those elegant cheekbones, even at her age. She's stopped performing her eccentric actions and has focused on me because I'm a writer and she imagines I'm writing a screenplay to cast her in a comeback role. Her agent doesn't return her calls anymore because he's dead, and her mind lives in a prior time, always expecting an old friend to show up at White Castle. *Maybe that could work!*

"What's it about?" Mildred asked.

She startled me despite her voice being low. My mind had been dedicated to the stab at the story of fictitious Mildred while my eyes were directed squarely at her.

"This story?" I asked.

"Yes."

I wasn't used to anybody ever giving a crap about what I was writing back at that time. *Aha! See, she is a fallen movie star looking for a script.*

"Before I tell you about it, would you like another burger or two? Cup of coffee or other drink? I really don't mind getting it for you."

"Yes. A coffee and two burgers. Just the bottom of the buns would be fine. They're so good. Aren't they?"

"Of course. My pleasure." I turned around to head for the counter just in time as a huge grin burst across my face. *Another bottom-of-the-bun lover. Who'd have thought?*

I returned with two WCs and a coffee for Mildred, and two WCs for me to replace the two I had initially given her to shut up the kid's mother.

"Should I sit at your table while telling you about the story?"

Mildred looked down for a second. "I'd like that, but it might not be a good idea. We might be seen."

I didn't know how to respond to that remark.

"Even now, I could be seen talking to you. But it's still early."

"Still early for what?"

"For my son's driver."

"Oh?"

"He's my driver, too… and looks after me. Just don't tell him, or anybody else that I spoke to you … or ate anything. My table has to be clear in an hour."

Chills down my spine. She was serious. Was she real?

"The story," she said. "What's it about?"

"Two guys—the friendship between two guys, beginning back when they were both eight years old, living in the same building. On the surface, their lives looked very similar, but behind closed doors, their lives were not at all alike. As they grew older, they pursued totally different careers, and led equally different lives. But the one thing that remained a constant was their bond, and how they always reached back to each other when one fell down. That's what drives the story. Their friendship. Of course, the events are what make their individual traits, and the nature of their relationship, play out."

"I like it," Mildred said, "It's not about guy chases girl, guy gets girl, another girl steals guy, guy and girl rob a bank."

"There are girls in it," I said with a laugh. "And relationships, good and bad. Successes and failures."

"But real life," Mildred said. "Not only slick shtick."

Slick shtick? "Right. Though there are some Hollywood-style feel good scenes. I think readers like that. Well, I like it. And I write for myself as well as for readers. But yes, you summed it up."

Damn right I was writing for myself, and also hoped that readers would like it, too, of course. At the time, I was working fifty to sixty hours per week as Controller of Mankado Consumer Products, and those hours sure weren't spent pleasing myself. Sunday afternoons were my escape time to create a world in which characters played by my rules—much more fair and reasoned than the rest of the week.

Mildred was not only capable of hearing and speaking, she was clearly quite capable of understanding paragraph-length conversation, and of responding. Did she have an in-and-out problem?

"Would you want your story to be in a movie?" she asked.

"Sure, I would," amusing myself with the possible motive for her question—a supporting role. "But I think the time frame of the story might be too long. Twenty-seven years. It would probably be too hard to do without a lot of flashbacks, and I think a movie often gets scrambled up that way."

"You might be right," she said, taking a first bite of her new WCs. I notice you here often. Only Sundays, though," she added.

Geez, she really is aware, I thought. Did I say she was always looking at apparently nothing?

"Yes, that's right—only on Sundays. And you? How often do you come to White Castle?"

"Nearly every day."

"But you usually don't eat anything. I've never seen you eat anything before today," I stated.

"I'd have to order the food."

I looked at Mildred questioningly, even though I felt that I knew the answer.

"I would have to speak if I ordered food," she said.

"Yes, of course. And you never speak when you're here."

"I never speak anywhere. Haven't for two years. If it was known that I could speak, and *hear*, he'd be coercing me to do something I don't want to do."

"He?"

"My son."

"I see. That's why you don't want your son's driver to see you speaking to me or eating burgers."

"You'd be a good reporter."

"Well, why did you speak to me? After two years of speaking to nobody, why speak to me?"

"I was interested. I'd been watching and observing you for a while."

I had an internal belly laugh. Mildred had been observing *me*.

"And I was curious about you," she continued.

Curious about *me*.

"You took a chance, I said.

"I didn't think so. Remember? I can hear. How you reacted with that girl, and then her mother. You're not a person who would turn me in. I know."

"Why White Castle? Why not some other place?"

"I met Albert at a White Castle in The Bronx seventy years ago when White Castle burgers were not even ten cents," she said, eyes twinkling. "We courted for two years, got married in a nice catering hall, and honeymooned in Niagara Falls. It was so lovely. Albert and I came to White Castle to celebrate our wedding anniversary every year … until I lost him four years ago."

"That's a lovely story," I said in a low voice.

"Yes, it is. Thank you… I have a friend you'd like to meet. Write down this name—Ronald Harvey. He's the chief editor at MacMillan Publishing. You tell him that his old friend Millie asked that he see you, and read your manuscript when you think it's ready."

Millie?

"That would be a great introduction. Thank you very much," I said, reeling from the coincidence of her name and wondering a bit if she might be pulling my leg, or living in her own alternative universe. "Will that ruin things for you? Not speaking?"

"Don't worry about Ron. Just tell him you met Millie at White Castle. He'll get it."

"He knows you as Millie?"

"Yes. My name is actually Mildred."

Mildred, Mildred, Mildred, kept echoing in my head.

"And what's your name?" she asked.

"Mitchell. Pleased to meet you, Mildred. Would you mind if I ask you a question about your lipstick cases?"

"What lipstick cases?"

I looked at her, saying nothing.

"Gotcha there, didn't I?" she said, laughing for the first and only time.

"Yes, you did," I replied, laughing too.

"Sorry. I don't otherwise get a chance to do anything like that. The lipsticks provide me comfort, and concentration. Ends up that they're a good cover, too."

"Yes. If you want to cover something."

"You saw *One Flew Over the Cuckoo's Nest?* "

"Yeah. Like *Chief,* in the movie, you don't want to talk to anyone anymore—for some reason."

"That's right—except for you, if nobody's watching. Don't lose that name I gave you. Maybe some other time I'll be able to read pages of your manuscript. Now, I had better stop talking. He could come early."

Out came the lipsticks, and I returned to my work.

An hour later, a nicely dressed black man in his late fifties came into White Castle and walked directly to Mildred's table.

"Here you are, right where I left you, Mrs. H. Guess I knew you would be. It's just you and me, like old times. Really wish you'd say something to me, Mrs. H." he said with a sigh. "Well, I'm going to get myself a couple of burgers before I take you back. Some for you, too, in case you're hungry."

I pretended to be involved in my work while I was listening to this man, and watching Mildred after he walked to the counter to place his order. She didn't transgress from the image she displayed prior to our conversation.

He returned to Mildred a few minutes later with a tray of burgers, a coffee and a cold drink. She had begun lining up her lipsticks, so he didn't have a chance to decide whether or not to sit at her table. He placed two W/Cs and a coffee on her table, and sat down at the one to my right. Our eyes met and we both nodded.

"Mind if I borrow your newspaper?" he asked.

"Not at all," I said, handing him the main section of the *New York Times*. "I'm finished with it, and just working on stuff I'm writing. You can keep it."

"Thanks. Stuff you're writing? For business, or like as an author?"

"As I was telling, uh, someone last night, I'm trying to become a writer. Yeah, I am a writer, but I'm the only person who knows that I am."

He laughed out loud. "You should be a comic. I'm Roy. What's your name, sir?"

"Mitchell. Nice to meet you."

"And likewise. Too bad the lady at the next table wasn't a friend of yours two years ago."

"The lady you were talking to before?"

"Yes. Mrs. H. Wonderful woman. So nice, and so dynamic. She didn't always spend her days looking over the lipsticks in her bag."

"No?"

"Ah-ah. She's Mildred Hendricks."

"*The Mildred Hendricks?* The Pulitzer Prize-winning author, Mildred Hendricks?" I asked, tipping over the remainder of my drink into my tray.

"That Mildred Hendricks—the author of fifteen number one best-selling novels. Mildred Hendricks, wife of Albert Hendricks, winner of seven Emmy awards for screenplay writing. I always called her Mrs. H, out of respect, but she probably wouldn't have cared if I called her Millie, like her husband did."

"I overheard you speaking very warmly to her, even though she doesn't seem to comprehend. Sorry, writers always have their ears tuned in to the people around them, even when their eyes are on the pad in front of them."

Roy gave me a short grin and a nod. "She's a wonderful lady. I'll stay with her as long she needs me. Except Wednesday nights—poker night with my high school buddies every week for the past thirty years."

"Are you ahead or behind over those years?" I asked Roy.

"Depends how you look at it. We just keep a running tab, nobody pays up, and we argue about the accuracy of the totals," he said, his hand slapping the table as he laughed.

"Who, besides you, looks out for your Mrs. H?"

"Her son, Martin, is legally responsible. He usually comes over on my night off. I wish he made other arrangements. He's been really ticked-off at Mrs. H for a while because she didn't do something he wanted her to do. So I'm always uncomfortable with his attitude when he's around her."

"How long has that been going on?"

"Oh, a bit longer than a couple of years—not long before Mrs. H stopped speaking, or hearing, or writing."

"He's ticked at her even now, though she can't speak or hear?"

"Does anybody in your family have lots of money? Lots and lots of money?"

"No, I'm sorry to say."

"Don't be so sorry. It can be a sorrow."

"I'd risk it."

Roy chuckled."I didn't mean it was all negative, especially if you made the money. But it can tear relatives apart."

"Like brothers and sisters," I said.

Roy nodded.

"Or even mothers and sons," I added.

"You bet," he said, before taking a bite of a WC burger.

"So that's why Junior is mad at Mildred? She hasn't turned over her money to him, and he has to wait till she dies? How does she communicate with you?" I asked.

"A look, smile, touch. She can't read."

"She can't? She can't read?"

"No. Even though she can see, she can't focus to read. Most of the time she stares blankly at nothing in particular, or lines up the lipsticks in her bag on a table."

"I've noticed. So she probably really couldn't update her will or any other document, could she?"

"Nope," Roy agreed, reaching for his soda. "How's that for the beginnings of a story for you to write?"

"Beginning and middle."

We chatted on about the merits of the latest trade made by the Yankees, and the role of religious institutions in helping poor people, until it had become past time for him to head home with Mildred.

Roy assisted Mildred to her feet, and said good-bye to me. As they turned to the door, I caught a glance from Mildred and a barely perceptible smile.

* * *

I followed up on Mildred's suggestion that I contact Ronald Harvey at MacMillan Publishing—for more than one reason. Using Mildred's name got me an appointment for a meeting remarkably soon. I brought my manuscript-in-process, as well as a story outline and an inquiry letter.

"So, you're a friend of Millie Hendricks. How do you know her?"

"From White Castle."

Harvey let out a big laugh. "I know that she and her husband celebrated their wedding anniversaries at a White Castle. Did you meet her with Albert? How long have you known her?"

"Well, I've noticed her for months," I said, "but we actually met only last week."

He gave me a questioning look. "I've been told that she can't speak—or hear. You come here saying that she referred you, and that you met her *last week*."

"If you asked other people around her, you'd have been told that she also can't read or write. Well, I can tell you she can speak, hear, read, *and* write. I wouldn't tell you this if she hadn't told me it was okay to trust you. I raised that with her when she suggested that I contact you, using her name. I said to her 'but you're not supposed to be able to speak or hear.' She said not to worry about that with you."

Ronald Harvey leaned back in his chair and studied my face.

"She liked that I didn't have any *boy chase girl, boy catches girl schtick,* in my story."

"That's what she said?" Harvey asked with an inquisitive smile.

"Yeah."

"Hmm. The phrasing sounds like her alright. But still, not much motive for her to refer you."

"I guess she was grateful to me."

"For?"

"I bought her a few White Castle burgers and coffee because she couldn't show herself as capable of getting up from the table and ordering."

"Because she supposedly can't speak or hear? It's her ruse. Is that what you're implying?"

"Yes."

"Then why do you know the truth? Why did she trust you to speak with?" Harvey leaned forward, elbows on his desk.

I described the incident with the ten-year-old girl and her mother, and Mildred's twenty-lipstick routine.

"Tell me, did Millie confide in you the reason why she's been conducting this *hear no evil, speak no evil routine?"*

"No. I was stunned when I heard her speak to me the first time, and trust me with that. And I was also very surprised that she said it was okay if you knew. As for the *motive* for her charade, I have no idea," I made believe. Jarred loose by the information I'd brought to him, Ron Harvey shared stories about the Hendricks family. Ron Harvey had been both professionally and personally close to Mildred Hendricks for decades. Millie complained that her son Richard was an extravagant spender, though a not very successful movie producer. Richard was divorced from Karla, his wife of nineteen years, to whom he had paid a handsome amount of alimony until her death two years earlier.

Mildred and her husband Albert had combined eighty percent of both their accumulated funds into a fifty-million-dollar trust fund which was divided into two equal parts. The annual income of Fund

A, plus half a million dollars, was available for the living expenses of the married couple or surviving spouse. Fund B could be spent, up to four million dollars per year, to finance deserving projects of worthy independent film or theater artists. In his own will, Albert Hendricks bequeathed two million dollars of his assets, outside the trust, to Richard, and the remainder to Mildred.

"Nobody knows the contents of Millie's will," Harvey told me, "much to Richard's consternation. And he's perpetually on the brink of being broke."

"Even after his father left him two million bucks?"

"That's right. He's a man who lives with the sense that money is obtained to be spent. Always irritated Millie. She's got the big house, and Roy, but otherwise she's lived modestly, using much of her money for charitable purposes."

I kept listening.

"Roy's salary is funded for life from a sub trust of the master trust fund. Albert and Millie wanted to be sure that he was okay, and not left to Richard's whims if they were incapable as she's pretending to be now. She must be doing quite an acting job to put all this over on Roy."

"Now that Richard is not paying alimony since his ex-wife died, he should have been having less trouble with money. How old was she?"

"Late forties. She was murdered."

"Murdered?"

"Yeah. A couple years ago. I was shocked when I heard about it on the news. I remember it clearly because the news was right after *Dancing With The Stars.* I always watch that show with my wife—one of her favorites. And a few minutes after the show ended, one of the news stories was the murder of Denise Hendricks, former wife of the son of Mildred Hendricks."

"Wow. Did they find the killer?"

"Not even any leads. Of course Richard was a suspect."

"Yeah ... but?"

"He was with Millie that night."

After more inside stories about Millie and the Hendricks family, Ronald Harvey and I actually did discuss the synopsis and outline of my manuscript that day. He also was good enough to spend much time explaining how the publishing industry works, as well as the publishing process.

* * *

I arrived at White Castle mid-afternoon, the following Sunday, well before Roy would arrive to pick her up. Sure enough, she was at the usual table, her back against the wall, cosmetic bag in front of her. I dropped my jacket and writing pad on the opposite table, laying my claim to it, and went to the counter to order. *Ten White Castle burgers on four plates, one cup of coffee, and a Diet Coke without ice, please.*

I placed five WCs and a coffee on Mildred's table before sitting down at mine. She looked up at me with a smile on her face.

"Thank you. That's so kind."

"You're welcome. Not a big deal. How are you?"

"Good. How's your story going?"

"Okay, but I've been working on something else. Another story, you might say. I met with your friend, Ronald Harvey."

"He saw you already?"

"When your name is dropped, people jump."

A hearty laugh displayed her amusement.

"He was very nice. And he was surprised that you presently speak and hear. We talked about my work ..."

"And about me," she said.

"Well, yes, of course. You're our common denominator. He told me about the trust fund and foundation you and your husband set up. And that the terms of your will are a secret."

Mildred didn't say anything. She took a sip of coffee and a bite of a WC.

"You're a mysterious lady. He also told me that your son had been pressing you to sign something. Since he's on shaky financial ground—little cash, not a very successful career, and previously had big alimony payments—we assumed that it was a version of a will he had drafted and that he wanted you to sign."

"Ron Harvey has a big mouth. What a gossip."

"You said it was okay for me to tell him that you could speak and hear, essentially telling him that you're faking it. I guess he assumed that it was okay to tell me stuff. I'm not so certain now that a will is the only thing your son wanted you to sign."

"Now you're writing a new mystery?"

"Roy mentioned to me that he has a steady poker game every Wednesday evening. Had it for the past thirty years."

"Are we playing trivia?" she asked, biting into the oily beef juice and onions stuck to the bottom of a WC bun.

"Do you want more ketchup for your burgers?" I asked.

"No, they're fine."

"Ron mentioned to me that your former daughter-in-law is deceased. And that you were close to her and maintained contact after the divorce."

"*We* didn't get divorced. Are you writing a social column?"

"She was a homicide victim. I did some research on the Internet, and learned that she was killed near her home in New Jersey at around nine o'clock in the evening."

Mildred did not add anything.

"Ron recalled hearing about it on TV, not long after *Dancing With The Stars* ended. Funny how people make connections like that in their mind."

"You've been writing a script for a *James Bond* movie. Go on."

"*Dancing With The Stars* is aired on Wednesdays."

"You have a TV Guide."

"Same day as Roy's poker game."

"Chance out of seven."

"Point is that Roy wasn't home."

"Are you accusing Roy of murder?"

"No, no."

"Articles in the newspapers online stated that the ex-husband of the deceased claimed an alibi: he spent the evening visiting his mother at her home close to the Queens/Nassau County, Long Island border. Now, it so happens that Roy could not contradict that because, as the ex-husband of the deceased who previously lived in the home for years knew, Roy has a poker game every Wednesday night."

Mildred grabbed her cosmetic bag and began taking out lipsticks and lining them up on the table.

"I called your home this past Wednesday evening, when I knew that Roy would be out and your son would answer. I told him that I was the manager of the security film company that installed four film systems in secret locations, at your husband's request, nearly five years ago, focused from different angles at the two entrances of the home. I also told him that payment for service was made in advance for five years upon installation as part of the initial deal, and that additional payment needed to be received for filming to continue—though all past recorded film would be maintained.

"He wanted to know the secret locations of the cameras, and I told him that I could reveal that information only to Mr. Albert Hendricks, or Mrs. Mildred Hendricks, or the police. Then he said all the past film should now be destroyed, and I told him that he wasn't authorized for that either. He had a fit. Very nervous and irate."

She continued taking lipsticks out of the cosmetic bag until all twenty were lined up, side by side.

"I don't think he was with you at your house the Wednesday evening that his ex-wife was killed—and Roy, as was his known custom, was conveniently not home. And if there really were secret security films still available from that night, they would show that Richard never arrived at your home. That's why he panicked when I told him my made-up story."

"This coffee is a little bitter."

"That night was twenty-six months ago. Ron Harvey and Roy both told me that your supposed disabilities began two years ago. I think there's something more than a will that your son was pressing you to sign."

Mildred looked right at my face.

"I've come to believe that it was an affidavit attesting that he was with you that night—when his ex-wife was killed—and you couldn't do it. You couldn't tell the police the truth, and you couldn't bring yourself to tell the lie and cover up the murder of your daughter-in-law. So you presented yourself as unable to do either."

Mildred waved her hand, and slammed down all the lipsticks.

"What would *you do*?" she asked.

"If I were you?"

"Yes."

"Maybe something achieving a similar result. And if you were *me*? What would *you* do?"

"If I were *you*," she said, "I'd go to the police. Don't forget that you figured it out. I didn't tell you!"

* * *

Both the trial and sentencing of Richard Hendricks made front-page headlines in the *New York Times* Metro section. Mildred Hendricks's next novel, *Speak No Evil,* was #1 on the *New York Times* Best Sellers list for twenty-four weeks.

NOT NEAR HALIFAX

It was a coincidence of fate that she chose me to tell her story. I was sitting in Gretzky's Sports Bar in Toronto, my mind tuned out from the hockey game on the big television screens surrounding the place. I estimated her age to be thirty-five, but couldn't tell for sure because she was so gaunt.

"When are you going back to New York?" the bartender asked me.

"Day after tomorrow."

"Add that to my tab," she said to him, before turning to me. "Do you know any famous people in New York?"

"No. No, I don't," I replied, surprised at the question.

I later learned that she liked knowing famous people, or people who knew famous people. Tiara once met an assistant film director who had just finished working with Al Pacino. She also met a famous casting director whose name she had not heard before. Tiara's real name was Diane, but she liked being called Tiara.

"Do you think you can help me get my story told?"

"I don't think so."

"But you're from New York. You must know people. Publishers, TV producers. I'd like to go on *The Johnny Carson Show* and tell my story. Or give it to a television producer. I bet you know somebody."

Weird as it sounded, she seemed serious.

"I once took an acting class," I said, suppressing a smirk. "But I didn't meet any famous people. The guy who taught the class once understudied Jason Robards on Broadway, but that was his main claim to fame."

"Are you an actor?"

"Me? No."

"Why did you take an acting class?"

There was a legitimate question. "To help my writing and to mix with people with similar interests."

"Are you a writer?"

"Kind of."

"Have you published famous books?"

"I'm a fledgling writer. Nothing's been published," I said, and took a sip of Diet Coke.

"So what do you do for a living?"

"I'm the corporate controller of Mankado Consumer Products."

"I never heard of that company. Is it big?"

"It's very big, and you've heard of our products," I defensively added. "Our sales are over ten billion dollars per year." I turned and fiddled with the change left in front of me by the bartender.

"Ten billion? That's a lot," she said, her voice rising to compete with a roar from bar patrons. The TVs on the walls had shown the Toronto Maple Leafs scoring a goal. "What do you do at this Mankado place?"

This woman really is nosy, I thought. "Different things relating to handling the money."

"That must be exciting."

"It's okay. It was more exciting at the beginning. Not so much now." I leaned back and exhaled. She had struck a nerve.

"Why?"

"Just isn't. Very disconnecting. Emotionally."

"Are you a good writer?"

"I like to think so." The question mattered more to me than the fame of Mankado Products.

"What do you write about?"

"People. Basically about people and what makes them tick," I said, turning to face her directly.

"Maybe you could write my story."

"I don't do biographies. I write fiction." I knew I had put my foot in it.

"You can try it."

"I don't know your story and I'm not a biographer."

"It's very important to me to tell my story before I die. You might be my chance. I'm sick. I have just six months to live … maybe less."

"I'm sorry to hear that. It's definitely incurable?"

She nodded her head and looked down at the floor.

Tiara told me that she grew up in Nova Scotia in a fishing village not near Halifax. The only place I knew of in Nova Scotia was Halifax, so when she told me that where she grew up was *not near Halifax*, I didn't really know where she grew up.

Tiara's father had left her and her mother when she was five years old, fleeing the day in, day out grind of life on the boats—nothing to see but water each day. The nets, the boats, and the harshness of the days broken only by the incessant tales of success and danger on the sea.

Her mother, Helen, worked low-paying jobs, doing the best she could, until she started hearing sounds that nobody else could hear, and speaking to guests at their home that nobody else saw or heard. Mother and daughter moved into Grandma Kate's little shack in the fishing village somewhere not near Halifax.

A stern and salty old woman, Grandma helped care for Tiara. But when Tiara was fourteen, her grandmother died and it was up to her to care for Helen. She did it out of duty and frequently let that be known, just as Grandma Kate had let her feelings be known about unwelcome burdens of life. One night, Helen went over the side of a cliff, fleeing a violent argument with one of her illusory friends.

Six months after Helen's death, Diane attended her high school graduation ceremony by herself, and went directly from it to her job at the general store. She called her father later that evening for the first time in eight months, and told him all about the graduation ceremony and the diploma with her name engraved on it. He told her that was very good and that he would send her a gift.

Tiara and I were sitting alone at a table at this point in her story.

"Who did you live with after your mother was no longer around?"

"Myself. I didn't want anyone to take care of me. I was already taking care of myself— and my mother before she jumped off a cliff."

"Your drink is almost finished," I pointed out.

"Thanks. I'll stay sober for the story."

Diane worked at her jobs for the next six months and, freed of school, she began spending time attracting the local fisherboys, doing what was needed to get their attention. She took up with Gilman who promised a home, and together they dreamed of a lovely white picket fence and a fireplace. They saved for it together until Gilman got Lucille Farrington pregnant.

It wasn't long before Diane, like her father, felt worn down by the harshness of each day even though she wasn't out on the sea. She'd heard stories of the big Canadian cities—Toronto and Montreal— where the lights were bright and anything could happen. Diane withdrew the small sum she'd saved for the house and headed for Toronto to become Tiara and make her mark.

I didn't want to interrupt this story, but my bladder was insisting on an intermission. I excused myself, headed around the corner toward the men's room, passing the giant video screen. The men's room was unoccupied and I was alone with my thoughts. *I've just met this woman and she's pouring out her life to me, wanting me to write her biography.*

I'm not used to writing about an actual person. I always thought it was, on one hand, a cousin to gossiping, and on the other hand, an endeavor that requires a great degree of accuracy. And I really never wanted to write with exactness, tied down to facts. It's too tedious, too demanding, and would frustrate my desire to let my mind wander free wherever it will take me. Worst of all, what I say might be proven wrong.

Tiara intrigued me. Or I was intrigued by her own intrigue with her story. I grew up in a standard way. A father, mother, sister, and brother in a standard kind of apartment. I didn't go to the bright lights of Toronto after I graduated high school. I went to college to obtain a degree in business administration so that I could spend my days ministering to the business details of rich people and corporations. And that is exactly what I did until the need became great for my mind to escape and wander from place to place. I wondered if that was what

Tiara's mother had done, and warned myself to be careful not to get on the page with my characters and quarrel with them.

But there is never any need for me to quarrel with my characters because, as their creator, I'm in charge. And maybe that, too, was causing me to feel off balance in our discussion. Right then, Tiara was in charge and I was her tool. Her manner surely was compelling. And the story of her childhood made me root for the underdog. But, then again, she did say that she was going to die soon. So how the game ends is already known.

There was a fresh drink at my spot when I returned to the table. Having tired of Diet Cokes an hour earlier, I had switched to light beers. My appetite was stimulated from the smell of grilled beef and I ordered burgers for us both before Tiara continued with her story.

When she arrived in Toronto, she had a few hundred dollars in her pocket, and that didn't go far. Her first job was at Mario's Bar and Grill where she met up with Sarah, also a Nova Scotia fugitive, who had arrived in town three years earlier and introduced the girl who was then Diane to life in the fast lane, helping establish her new identity as Tiara. *A new identity*. The thought fascinated me.

"Sarah took me to nightclubs and introduced me around. I had no money for that, but she taught me how to have guys pay for all my drinks and even my admission. Grass was free. Everything was free. We had a wild time," she said, wistful but with a tinge of regret. With a laugh, she told me that "one time, me and Sarah went off for a long weekend with nine guys. I'm not bragging, but I always got the extra fifth guy. Just kidding. Did you ever try that scene?"

"No, I haven't."

"You should. Once, anyway."

"Maybe someday."

"Neil—the guy I lived with when I was in Toronto for a year— liked that. He was a rich guy. Not famous. Not famous at all. But he had lots of money. And lots of money was what I needed when I got out of the hospital. I had what was described as an accident."

"What kind of accident?"

"The kind where you get hurt bad."

"How bad?"

"Fractured pelvis, broken leg, dislocated shoulder, and a concussion. Bad enough, aay?

"Yes," I agreed. "How'd it happen?"

"We'll get to that another time … if you're still interested. But, anyway, you should try it. The *scene*. The *multiples scene.*"

"Do you like it?"

"I used to love it. The attention. The power. I had the power and I could direct. Don't do it anymore, though."

I was quiet.

"You want to know what the accident was about. You think it had something to do with the *scene*. It didn't. It was something else. We'll get to it."

"What happened to Sarah? Are you and she still friends?"

"No. She died five years ago. Drug overdose. We were no longer close friends."

"How come?"

"Competition. Women kind of competition. I sometimes beat her out for the attentions of a man. Perhaps she sometimes beat me. But it became more of a strain on our friendship when I moved in with Jean-Paul Artiste. His real name was Henri Rembarde. He was a painter, very much in the image of the struggling young artist: intense, interesting, charming, and starving. So Sarah and I nicknamed him Jean-Paul Artiste."

"How did you live if he was starving? You had no money."

"I wasn't poor anymore. I learned how to make money. Lots of money sometimes. Sarah had taught me. And I was able to care for Henri's financial needs."

"That was a turnaround."

"Yes, it was. But he took care of my spiritual needs."

"And…?"

"Yes, yes. All my needs," she laughed.

"No *multiples scenes*?" I dared to kid.

"No. Not with Henri. You are curious about the *scene* I see," she kidded back.

I didn't respond.

"Henri was his own scene. Poor boy. Too bad he couldn't sell his paintings. He tried so hard. He really did. I attempted to help him, too, going from gallery to gallery."

"But you didn't really need the money."

"The money couldn't feed his ego. His ego got lower and lower, and he became resentful of me for supporting him. Then he started asking more and more questions about how I made so much money. The more support I gave him, the more enraged he became. Finally, he went back to Quebec. Brokenhearted."

"Did you ever hear from him again?"

"Sporadically, for a year."

"And then you lost contact?"

"No. And then he killed himself. A bullet to his head."

I felt myself wince and remained silent for several seconds. "I'm sorry."

Tiara nodded. "I too am sorry. Poor Henri."

"You loved him."

"Yes."

"What did you do after Henri went back to Quebec? You were no longer friends with Sarah, and now he was gone."

"I did nothing much. I had some new friends, but most of them were Henri's friends. After he was dead, I withdrew from them. Or they withdrew from me. The thought was that I had let him down."

"Their thought or your own?"

"I thought it was their thought. Or I feared it was. But partly it was my own."

"So what did you do?"

"I continued with my work. The people I met at work became my social support and my sources of interest."

"What was your work?"

She smiled. "Sarah had taught me to make lots of money."

"I see."

"One of my friends from work was a Brazilian business hotshot. He took me to Brazil where I stayed with him."

"What did you do in Brazil?"

"I entertained Raoul. My friend. And he entertained me. Raoul liked to show off, taking me around to all his business holdings and homes. He liked to show me off to his friends and acquaintances in the evenings. I was younger ... and not sick. I could be shown off back then. And Raoul took care of all my needs."

"All your needs?"

"Nearly all."

"And you took care of ..."

"Of course. Yes, I took care of Raoul's needs. That was the arrangement. And one of his needs was to take care of my needs. And if I had any need that he could not satisfy, he would see to it that someone else satisfied it."

"He was devoted to you."

"Raoul was devoted to his devotion."

"How long were you in Brazil with Raoul?"

"For eight months."

"What ended it?"

"Raoul was assassinated."

"Oh." I was beginning to feel uneasy. Her mother went over the side of a cliff. Sarah overdosed on drugs. Henri committed suicide. And then, Raoul. "Who assassinated him?"

"Enemies. I'm told that business is very corrupt. And business in Brazil is extra corrupt."

"Was Raoul corrupt?"

"Of course."

"What did you do after his death?"

"I was very broken up."

"You loved him?"

"No. Not really. I was dependent on him. I'd become dependent on him to provide a lifestyle that I couldn't replace even if I were working. I felt threatened." She paused. "You think it was callous."

"I didn't say anything."

"Your face speaks."

"Oh."

"I cared for Raoul. One does care for someone who cares for them. But I was not in love with him."

"Did you resent him?"

"Maybe. But my reaction to his death … it was not mournful … it was fright. What would become of *me?*"

"You could have gone back to Canada to work."

"And I did. You are wondering—"

"Am I?"

"Yes. Is your pen is as expressive as your face?"

"I don't know."

"I believe you don't."

She told me that after she returned to Toronto and her work, she met Chad—a nice guy, recently separated from his wife, Victoria. He had a ten-year-old daughter, MaryAnn. Tiara often accompanied Chad on his Sunday visits with her. Trips to the zoo. Rides in the country. Tiara canceled her work when MaryAnn was sick to in order to stay with her if both Chad and Victoria could not, and bought MaryAnn a beautiful bracelet when she graduated from grade school.

Chad was a fireman and loved his work, but the money didn't go far enough to support two households and also save for the home he wanted to buy for himself and Tiara. He would not accept the financial help she offered. Tiara's devotion to MaryAnn became a source of contention with Victoria, who had become fearful that now that Tiara had her man, she would also take her daughter. There were many emotional fights between the two women.

MaryAnn stayed with her Grandma one night. Chad was shot to death in his car that evening. Tiara cried for weeks. She frequently called MaryAnn until Victoria took her off to Vancouver and assumed a new identity for both of them. Tiara had been unable to locate MaryAnn ever since.

It occurred to me that Tiara had done everything. Her relationship with men had touched all bases. The puppy love with Gilman. Frolicking sex with anonymous men. Infatuation for the starving, intense young artist. The pragmatic relationship with the wealthy Brazilian. And finally, loving affection for Chad and his child. She'd had so many lives.

We continued to meet in bars for several nights. One night, I sensed a sadness in her. Not the sadness of a woman with a limited time to live. I tried to reach out to her.

"You never say anything about yourself," she said to me.

"This is about your story. Your life."

"Well, now you're part of it. And I only know that you handle money for a very big, but not famous, company and that you like to write. Fiction. Not biographies. You never say anything about your life."

"Oh … I didn't think … I don't know."

"Didn't think it mattered?"

"Something like that. And there's not much to say."

"How can there be not much to say?" How old are you?"

"Forty-five."

"Do you like your job? No. You did say it was … emotionally disconnecting. That's what you said."

"And it is," I responded, surprised that she remembered what I had said. "Maybe that's why I don't talk about it."

"Do you have a family?"

"My parents, a brother, and a sister."

"Ever married?"

"Briefly. No kids."

"Any girlfriend in your life?"

"Not right now."

"Why do you stay in your job? It's disconnecting."

"The money, for now. I help my parents. They're elderly and my father's pension isn't much. I help my sister. She's divorced and her husband doesn't pay the alimony, or the child support. Her daughter's in college."

"What does your sister do?"

"She works part-time as a bookkeeper in a doctor's office."

"I thought you said you weren't into the multiples scene."

"What?"

"Nothing. I spoke nonsense. None of the things you've written have been published?"

"No, not yet."

"If you have any stories with you in Toronto, I'd like to read them."

"I have a few. I'll bring them tomorrow."

"I'll look forward to it."

"Why do you want to see them?"

"Because I'd like to. Why would I not?"

Her spirits lifted and we briefly went on with her story before she switched gears, telling me the gossip about each of the regulars in the bar. I told her about the people in my company and their personal quirks, and about how business was conducted.

"I thought big corporations were corrupt, not stupid," she said, laughing.

I brought copies of six short stories my last night in Toronto and, sitting at a corner table, we talked more about her life, and TV shows, over hamburgers and beer. Tiara gave me her number so I could contact her upon my return for business the following month.

* * *

Back in New York, I often thought about Tiara and her life. I didn't know the nature of her earlier life accident or her present illness. It seemed curious that she wanted to know about me—not just name, rank, and serial number. And it seemed even more curious that I didn't know what to tell her.

I worked at a job. Had a good career. Made money. Had elderly parents, a divorced sister, and a brother. I had never been to Brazil, or even to Nova Scotia. Nor had I smoked grass and gotten other people to pay for everything. I'd never loved a struggling artist or another person's child. And I'd never participated in the multiples scene. Nine guys and two girls—I could only imagine. She read my face. Tiara was right when she noticed a reaction. I was surprised that she observed me enough to read my feelings. I was not aware of that ever happening before. And she wanted to read my stories.

Despite many late nights at the office the following month, I continued working on a play I'd previously started, but frequently jumped off to write notes about Tiara's life. After a while, I realized that I didn't need notes. Her story was burned into my consciousness.

* * *

I called Tiara when I returned to Toronto, and she suggested that we meet at the Idler's Pub rather than Gretzky's Bar.

Tiara was already seated at a table for two and waved to me as soon as I came through the door. She looked a little more gaunt, but still lovely.

"Hi," I said, taking her hand. I was conscious of the fact that it was the first time I'd touched her. Not knowing what her terminal illness was, I'd been a bit queasy about physical contact. I came to the conclusion that it was not contagious by casual contact, or else she would have told me.

"Sit down."

"New location."

"I thought you'd like it. Lots of writers, artists, and other creative people hang out here. I figured you'd fit in well."

"Don't know about that, but it can be an interesting experience."

"Read your stories. They were terrific. Blew me away."

"Really?"

"Where did you ever get the material?"

"I don't know. It's from when I let it go in here," I said, touching my head, "and float away," gesturing with my hand.

"Well, now I know where you go when you're not disconnected, because it's all really very connected—in a disconnected way," she laughed.

"Thank you. I think."

"They really should be published. I'm so pleased. They're so artistic, yet so down to earth."

"You make me blush. And how have you been?"

"Oh, couldn't be better ..." her voice trailing off, and her eyes briefly looking down at the table. Instantly, I regretted the question.

She'd been feeling ill for several days. Her doctors had started her on an experimental medication with the hope of slowing down the progression of her symptoms. Upon closer view, I could see that she looked washed out. I didn't say anything and, conscious that my face speaks, wondered if she saw my observation.

Tiara pointed out several writers and artists and called two of them over to our table. We chatted for a while. I later asked her how she knew them.

"They've achieved a degree of success, and they have a bit of money," Tiara said with a soft, brief grin.

She'd been trying again to locate MaryAnn, but had no leads. It had been five years, and she yearned to see her. Fearful that she would never see her again, she had begun writing a series of letters to MaryAnn and hoped that someday the collection would find its way to her.

Tiara hadn't loved any other man after Chad was killed. Though she had cared for several, she had had her last love. A year after Chad's death, Tiara started a business, employing young girls who were on their own and having a tough time of it. She taught them how to make money, though not how to get drinks and grass for free. And she looked over them for one year; one year was the individual limit.

Each girl was required to enroll in school at the time Tiara employed her, and had to prove to Tiara each month that she was saving enough money to finish school. She never initiated contact with any of her girls after their year was up, but many of them called or wrote to her from time to time. Jennifer had become a bookkeeper, Monique was attending medical school, and Robin had become a chemist. Claudine met Bernard while working for Tiara, of all places, and was a third-grade teacher and the mother of a two-year-old girl. And so on. Tiara's illness was not known of by any of her former girls.

Tiara suggested that our next discussion be at her apartment. I thought about it and she noticed my hesitation.

"It will be a home-cooked meal," she said. "I'm a very good cook."

"Okay, you're on."

We paid the restaurant bill, splitting it down the middle as she insisted.

I didn't know what to bring to her home. Liquor? I thought not. Flowers? Not appropriate. Something decorative for her apartment? I didn't know what would fit in. And would she think it silly? She wouldn't have it too long.

I stopped on my way and chose a box of gourmet chocolates. I questioned my prudence going there. I was always very prudent, and here I was going to the apartment of a dying woman that I'd met in a bar. A woman who had a number of people in her life die in bizarre and mysterious ways. It was not prudent. But I went.

* * *

Her building was in a decent part of town. It had twelve floors, and her apartment was on the top. Her voice on the intercom told me to not take the main elevator. Instead, I was to ride the back elevator all the way up. It was waiting for me.

The only button was for the twelfth floor. I pressed it and the elevator rose very slowly up the shaft. I didn't actually time it, but I guessed it took a full minute. The elevator door opened and I stood five paces before the only apartment door on the floor. Tiara opened it, held out her hand, and ushered me in.

She took my coat and hung it in the closet near the doorway. I handed her the chocolates.

"Thank you. That wasn't necessary."

I didn't respond.

"But thoughtful. Can I offer you a drink?"

"Okay."

"Diet Coke with no ice? Or would you prefer something else?"

"That's fine," I said, while I was thinking how ill she looked. Yet a spark of radiance showed through.

"I hope you like roast duck. It's a special recipe I got from a friend. I also made a vegetarian dish. I won't tell you what it is. It's a hodge-podge surprise."

"I like hodgepodge."

"Great," she said with a laugh. "Come, have a seat," she offered, leading me to the living room.

My eyes took a tour. The living room and dining room were tastefully furnished; there was a lot of artwork on the living room walls and many books on the shelves. I was surprised. I didn't know why, but I didn't expect to see that. There was a hallway to the side of the kitchen that led to a row of closed doors. Six or seven doors. I couldn't tell precisely on first glance. I wondered what was behind them.

"You have a very nice place."

"Thank you. You're wondering about all those other rooms. I'll show you later."

"You look very nice, too."

"I look sickly. But thank you ... I have not been well. The illness is progressing."

We chitchatted for a while and then Tiara retreated to one of the rooms and was gone for several minutes. She returned with a box full of photographs, and we looked through many of them. One was a picture of Tiara a few months after migrating to Toronto from Nova Scotia.

"I was really pretty then," she said.

I nodded in agreement. Actually, despite the effects of her illness, I could still see her very attractive features, but I didn't say it, anticipating that she would wave it off.

I saw photos of Jean-Paul Artiste, and of Sarah. There were also pictures of Raoul and Tiara in Brazil. She looked very beautiful, and I told her that. She didn't respond. Then pictures of Chad, and of Tiara's mother. I started having an eerie feeling as though I were passing through a cemetery.

We came to a few photographs of Tiara and Sarah and a bunch of guys outside a country cabin. I picked up a photo from the bottom of the pile. It was a black and white of a man standing by the sea; his face was cut out. I was startled. She took it from my hand and put it aside.

"That's my father," she said. "More about him another time." There was an obvious edge in her voice.

We went through a group of more recent photos. Some were of her girls. She didn't tell me their names. At least not their real names, explaining that the real names were not relevant to anyone but her, and that they'd all gone on with their lives. There weren't any pictures of other friends because they were all male business friends and, as should be understood, pictures would not be a good idea. However, we spoke of her fondness for them. She was especially fond of "Eric," a burly veteran police captain who stayed on the job long past his own wishes in order to financially help his youngest daughter and her kids.

"It's time for dinner," she announced, and directed me to the first door in the hallway to wash up. That was my chance to count the doors. There were seven, and I wondered about them. We talked throughout dinner. The goose was delicious, and so was the vegetarian dish. Once again, I was surprised. I thought she knew that, and took delight in it.

"You're wondering about what's behind the doors, aren't you?" she asked after clearing the dessert dishes from the table.

I responded only with a half smile.

"Would you like to see?"

"Okay."

"Only if you want to. You don't have to."

"I want to," I said, standing up from my chair.

Tiara stood and led me to the first door on the left, opened it, and nudged me inside. I jumped. There was a nude torso in the middle of the bed, and skeletons standing at the corner. Shocked, I drew back.

"It's not real," she said. "I should have told you before you were inside."

It was a woman's torso. Very pale, but very voluptuous. The lips were a dark color.

"You can touch it," she said.

I hesitated. She gave me time. I moved forward and touched; it felt like flesh.

"It's very expensive," she said. "Some people really like her. Would you like to mount her? It's cleaned after each use."

I shook my head.

"That's okay. "I don't care for it either. Even if it had a penis. Come, we can leave this room."

We went to door number two. I flinched as she opened it. But there was no reason, other than the startling effect of the mirrors on three walls and the ceiling. The domino mirror-to-mirror views made me see dozens of my and Tiara's images.

"Nothing extraordinary here," she said. But it's a popular room. I always liked it."

"Have you used it often?"

"Of course," she said. Hundreds of times. Maybe a thousand times."

"How long have you had it?"

"Four years."

"So ..." I started to mentally calculate.

"Yeah," she said. "Probably once a day, five days a week."

"What do people ... men ... like to do in here?"

"Mostly?"

"Yeah."

"Mostly, they like the girl to get on top, and they watch her in the mirrors."

"I see."

"Have you ever done that?"

"No."

"You should some time ... I don't mean with me. Not anymore."

I looked at her but didn't say anything.

"Come. I'll show you the next room."

Once again, I was startled and drew back. The center of the room had shackles for head and limbs. Chains and whips hung on the wall to the right. There was a rack on the left side of the room, the kind used in medieval times to stretch a man's body.

"The S&M room," I stated.

"Yes. So, you've been in one of these?" Tiara kidded.

"No."

"I didn't really think so. You're not the type. This is not for you. I don't like it either, really."

"Why do you have it? Is there really a demand for it?"

"Oh, you'd be surprised. But we don't really use the whips and chains. They're just for dramatic effect."

"The rack?"

"Yes, it's used. But lightly."

"Do guys actually, uh, you know ..."

"Do guys actually what?"

"Get off on that?"

"Usually not. Sometimes with a bit of help," she said.

The next room was very dreary to my eyes. Just a double bed with an old metal headboard, and an old scratched wooden night table. I looked at it, puzzled.

"Some men like it the old fashioned way. Stark. It makes them feel primitive. It works for them," she added matter-of-factly. "Time for the next room."

Tiara opened the door. The room was much larger than the others. It had three queen-size beds, several mirrors, two couches, and a movie screen. She knew I was stunned.

"The orgy room," I said.

"The *multiples room,*" she corrected.

"There are three beds," I pointed out.

"Yes, sometimes we have three or four girls in here. Other times, the beds can be pulled together for one or two girls."

"The couches?"

"The guys' bullpen," she replied with a laugh.

"I see."

"It's great."

"What about the other way?"

"There are lots of other ways," Tiara said, having fun by not making it easy for me.

"I mean one guy."

"I like sex with one guy, too," she said, likely pulling my leg.

"I mean this room."

"Oh, sure. It can be one guy and two or three girls. That appeals to you. Have you tried it?"

"No."

"You should. You will."

I couldn't answer.

"Come. Let's go to the next room. I have a feeling you'll never leave it."

We walked down the hall to the last room.

She flung the door open and nudged me in. "The honeymoon suite at the Tiara Hilton," she announced. It had a ceiling fan above a king-size bed, silk drapery, fine furniture, and a Jacuzzi for two.

"I like it."

"I knew you would. You're a lot like Chad. He liked this room, too. It's the only one of the rooms he was even in."

"Really?" I didn't know how else to respond to that bit of information.

"Yes. Most of the other rooms wouldn't have been for Chad. I offered him a visit to the multiples room, but he declined."

"You offered that to *Chad?*" I asked, astonished.

"Sure. Him and a few girls. I wanted to treat him. I would have been with him, of course."

No response from me.

"He said 'no.' He was being polite, I'm certain… He was a lot like you."

"Any other room?"

"Just the wash rooms. And my bedroom at the other end of the apartment."

The bedroom was plain modern. Tastefully done. I was saddened to see the dresser covered with pill bottles, and a plastic basket on the side of her bed. She didn't say, but I imagined that the plastic basket was to vomit in when the nausea from the medication was more than she could handle.

We sat at the dining room table for an hour, indulging in second desserts and chatting about the works of famous authors. When I left,

I thought about the various rooms and how open she was about them. I wondered why. I also wondered about the picture—the one of her father with his face cut out. But she said she would tell me about it some other time and, in accordance with our unspoken contract, I asked nothing further than what she offered. She escorted me to the elevator entrance, and I thanked her for a delicious meal and an interesting evening. Then the slow ride down to the back of the lobby.

* * *

I returned to New York, and my job at Mankado Products, two days later. In my spare time, I worked on the play that I had started prior to meeting Tiara. There wasn't a lot of time for that because Mankado was bidding to take over Eastern Merchants Corp., and there were mountains of computer tabulations and contracts to review—usually until eleven o'clock each night. It was necessary to be sure how the takeover would be affected by local property and income tax allocation formulas, federal pension regulations, capital loss carryovers, consumer product liability insurance, and by federal anti-monopoly laws. Yes, it was necessary to consider those matters and anything else that could be thought of, or not thought of. Sometimes I stopped and thought of Tiara. About her rooms—all so straightforward and human, and in such a direct and base way. No computer tabulations and no regulations. And she, herself, was so human. When the Eastern Merchants deal was finalized, and my evenings were free, I went full steam ahead on finishing the play. It was an expression of a part of me different from the intellect called upon for Mankado, and I was eager to show it to Tiara on my next trip to Toronto the following week.

Each time I called Tiara, I heard the same greeting saying that Tiara was not home and that the caller should leave a name and phone number, and that if it was a business call to press "3" to make an appointment. On my fifth call, and three calls thereafter, I left a message for Tiara to call me in New York. But she never did and I became concerned. Two days before my trip, I left another message advising her of the completion of the play and my expected arrival in Toronto.

It was a tough winter and Toronto was covered in snow, frozen over the snow from prior storms. The skidding bus ride from the airport was treacherous. I checked into the Royal York Hotel, unpacked my suitcase, and dialed Tiara's number. Again, she didn't answer, but this time the voicemail greeting was a recording of Tiara's weak voice.

"This is Tiara. I'm not home, and will be away for a while. Rather than leave a message, please call back in April. If this is Salinger calling, please press 3."

Salinger was a nickname she'd given me. Like the author, *J.D. Salinger*. I pressed 3 and heard the weakened version of Tiara's voice say, "Hello, Salinger. Sorry I couldn't return your calls. My story is nearing a conclusion, and I'd love to read your play. If you call 768-0900, you'll find out where I am. And if you'd like to see me, I'm in suite 1122. Only if you want to ... but I hope you do."

I dialed the number Tiara gave. An operator's voice answered, "Toronto University Hospital." Though not surprised, I was shaken.

"Do you have a patient there by the name of Tiara Conolan?"

"Checking, sir. Do you have a room number?"

"Yes. Room 1122."

"I'm sorry, sir. I have a Conolan in that room, but not with the first name, Tiara. Are you sure of the first name?"

"Oh ... do you have a Diane Conlan?"

"Yes, we have a Diane Conlan in room 1122."

"Can you tell me her visiting hours?"

"I'll check. Her hours are restricted, sir. Only from 1:00 to 3:00 P.M., and 6:00 to 8:00 P.M. And visitors are asked to not stay longer than one hour. Would you like me to connect you with the room?"

"No, thank you. Not now." I hung up.

I paced the hotel room floor for some blurred period of time. I never liked hospital rooms, or visiting hospital rooms. The issue wasn't simply that I didn't like being there; it was that it struck a chord in me. I don't know if it's of fear or depression. Due to the feeling of not being able to do something to help ... or maybe fear of myself being helpless. But I always intensely disliked that chord, and it would inevitably leave me in an emotional turmoil that would take days to shake. I stopped pacing around the room and stretched out on the bed. After a few moments of counting ceiling tiles, I flipped on my side and reached for the telephone book in the night table drawer. I looked up the address of Toronto University Hospital.

I didn't know what to bring her. Some small gift to cheer her up. Could she even eat chocolates? I had picked up flowers on the way, but when I reached the hospital I noticed a stuffed puppy dog in the gift shop window. It made me smile, so I bought it for her. I received a guest pass at the lobby desk and rode the elevator to the eleventh floor. It wasn't like the elevator in Tiara's building. It moved quickly, and the doors opened on nearly each floor, hospital staff getting on and off in an official way, conducting business. Each had a photo ID on his or her uniform. I went down the hallway, looking for her room. A nurse addressed me, asking what room I was visiting.

"Room 1122. Diana Conlan."

"Right around the corner, sir. Please try to keep your visit short. There might be a procedure being performed in the room. If there is, please wait for the doctors to finish before announcing yourself."

"Okay."

I went around the corner and, as warned, there was a procedure in process. The door was partly ajar, and I could see a curtain pulled around the bed. I heard the voices of medical staff. I heard Tiara moan. It shook me. I sat in a nearby chair and waited for it to be over. After the doctors came out, I waited ten minutes, put my coat back on, and tapped at her door as though I had just arrived. It was a warning tap. I walked in without waiting for a response.

"Salinger." She smiled.

"Hi." I leaned over and gave her a gentle hug. "I just got here," I added. "Sorry I didn't get here sooner."

"You look terrible, Salinger. Are you okay?"

"Yeah, I'm fine."

"Let me feel your head."

I hesitated.

"Give me your hand," she said. "It's not even cold," she stated, as she held my right hand. "Not cold, not hot. Perfect room temperature." She smiled again. "Please don't be so upset, Salinger. Thanks for coming."

I nodded. "Are they treating you well?" I asked.

"As well as they can. Are those for me?" she asked, pointing to the flowers.

"Yes," I answered, placing them just below her chest.

"They're beautiful."

"This is for you, too," I added, giving her the stuffed puppy dog. "I saw it downstairs in the gift shop on my way in. I thought you'd like it. Silly, heh?"

"No, not silly at all, Thank you. It's adorable," she added, wiping some moisture from her eyes. "You've gone to too much trouble."

"Not much trouble," I mumbled. "Really. Not much trouble at all," I said again, self-conscious at how little trouble it really was.

"Did you bring your play?"

"Yes, I have it here," I said, pointing to my brown portfolio bag. I took it out and handed it to her.

"Wonderful," she said. "I'm so tired of TV. I'll start it tonight."

For some reason, I didn't know how to react. And I didn't know how to ask about her condition. Or if I should ask.

"They've stopped giving me chemotherapy," she said. "I didn't want it anymore. I'd like to be comfortable. I only have about a week left."

I nodded. "I understand. Is there anything I can do for you?"

"Yes," she told me. "There are several things you can do for me, but I don't know if I have the right to ask."

"Sure. What are they?"

"First. At my apartment. There are letters and tape recordings in the top drawer of the bureau in my bedroom. They're for MaryAnn. Could you take them, and, if at all possible, please try to give them to her? I know she can't be found now. But if you would register a search, and hold on to them in case she is ever found."

"Yes. Of course."

"Some of the letters are dated for the future. For her to open on her birthday and graduation dates. Those letters have little gifts in them so she'll always feel remembered on her special days. I'm sorry to put you to so much trouble. But it would mean a lot to me."

"I know. I'll do my best. I promise."

"My will is with a lawyer. His name and address are in the second bureau drawer. Can you advise him when it's time?"

"Yes," I said, glancing at the floor.

"In that same drawer is a list of names and phone numbers. My girls. And a small number of my former girls. Actually, their working names, rather than their real names ... you never know who might pick it up. Would you let them know when the time comes? They might be wondering— I haven't been returning their messages. The former girls don't know about my condition, and I don't want them to think I've deserted them. You know, moved on and forgotten them. Please call them before the lawyer calls some for the reading of the will."

"Okay. Tiara ..."

"Yes?"

I couldn't speak.

"There are still two more things I ask of you."

I looked at her and nodded.

"First, could you read your play to me? Not right now. I know they won't let you stay long. But if you could come back a couple of times and read to me."

This request put me over the edge, and tears slid down my cheeks. "Is that important to you?" I asked.

"Yes. Very important."

There was a big lump in my throat. After regaining my composure, I asked, "What was the other thing? You said there were two things."

She hesitated. "I know this is asking more than I should, and I'll understand if you can't. Would you lie down and hold me ... just hold me. Play act for me. Hold me like you love me." Tiara began to cry for the very first time since I'd known her.

I slowly adjusted her legs, then her shoulders, making room on the bed. I looked around, noticed the door was open, walked over and shut it. I returned to the bed, lay down, and slipped my arm under her shoulders. I turned to Tiara and pulled her close to me. She nudged her head into my chest and I wrapped my other arm over her. I kissed her forehead and then her cheek. She trembled. Her arms clutched me tightly. She sobbed and held me even tighter. Saying nothing at all, I drew her still closer to me and stroked her head. After a few moments, she stopped sobbing and just lay in my arms. I draped my leg around her and continued to hold her close.

I'm not sure how long we were lying there like that before there was a soft knock on the door. It was a nursing aide. She opened the door and said that visiting time was over. "You can stay a few more minutes," she added.

After those few more minutes, I got up, tucked the blanket around Tiara, and kissed her. She smiled at me and closed her eyes. I picked up my coat and left.

I returned the next night, and read aloud the first forty pages of the play. Tiara especially liked when I acted out the role of each character, changing my voice and persona for each line.

"Salinger, like we talked last night? The things in the bureau drawer? These are the keys to my apartment."

I nodded and took them.

"I never told you about the accident I had years ago," she said.

"No, you haven't."

"It's in my diary. April 1981, if you want to read about it. The diary in is the third bureau drawer, under the clothing. Only if you want to. It's not pretty, Salinger, she added, and held out her arm.

I closed the door and lay down in her bed. We held each other for nearly thirty minutes. She didn't cry. I drew her close to me and kissed her. I kissed her again.

"I think you might be aroused," she laughed. "I wish I could satisfy you ... but ... " She held me closer and kissed my face.

After I closed her door behind me, I left the hospital and headed back to my hotel. En route, I changed my mind and went to Tiara's apartment. I decided that I didn't want to wait a year, or even a month, to read the diary. I went to her room and took the diary from the third bureau drawer.

"April 4, 1981 – I want to see my father. I called him this morning. We talked for a bit. I said I planned to visit next week. He said okay, but he sounded tense. I don't know what he thinks I want. Haven't seen him for years. I called him when I graduated high school and he said he would send a present, but I never got it. I wonder if he sent it, and I just didn't receive it. I'd like to ask him. I don't want to get him angry, but I just want to know if he tried to send it.

I don't remember what he looks like except for the photograph I took from my mother's things. It's a picture of him standing down by the sea. I'd really like to ask him things about leaving me and stuff, but I don't want to get him mad right away. I want to know him. To be able to visit once in a while, like other people visit their parents. It's lonely here in Toronto, even though it's fun. I'd like to have my dad. A dad. I know he probably doesn't want me, but maybe he'd change his mind. I hope so.

April 11, 1981 – I arrived at my father's place today. It's not much. A two-room shack and a tool shed where he works. But it's okay. There are some chickens in the coop, and barbwire fence around most of the place. He's older than I thought he'd be. That's okay. I didn't know what to talk to him about. He looks at me funny. I guess he doesn't know how to deal with me being here. He says I look real good. Like a healthy young woman. It seems so lonely here. I don't know how he stays here all alone. I don't know if he goes into town much. He didn't say.

April 12, 1981 – I did some errands in town for my dad. Then I made us lunch. We didn't talk much. But I liked it. He said again how healthy I look. Maybe he's surprised. But I think he's pleased. I didn't ask him yet about the graduation gift.

April 13, 1981 – Last night, my dad said I should sleep in his room. I said at first that I didn't feel comfortable about it. But he seemed mad, so I slept there.

"April 14, 1981 – I asked Dad about the gift. He said he didn't remember sending one, but wasn't sure. Maybe he did, but just didn't remember. He seemed angry. I won't ask about it again.

April 15, 1981 – He went out after dinner and came home real drunk. He started yelling at me. I went to the tool shed. This isn't how I pictured things.

I went back inside an hour later. He sobered some. I put up some coffee. He came behind and put his hands on my breasts. I pulled away and he grabbed me by my butt. He squeezed me all over. I just stood there at first. He kept doing it so I yelled and scratched at him. He cursed me and said I was a miserable little bitch, like my mother. He lunged and hit me. Then he pulled at my underwear with one hand, and choked me with the other. I pushed him off me, and he picked up a metal rod and hit me across the face with it, and then he punched my face. I was crying real badly. He punched me again. Finally, he stopped. Said I wasn't worth fucking, and he walked away.

I went outside and back into the tool shed and sobbed. I was so angry. But I couldn't just sit there. He didn't even send me a gift!

I took a hammer and an old sickle out of the tool shed and headed back to the shack. I was in a rage. I burst in and went after him with the hammer first. I landed a good blow to the side of his face. We battled furiously for I don't know how long. Somehow, we both ended up on the ground, under a broken banister of the shack. At first, I couldn't move. But I had to. I saw the sickle about ten feet away. And I saw him start after it. I lunged for the sickle and then lunged at him.

I cut off my father's miserable damn head. Blood gushed all over, and I just kept chopping at it. Chopping, chopping. Then I started to cut off his penis, but stopped and screamed at his dead body that it wasn't worth cutting off.

I passed out. When I came to, I put his body in a trash bag, where it belonged. I realized how badly I was injured. I needed help. I couldn't call the police. I crawled to the phone inside and called Toronto.

I was just lying there, waiting. Nobody there knew me. I hoped I could get away without anyone ever knowing that his daughter had visited. I wondered if he told anybody about me, and thought I could take comfort in the certainty that the bastard never did."

The next entry in her diary was not until August. It made no mention of "the accident," nor did any subsequent entries during the next year. I felt I had been given that liberty, but not the liberty to divulge any of what she hadn't specifically told me herself.

* * *

I visited Tiara in the hospital in both the afternoon and the evening, the next day. I read the remaining pages of my play aloud, acting out each role as I had before. She again enjoyed it. At night, I lay down next to her and held her close. Very close. I stroked her hair and her head for a long time. She was very weak.

"You read the diary last night," she said, her head tucked in my arm.

I didn't answer.

"You didn't have to," she added, as though seeking acknowledgement of what she already knew.

"I know I didn't have to."

"You didn't have to do it now, for me. You could have waited till after."

"I didn't want to wait." I could feel her grin against my neck.

"I love you, Salinger."

"I love you, Tiara ... Diane, too."

"I know," she said. "I know." I felt a tear roll on my hand.

We lay in the bed for a long while. The nurse tapped on the door and came in. I feared reproach for my position but there was none. When the nurse closed the door behind her, I kissed Tiara's head and she kissed my neck. Again, I held her close.

A few minutes later, I felt her hand loosen its grip on mine. Tiara's story was finished.

* * *

The reading of the will was just two days after the funeral, as the lawyer stated she had requested. Several of the people were visually familiar from the funeral. Tiara had left a fair sum of money for MaryAnn, to be held in trust until her whereabouts were determined, and until she attained the age of eighteen. Two men were left modest sums of money and a personal item. Five young women were each left sums of money, and were individually handed sealed envelopes to be opened at another time. I presumed that there were personal notes in each one as there was in my envelope.

* * *

The next day, I returned to the apartment to tend to a personal matter, as requested in Tiara's note to me. I was to help by just following instructions when I got there. I entered the elevator and the car took its time ascending the shaft. When I reached the twelfth floor, I knocked on the door and was greeted by an attractive woman.

"Hi, I'm Jennie," she said. "I know who you are. Come on in."

I answered by complying with her request.

"Tiara asked only a few people very close to her to tend to something. Please come this way."

I followed Jennie to Tiara's row of rooms, and into one of them. It was the multiples room. Jennie and four other beautiful girls stood before me.

"This is Monique, Stephanie, and Robin," she said.

The fourth girl, the youngest, and extraordinarily pretty, wasn't introduced. She sat down on one of the couches and didn't speak.

"We're all friends of Tiara," Stephanie explained, "and this is the multiples room. We're going to have a good time this afternoon. A very good time," she added with enthusiasm.

"We'll each get comfortable, and then you can, too." Jennie told me.

One by one, Jennie, Stephanie, Monique, and Robin removed all their clothing. Then they all removed my clothing and coaxed me to the middle bed. They decided to put the three beds together. One by one, they each pleasured me for five minutes. Then two by two. Then all four at once. All while the youngest girl remained fully clothed and watched. Eventually, she came over and kissed me while the other four continued their ministrations. Their objective was achieved a few minutes later, and they each kissed me. The four got dressed, kissed me again, and thanked me for being Tiara's friend.

I was left alone with the fifth girl. She came over and gave me a little hug. Then an affectionate kiss.

"Come with me," she said, and led me to the honeymoon suite. "We're going to spend the rest of the day and night here," she said, with a sweet smile. "Make yourself comfortable on the bed," she suggested. "Are you hungry?"

"Not now."

"Whenever you're hungry, we can order room service." She smiled again. She removed her outer clothing, remaining only in matching blue silk panties and bra. She crawled next to me on the bed and kissed me, stroking my body all over with her hands.

"You can do that to me, too, if you want. I'd like that," she said. So I did.

We lay there quietly for a while, stroking and caressing each other.

"What's your name?" I asked.

"Diane."

"That's a nice name. Where are you from?"

"Nova Scotia. I came to Toronto four months ago."

"Where in Nova Scotia are you from?" I asked.

"A small town. You probably never heard of it."

"Is it somewhere near Halifax?"

"No. It's *somewhere not near Halifax.*"

We dined on seafood and Diet Cokes, and made love through the night even when I no longer could.

* * *

Tiara's financial bequest to me was used to market an anthology of my short stories, enabling it to become a best seller, and me to be hailed as an up-and-coming writer, putting me on the map. I knew that would have pleased her very much. I left Mankado Consumer Products shortly after, but I still go to Toronto from time to time, and each time I visit Tiara's gravesite and place flowers next to her tombstone. It reads exactly as she wrote it.

TIARA CONLAN
May 15, 1960 – February 10, 1998
DEAR FRIENDS,
VISIT ONLY IF YOU WISH.
PLEASE REMEMBER ME ALWAYS.

DENNIS AND THE BAD GUYS

Dennis and I first met as I was sipping a Diet Coke in an Amtrak lunch car. I was en route to New York City from Washington, D.C., the location of the story I was working on at the time and where I'd spent the prior week familiarizing myself with its color and details. Sipping my beverage very purposefully was a ritual that I convinced myself would assist me in mustering up the level of concentration needed to tend to the rough draft manuscript on the table in front of me.

Still unable to focus, I retreated from the page and looked up at the passenger who had sat down opposite me. He had a moderately full face beneath a crop of curly black hair. I didn't notice the expression in his eyes right away because my attention was drawn directly to the shape of his mouth as he grinned at me. I returned a smile, as one automatically does.

"Hi, I'm Dennis," he announced.

"Hi."

"I'm going to New York," he said and looked at me questioningly.

"I'm going to New York, too."

"I'm visiting my aunt. Why are you going there?"

"I live there."

"Really?"

"Yeah," I answered. I studied him for a moment, guesstimating his age to be about twenty, twenty-two, although his juvenile exuberance made him seem much younger.

"Watcha lookin' at?" he asked with another grin.

"Nothing."

"Nothing? My mom looks at nothing, too. She's my aunt's sister. My Aunt Margaret, in New York. Margaret Patortney. Do you know her?"

"No, I don't," I said and looked back down at my manuscript.

"You don't? She's a nice aunt," he assured me in a voice louder than necessary. "She always talks to me, and last time I was in New York she took me to lots of places. You wanna know where she took me?"

"Yeah," I responded, laying down my pen. "Where did she take you?"

"Radio City Music Hall. We saw a live show on stage. And then a movie. After that we went to the ice-skating rink at Rockefeller Center. Did you ever go to the ice-skating rink at Rockefeller Center?"

"I've passed by and stopped to watch the skaters, but I've never skated."

"I didn't skate, either. I tried, but I fell." He laughed and hit the table with his hand. "And then Aunt Margaret took me on the subway train to the museum. Did you ever go on the subway?"

"Yeah. I live in New York. I go on the subway all the time."

"It's crowded, heh?"

"Yeah. During rush hour."

"Rush hour? Do you believe in Superman?"

"What?" I asked, suppressing a laugh.

"Do you believe in Superman? Do you think Superman is real?"

"Well …" I pondered what would be the right answer for Dennis. I didn't want to burst any illusions, remembering back to when I was five-years-old and learned that there was no Santa Claus. But after all, this was not a toddler sitting in front of me.

"I suppose it's possible," I answered.

"So why does kryptonite hurt him?"

"Uhm … I think he's probably allergic to it."

"Yeah? But how come he's the only one allergic to it?"

"Because he was born on planet Krypton," I began explaining in a patient, professional manner," and that's where kryptonite comes from. So kryptonite doesn't affect other people on earth because they're not from Krypton." I couldn't believe that I was providing the rationalization, but my intent was to protect Dennis from the truth.

"You think so?"

"Yeah, that must be it."

"But if nobody else is from Krypton, how do they get the kryptonite? I don't think he's real," Dennis declared. "I don't think Superman is real."

"Well, you could be right. I never thought of it that way."

Dennis fell into silent thought, and I turned my attention back to my manuscript once again. The train tilted as it rolled on a turn in the tracks and Dennis's curiosity began to flow again.

"How come Robin always gets the crap beat out of him and Batman has to come to his rescue?"

I wondered for a moment how to handle this second riddle.

"Maybe it's because Robin is like a scout for Batman, and he gets to the bad guys first, so he's outnumbered till Batman gets there."

"Nah. I don't think so. I think it's cause Robin is a wimp," he said, laughing. "What are ya reading there?" he asked, pointing to my manuscript.

"It's a story I've written. A draft of a story. A first version. It has to be changed."

"Why you gotta change it?"

"Because I don't quite like it the way it is. I wrote it this way just to give it a try. To get the story down, and then go back to make it better."

"Is it gonna be a comic book?"

"No, it's going to be a short story. But right now, it's too long to be a short story and I don't think I can add enough to make it a novel." I saw a quizzical look on his face. "A book," I added.

"Oh. What's it about?"

"The main person in the story is a girl who grows up in New York, goes to school in Washington, and stays to live there after she graduates."

"Oh. What school does she go to?"

"Georgetown University."

"What's the girl like?"

"She's a very nice girl. But a little bit confused."

"What's she confused about?" Dennis asked.

I wondered how to explain a psychologically driven story to Dennis. "About other people and how they act. How they act with her."

"Whatta ya mean? Like when people aren't nice to her?"

"Something like that."

"Sometimes people aren't nice. How come?"

"It doesn't always have to do with the person they're not being nice to. It's often because of something else."

"Yeah," he responded, his eyes fixed on something not visible to me. "Sometimes people treat other people like they don't matter."

I felt the hollow well from which Dennis was speaking. No doubt he'd felt dismissed by people over and over again. Maybe even ridiculed. I thought about how I initially felt like shrugging him off until I found his simplicity to be engaging.

"That's not right, is it?" he asked.

"No, it's not."

"Why do people do that?" he asked, his face colored with a sadness that touched me.

"Dennis, sometimes people aren't thinking."

"Yeah. You want to see the autographs I got when I was in California last year?"

"Sure," I said.

"I have two of them in my pocket." He fumbled for a moment and fished out two yellow pieces of paper. "This one's from Hulk Hogan, the professional wrestler. Here, read it."

"To Dennis," I read out loud. "*To Dennis, Good meeting you. Lots of luck in your wrestling career. Your pal, Hulk Hogan.* He sounds like a nice guy," I said.

"Yeah, he is," Dennis blurted, the childish smile returning to his face.

"How'd you meet him?"

"He was signing autographs and we got talking."

"I see. So, you're going to be a pro wrestler?"

"Yeah. Someday, maybe," he said, his eyes cast downward. "Here, look at my letter from Dale Earnhardt." He handed me another folded sheet of yellow paper.

"Who is that?"

"He's a race car driver. We were talking at this show. This race car show. Read it. What does it say?"

"It says, *To My Pal Dennis, Good talking to you. Hope you enjoy California. Glad you came to the show. Dale Earnhardt.* He sounds like a good guy, too."

"Yeah. We were talking at the race car show near Los Angeles. That's in California. So, why'd you write the story about the girl?" Dennis asked, shifting subjects in mid-sentence.

"Well, because I wanted to create it. I'm a writer."

"Why? Why'd you become a writer?"

"Because I can set the stage the way I want."

"Like at Radio City Music Hall?"

"No, Dennis. It's a different kind of stage. It's not really a stage. It's just a figure of speech. I mean another way of saying it. I create the characters and I direct what they do."

"Oh. I have to go to the bathroom. I know where it is," he added, getting up from his seat. "I've been on this train lots of times. I'll be back. Save my seat," he called over his shoulder. "Okay?"

"You got it."

"Dennis asked why I became a writer. It certainly wasn't for the money. I gave up a job as the controller of Mankado Consumer Products in order to pursue a career as a writer. It was to escape the confinement of the boundaries drawn around my life by the demands from and deadlines set by the powerful who yearn to feel their power by exerting it. As a writer, I have a feeling of power—the power to ride a magic carpet through the lives of my characters and travel through one life after another like a tour around the world. At least until my carpet lands in the offices of publishers and editors where my itinerary is changed.

I thought that Dennis might be a wonderful writer. Or, at least, a wonderful storyteller as he knows nothing of borders and his mind travels wherever it wishes. Though I'm not certain that any of his stories would have a plot or an ending, his style might have a refreshing charm, with honesty in the author's voice, even if the stories come more from observed experiences of others than his own. Observed from television, movies, comic books, and stories told by whomever he'd engaged in conversation on a train.

I later learned that very few of Dennis's stories were true. He had never been to Radio City Music Hall, nor had he skated at Rockefeller Center. But he had taken several rides on the New York City subway with his former case manager, a social worker named Margaret Patortney. She was a sincerely interested lady who, indeed, was to meet Dennis at Pennsylvania Station in New York as she had done a number of times since moving from Washington to New York. Dennis had two younger brothers at home. Michael, the eighteen-year-old Romeo, was adopted when he was one year old, and fifteen-year-old David was an honor student in his second year of high school.

Putting aside the hurts that must come his way, I felt a curious envy for Dennis's simplicity. No need to wrestle with anything more complex than the questions of Superman's authenticity and Robin's inferiority to Batman. He was exuberant about what I then thought were real experiences at Radio City Music Hall and the Rockefeller Center skating rink— an exuberance of youthful pleasures that I had left behind me when I entered college to study business and finance. Very serious stuff. Even more serious when I actually entered the business world and was dipped into a boiling pot of long hours, marinated in a thick sauce of responsibility and then sautéed in a Horatio Alger work ethic.

I was forty-five years old when I jumped ship and pursued a career as a writer, aided by the encouragement and largesse left to me by an extraordinary woman named Tiara. But that is another story. I envied Dennis for his ability to go from place to place with no apparent intervention. But I also realized that Dennis, too, was burdened ... by the feeling of being discounted in the real world.

It took Dennis more than ten minutes to return. I'd just become focused on my manuscript when he slid back into the seat opposite me.

"Hi. I'm back," he announced.

"Hi."

"Did I take long?" he asked. He seemed a bit flustered, causing me to wonder about the successful completion of his mission.

"You were gone a while," I acknowledged. I didn't want to embarrass him by asking him about it.

"Yeah? You'll never guess what happened," he said.

"Really?"

"Should I tell you?"

"If you want to," I said, realizing that the choice would actually not be mine.

"Okay," he said, leaning forward over the lunch table between us, his face lit with excitement. "When I went to the bathroom, I found dynamite next to the toilet, and then there was a knock on the door. I just called out 'yeah,' but I didn't open the door cause my pants were down. Then I heard somebody tryin' to open the door. Ya know, tryin' to turn the doorknob? And then they banged on the door, and this guy starts yellin' that he's gotta get in the bathroom right away, and I better get out. So I called through the door that my pants weren't on, ya know, and I'd hurry out soon. I heard a gun click and I pulled up my pants and got out as fast as I could. I didn't even wash my hands."

"And then what happened?" I asked. "Did the guy go in right after you left?"

"When I got outta the bathroom, there was nobody waiting. I looked around and there were people sitting at tables. A coupla guys looked at me when I came out."

"Was one of them Robin?" I asked, trying to find out whether Dennis's mind was again floating free.

"Nah. Robin wasn't there. Just the people at the tables."

"And the dynamite? Is it still in the bathroom?"

"I left it there. Ya think one of the guys went in and took it?"

"How do you know it was dynamite?"

"It was. There were four sticks wrapped together and there was a fuse."

"One fuse?"

"Four fuses, but they came together into one fuse."

"Four sticks just sitting in the bathroom? Wouldn't people have noticed somebody carrying around four sticks of dynamite on the train?"

"It was in a case. Like for a camera."

"You opened the case?"

"Yeah."

"You were looking for kryptonite?" I asked, still testing.

"No. I had nothing to read and I couldn't go right away. So I started foolin' around with the case and I opened it up. Do you think they're gonna blow up the train?"

"I studied Dennis's face for a moment. "Did you close the case before you left the bathroom?"

"No. I was in a hurry. I told ya I didn't even wash my hands. Do ya think they know I saw the dynamite?"

"I suppose they do."

"Gadzooks!"

"Are you scared?"

"Yeah." His eyes wandered and, a few seconds later, his face lit up again. "Hey, you see that girl standing over there?"

"Is it okay for me to turn around?"

"Yeah. She looks like Brenda. My girlfriend."

Your girlfriend," I repeated as I turned to look.

"Uh-huh. Brenda's in one of my classes in school. I don't see her every day, though. You know why? Cause she works in an office two days a week, so she's not in school. You know what I like to do with Brenda?" he asked, a silly grin on his face.

"What?"

"I like kissing her. And you know what else?" He turned his face sideways and blushed. "Nah. We never did that," he said, laughing. Her parents are always with us. Did you ever do that? You know. It's fun. Right?"

"Yeah," I mused. "How old is Brenda?"

"She's twenty. She's pretty. And you know what? She's got a big pair." He giggled, thrusting his face slightly forward.

I had not expected this from a person who previously rapped with me about the authenticity of Superman and the inferiority of Robin. It was like talking to Big Bird about the Happy Hooker or the Mayflower Madame. And he'd just been telling me about sinister guys who could be preparing to dynamite the train. Did any of it come from actual experience? Should I have been concerned about being dynamited into oblivion?

"Dennis, if Brenda were on this train right now, would she be in any danger?"

"Whatta ya mean?"

I hesitated, trying to word the question in a way that addressed my concern, but yet stayed on the subject of Brenda, which was absurd because staying on the subject was of no concern to Dennis. "If Brenda had used the toilet in the next car, what would she have seen there?"

"A black case with four sticks of dynamite in it."

"And what would she have done. About the dynamite, I mean?"

"Well ... she'd probably start crying cause she'd be scared that she'd get blown to bits."

"Would she really be in danger? If she were on this train, could she get blown to bits?"

"Uh-huh."

"Then could we ... everybody on this train, get blown to bits?"

"Yeah. I told ya. Don't ya believe me?"

"Yes. Are you scared?"

"Yeah. Sure I'm scared. I can get blown up," he added in a loud whisper.

Was I to usher Dennis to the train conductor or to a motorman and have someone radio for help? Would he tell them what he told me? Or would he suddenly spot somebody that looked like Aunt Margaret and give that person a dissertation about her. I was losing patience with Dennis. Becoming serious and concerned, I reached over and tugged on Dennis's shirt collar.

"Dennis. What are you and I going to do about the guys with the dynamite? Are we going to tell the conductor to radio for help? Are we going to find the guys with the dynamite and take it away from them? Are we going to get off the train at the next stop and not worry about it?" That was an appealing thought. "Or are going to sit back and talk about Brenda's big tits and wait to get blown into the next kingdom? What do you think?" I added, loosening my grip on his shirt collar.

"I don't know."

"Do you ever want to see Radio City Music Hall again?"

"I never been to Radio City Music Hall. But I want to."

"What? Then do you want this train to blow when we get to Penn Station and kill your Aunt Margaret?"

"She's not really my aunt. But I don't want anything to happen to her."

"Dennis, is it dynamite that you saw in the black case?"

"Yeah, At least I think it is."

"Dennis, is Superman real?"

"No."

"Is there dynamite on this train?"

"Yeah. Are you mad at me?"

"Yes ... I don't know. How big are Brenda's tits?"

"Pretty big."

"Ever feel them?"

"Nah. She's my brother Michael's girlfriend."

"Dennis! Is there dynamite on this train?"

"Yeah."

"Shit!" was all I could say as it became apparent that the one thing that Dennis actually believed to be true was that there were four sticks of dynamite on the train. I thought about the possibilities. One, the train could blow up before I had a chance to do anything. It wouldn't be my fault, and I wouldn't have made the wrong decision. But I'd be dead. Two, Dennis and I could look for the men who were watching him when he left the bathroom. We'd spot the dynamite and overwhelm them. The positive of that scenario would be that I could write a story about it, but the possibility was much greater that the train would blow up before I decided. Three, I could make Dennis repeat the story to the motorman. In some respects, that seemed like the most difficult option to achieve. Four, I could get off at the next stop but it was an express train; the next stop was Newark and we wouldn't arrive for another eighty minutes.

"Dennis, do you remember what the guys looked like? The ones who were looking at you when you came out of the bathroom?"

"Yeah."

"Would you recognize them if you saw them?"

"Uh-huh."

"Come on," I said as I stood up, "we're going to the front of the train to tell the motorman about everything."

"What's the motorman gonna do?"

"He's going to radio for help."

"What if they already cut off his radio?"

"Dennis, let's go."

"Wait."

"What?"

"You never told me your name. Who are you?"

"Spiderman."

"Really? Okay, let's go. Hey, why don't we just jump those guys ourselves, Spiderman?"

"No, Dennis. The official way is to report them to the motorman."

With Dennis trailing two steps behind me, we headed to the front of the train, not bothering to excuse ourselves as we broke through a line at the lunch counter. We were near the front of the train when Dennis stopped short, pulled on my arm, and said, "I see the guys with the dynamite. They saw me."

Dennis turned and darted through the aisle in the other direction. Instinctively, I spun around and dashed in the same direction, two steps behind him. I'm not sure if I was trying to catch up with Dennis or pass him. He flung open the metal door as we got to the back of the car, not stopping to hold it for me. I caught it and kept pace right behind. But then he hesitated for a panicky second to look behind and I crashed into him. Like two fumbling fools, we continued scurrying through several more cars, never looking back. Finally, we got to the last car—the sleeping car. Dennis, panic-stricken that there was nowhere else to go, slipped into a sleeping berth. Equally panic-stricken, I ducked in with him.

"Did they see us?" he asked, panting.

"I don't know."

"Where are they?"

"I never even saw them," I answered. "I just kept running behind you. Did they follow us?"

"They musta followed. They saw me."

"Shh," I said, poking his arm. "Be quiet," I whispered. "They could be right outside."

Motionless, we lay there for nearly ten minutes, not daring to breathe louder than absolutely necessary. I thought about what a bizarre end I could meet. So quickly. So unexpectedly. All the unpaid favors I had accumulated could not help me and, in fact, all those uncalled chits would go up in smoke.

I thought about how foolish it is to spend our lives accumulating chits before we feel secure enough to call them in, and how we continue to accumulate as an end in itself. The favors I had done for my publisher's daughter—never cashed in. I never called on him to give me something in return. I hoarded the chits, never wanting to spend them, feeling their security like an FDIC-insured bank account. And the money we accumulate in our bank accounts—to feel secure enough to buy and do the things we want—we never use it; we come to associate the ownership of the money with the pleasures we originally planned to enjoy when we began saving.

In those moments, lying next to Dennis in the sleeping berth, I vowed to myself that if I survived I would spend all the chits I earned and never bank them again. Except for my chits with God. It then occurred to me that perhaps I had not accumulated enough chits with him, and I vowed to make him my only banker if I arrived in New York in one piece.

The ten minutes we lay there seemed like hours, and it occurred to me that the world had not come to an end. Nobody had found us; I wondered why. There couldn't have been more than eight cars on the train. It wouldn't have taken too long to search each car if they had really been on our heels. Maybe they were captured by undercover train security. Or maybe they were waiting it out until we pulled into Newark so they could quietly slip off the train—or blow up the

Newark station! Then again, maybe they never even saw us. But what if they had jumped off the train to safety, leaving the dynamite behind to do its job? Damn! Panic returned and I tugged Dennis's arm.

"Dennis," I whispered. "They haven't found us. Maybe they're not even looking for us."

"Think so?"

"Shh! Talk lower. They might not be looking for trouble by chasing us. Or they might have slipped off the train and left the dynamite."

"Why would they leave it?"

"They can't jump off the side of the train with it," I said.

"Yeah."

"Are you sure they saw you?"

"I think so."

"Maybe they didn't and they never even followed us."

"Should we just stay here?"

I considered our options.

"Whatta ya think? Should we go find 'em and jump 'em?" he asked excitedly.

"I don't think that's the first game plan. Listen, I'm going to walk to the motorman in the front of the train by myself. They're probably not looking for me, unless they spotted me running with you. But they didn't come after us, so I figure they probably didn't even see you. You just stay here."

"By... by myself?" he asked.

"Are you afraid?"

"Kinda."

"You were just talking about jumping them."

"That was the two of us together. Like Batman and Robin. Not by myself."

"Just stay here. If they're not even looking for you, they won't see you here."

"What if I have to go to the bathroom again?"

"Listen," I whispered. "You just stay put. I'm going to speak to the motorman." I stuck my head out of the curtain, checking to see if the coast was clear. "Stay put," I told him, poking him for emphasis, as I swung my body out of the berth and into the open aisle.

I looked in both directions, walked to the door of the car, and held my breath before entering the next car. I was trembling. *Into The Valley Of Death Rode The Six Hundred.* How brave I am, I assured myself. A great story in human history to be told by many generations. I entered the next car and began walking through.

I told myself not to walk too fast; I didn't want to attract attention. I studied each face as I passed by. *Don't be so obvious. You're conspicuous.* I had slowed down to observe the other passengers, so I increased my pace to one I believed to be exactly appropriate for a business traveler walking through a train car. *Yes, that's it. That's better.* I got to the end of the car. *Okay, you made it through one car. You're doing fine.*

I hoped that Dennis was staying put. If they caught him, they just might kill him and hide his body in the sleeping berth. And since nobody else would recognize them, they'd figure they could just safely ride the train to Newark, or even New York, and get off with the dynamite. I thought about sitting down in one of the open seats to wait it out. Nah. What if they decide to blow the train? *Keep going.*

I entered the next car and walked through the aisle at the precisely appropriate pace. I spotted a suspicious-looking guy sitting near the end of the car—next to the bathroom. He looked like a terrorist. A terrorist named Nicholi. He tapped on the bathroom door and sat back down as I walked through the car. He looked at me approaching; his eyes were sinister. *Just keep walking. Keep right on pace.*

I was five feet away when the bathroom door suddenly flew open; a guy came out and Nicholi sprung to his feet. Stunned, I fell back one step. Nicholi stared right at me and moved to the aisle.

"I'm next. I've been waiting for the bathroom," he declared.

"That's okay. I'll wait."

"I won't be long."

"Take your time.

He shut the door behind him. I felt like I needed to use the bathroom but I kept on going. The lunch car, where I first met Dennis, was next. I pictured him sitting in the same seat, asking whether I believed in Superman and why Robin always got the crap kicked out of him. That thought stopped me and I asked myself what I was doing. By this point, it was more real to me than to Dennis.

I saw the lunch counter guy and thought I could enlist his aid, but there were six people in line. I couldn't tell him anything with all those people standing here. It would cause panic. *What if one of them is a terrorist? I'll have to wait till the people are served.*

There was an old lady at the front of the line. She was counting out the exact change to pay for her coffee and donut.

"Two dollars and sixty-four cents. I have four pennies in here somewhere," she declared, fumbling through her wallet. She removed tissues, lipstick, and a small photograph book. "These are pictures of my granddaughter," she explained to the lunch guy, and opened the book.

"Excuse me," I repeated robotically as I went past each person on line. "Coming through, Excuse me." I got past the end of the line, but felt a pair of eyes on my back.

"Hey," a voice called out. I froze. "Hey! You made me spill my coffee."

"Sorry," I called back, and kept walking.

The next car was packed with people and I knew that everybody was staring at me. Any one of them could be Dynamite Man. There was a guy peering over his newspaper at me. The paper dropped a bit, and then he lifted it up. As I came closer to him, I could see that he had a beard. I was sure Dennis would have mentioned if one of the guys had a beard. *He's not a terrorist. Keep going. Not so slowly. Keep your pace fast enough so you don't look like you're looking for somebody, or like you're scared to death.*

The front car was next. *Just one more to get to the motorman. Almost there.* I was going to make it. When I reached the front car, my feet were moving fast—no controlling them then. Forget about looking like a casual business traveler. People were noticing me. I didn't care.

"Motorman, motorman," I repeated as I got to the front and started pounding on the door.

"Stop punching the door like that," a voice called from behind.

"Open up. Open up. I have to talk to you."

"Can't open up. Not allowed. Security reasons."

"There's an emergency."

"What is it?"

"I can't yell it through the door. People will panic."

"What? I can't hear you."

"I can't yell it through the door."

"I'm not opening it."

A voice was heard over the public address system. "Conductor. Please come to the front car."

Crap. He's going to alert the dynamite guys that something is up. I'll sit tight and wait for the conductor. When the conductor walked through the door I was disappointed. He was a pudgy little guy of around five feet, five inches. Say, sixty years old. I was hoping for Arnold Schwarzenegger, chest popping out his trainman's uniform, but I got Norm from *Cheers*. He approached the front of the car, eyeing me as I leaned against the motorman's door.

"What's going on here? Is there a problem?" he asked as he got to within ten feet of me.

"Yes. Listen. Come closer. I can't talk too loud." He drew nearer to me, still looking at me in a funny way. "I know this story sounds crazy, but I have reason to believe that there's dynamite or another explosive on this train. And it can blow at any minute. I think you guys ought to radio for help. Or instructions. Or something."

"Why do you think that?" Norm asked.

"Dennis saw it. When he went to the bathroom. It was there. The dynamite."

"Dennis?"

"Yeah. He's this young guy I met on the train. Anyway, he went to the bathroom and came back all scared. I asked him what was wrong, and he told me about what he saw, and that these guys were pounding on the door wanting to get in. Probably the guys that left the dynamite there. I was bringing Dennis to the motorman but those guys saw him and he ran to hide and I ran after him. They didn't find us. We were hiding in a berth in the last car. He's still there, I hope."

"Dennis?" the conductor inquired.

"Yeah."

"What does Dennis look like?"

"He has curly black hair. Early twenties."

"And he's visiting his Aunt Margaret in New York?"

"Well, she's not really his aunt ..."

"Listen. Dennis has been riding this train to New York from Washington about every month. He talks to anyone who'll listen to him and he has a tall tale for each one of them."

"I think he might be telling the truth this time." Norm gave me a blank look. "He told me that Brenda's really not his girlfriend, and that he never went to the ice-skating rink at Rockefeller Center."

"Oh?"

"You don't understand. He's being serious about this."

Norm tapped on the motorman's door. "Walter, this guy out here thinks the train is in danger. That kid, Dennis, told him there's dynamite on the train."

"Yeah?" said the voice from behind the door. "The kid's full of tales. He's playing out another fantasy."

"Call for help," I urged. "He's not in outer space on this. He's leveling with me."

"Walter, whatta ya think?" Norm called through the door. "This guy thinks it's serious."

At that moment, Dennis burst through the door at the other end of the train car, excitement all over his face. He saw me.

"Spiderman! Spiderman! Come quick."

I shrank about twelve inches. I did tell him my name was Spiderman, didn't I?

"Hurry," he called again.

"What is it?" I yelled to him.

"Hurry. Come quick!"

He turned and ran to the next car and I chased after him. I thought the conductor was following me, but I wasn't certain. The eyes of every passenger in the car were beamed in on me. I got to the end of the car and struggled to pull the door open, fumbling over my own hands. As I made my way into the next car, I could see Dennis way ahead. He turned around and yelled "Come on. Hurry!" and kept going. He was serious; of that I was certain.

I dashed after him. Heads turned and people stood up as I went into the third car, the fourth car, the fifth car. Dennis had entered the last car, the one with the sleeping berths where we were hiding earlier. I went through the door and saw Dennis standing over two unconscious bodies and a heavy-looking metal object on the floor. Dennis stumbled past them and picked up a black case on the floor.

"It's in here. It's in here," he yelled at me.

"The dynamite?"

"Yeah. It's in here."

"Be careful," I urged him.

"It's ticking!" he exclaimed.

"It's ticking? Like a clock?"

"Yeah. What should I do?" he asked. "Should I turn it off?"

"No! Don't touch it! Hold still!"

"It's ticking," he repeated and started running in my direction.

"Out of the way," he yelled at me. "Out of the way," he repeated, bumping past me.

Dennis headed to the car door, pulled it open, and heaved the black case high in the air and over the gully we were passing. I froze and listened. A loud blast pierced my ears and reverberated through the floor of the train car and up into my throat. The car shook, but stayed on its path. I looked at Dennis. He stood between the two cars, the wind blowing his curly black hair. He turned toward me and smiled.

"It exploded," he said with astonishment. "It exploded."

"Out there," I said. "Not on the train."

"Yeah."

"Dennis, you saved the train and everyone on it."

"Yeah. Like Batman, right?"

"Just like Batman. You're a hero, Dennis."

"Yeah, I'm a hero," he said, and grinned. "Like Batman," he added with great satisfaction.

The conductor came through the door of the car, followed by a half dozen passengers. Everybody stood guard over the two men on the floor when the conductor went to look for a ball of cord to tie up the bad guys. Dennis received congratulations from many thankful groups of passengers and repeated the story of how he jumped the dynamite guys with a heavy metal bar he had removed from the chain gate between the railroad cars.

The train was evacuated when we got to Newark and the two guys were arrested. The authorities questioned Dennis and searched for other explosives before the train was permitted to proceed to New York. When we did start the last leg of the trip, Dennis and I sat in the same car, at the same table at which we had met earlier.

"Could you tell my Aunt Margaret what happened when we get to New York? Tell her what I did?"

"Why don't you tell her yourself?"

"Nah. She won't believe me."

"Okay. I'll tell her. I'll tell her about how you saved the day. Just like Batman."

"Good. And could you tell my mom? And my brothers?" he asked. "Could you call them in Washington and tell them?"

"Absolutely," I assured him.

"That would be really great. Are you gonna finish that story you were writing?"

"Not today. When I get back to New York."

"Are you gonna write a story about me and what happened today?"

"Are you kidding? Yes. Definitely."

"Can I read it?"

"Of course you can. It'll be about you."

"What are you gonna call it?"

"Dennis and the Bad Guys," I answered.

Dennis sat perfectly still all the way back to New York, a contented smile fixed on his face and his eyes gazing off into his daydream. The sun shone down on Dennis all the rest of the day. All the rest of Dennis's special day.

BILLY STRUM AND ME

I knew that I had to meet Billy Strum and get his story the first time I saw him. It was in his jazz bar and restaurant on the South Side of Chicago. There was a plate full of Strum's famous ribs in front of me while I sat at the bar with a beer in my hand. It was my third or fourth. Maybe fifth or sixth.

Billy was on the stage introducing his jazz trio. "On my right, jazz guitarist, Danny Williams. And on my left is pianist, and my musical arranger for fourteen years, Jesse Johnson." He paused. "And me, I'm Billy Strum on the drums."

Billy had nearly white hair and an unforgettable, infectious smile. The sticks in his big black hands beat on the drum skins and cymbals, his body rocking to and fro.

During intermission, Billy made public relations rounds with the regular patrons and joked with the young waitresses. The stories of a lifetime showed on his face. I wrote a note for Billy on a napkin, explaining that I read him as a man with a colorful story to tell, and asked to interview him. My waitress passed the napkin to Billy and I watched as he read it with a suspicious expression, shook his head, and turned away. But fantasies I'd already drawn of Billy's life made me determined to interview him. For the next hour, I continued to study him. I envisioned the story of his life from the image he was projecting.

At the end of World War II, Billy turned eighteen and moved from Alabama to Chicago. He met up with Bobby Joe Turner, already a famous black musician from the thirties, and Bobby Joe taught him how to play jazz, whore around Chicago, and stay out of the white man's way. Billy later joined several bands that came unglued due to arguments related to musical egos, women, practice sessions, and money. In the early sixties, Billy finally formed his own band, which toured successfully in many cities across the country. The yield of that success included two illegitimate children that Billy had fathered … the only two that he acknowledges. That was a few years before he married Wiona, a preacher's daughter, to whom he has been married for thirty very happy years.

That's my latest version of Billy Strum's biography. He never grants me the interviews I request. But every time I'm in Chicago, he does read the then-current version of his life story that I've written, promising to acknowledge it if ever get it right. One day, I hope to reunite Billy Strum and Bobby Joe Turner and interview them together.

THE ETERNAL LEGACY OF WILBUR JONES

I was strolling through Washington Square Park in the center of Greenwich Village that sunny May afternoon. New York University students mimicked the actions of studying while they lay on the grass. Drug dealers were scattered at the central-west section, inquiring, "S*moke? Smoke?"* of passersby. Everybody knew who they were with the seeming exception of the police, who I've theorized often overlooked their presence because it seldom appeared tied to violence in the park or the surrounding area.

There were no main attractions of acrobats, comics or bands entertaining in the centrally located fountain roundabout that day, leaving it to be occupied by small ad hoc guitar and vocal groups. I had to dodge an oncoming student on a skateboard only twice.

I carried with me more than a handful of short story manuscripts. After several very commercially and critically successful novels, I wished to take a temporary lateral step, and work on short stories I'd had in the pipeline for a few years. Each one had a theme that made a point to me and, I hoped, would to readers as well.

My plan was to walk to the southwest corner of the park, as I generally do, to be entertained by the usual band of chess players waiting to be hired for a game. However, a pulled leg muscle got the best of me, and I flopped down on a bench. The older black man to my left, staring into space, looked very familiar—but from where, I didn't know.

"Hey pigee, pigee," the scruffy, blond, late-forties guy to my right called out to four pigeons waddling five feet in front of the bench. "Try this," he said, tossing a few scraps torn from his slice of pizza.

The pigeons ran to the spots where the scraps had landed and nibbled them apart.

"Hah, they love it, the little goombahs," he said to me in a raspy voice. "Watch this," tossing more bits of pizza with and without cheese. "See them go for it?"

"It proves that pizza is the universal food," I said, to humor him and be polite.

"Hey buddy," he called over to the pensive black man, "you see how those birds went for the pizza?"

The older man turned his head, gave a courteous nod, and returned his gaze back to nowhere. I continued to look at him, still wondering why his face was familiar. He wasn't dressed up, but his clothing was definitely not tattered—certainly not a homeless person as were many occupants of that section of the park. His face had an expression of both dignity and sadness. He turned slightly toward me, and he caught my glance. I smiled, and he returned a short smile and a nod. Once again, he shifted his stare straight ahead.

"Hey, buddy," the pigeon feeder addressed me, "what's your scene here?"

"My scene?"

"Yeah," he said, leaning closer to me, causing me to notice his lined forehead above his blue eyes and making him look older than I'd first estimated–early fifties. "What's your game or gig here?" he asked in a louder voice.

"My gig is watching pigeons eat scraps that people toss to them," I said.

"Yooo are pulling my leg. I know when my leg is being pulled. Ouch!"

I laughed. I couldn't not. "My scene, or gig, whichever way you put it, is *observation*," I said, purposely stopping with no further expansion, laying it at the feet of my newfound friend and waiting to see how he would ping-pong that.

"Observation? Hah. I know what you're doing. Sittin' around the park, watching all the freaks—like me," he said, laughing. "Right?"

I leaned toward him. "Do you consider yourself a freak?"

Head tilted, he paused for a thought. "Nah."

"Then why should I consider you a freak without even knowing you?"

He grinned. "Sometimes it's fun to act different. See how people react to ya. I guess I really am kinda different than most people, but I have fun exaggerating it and watching people's reaction."

"So, I'm not the *leg-puller* on this bench. You are. Right?"

"I'm guilty as charged," he admitted, "but so are you."

"I was just kidding you."

"We'll ask our bench neighbor. Hey, fella," he called to the older man to my left. "I know you've been listening to our conversation even though you keep looking straight ahead. I can tell by the way your head moves, just like any eavesdropper in the park."

I turned and saw a small smile on the older man's face.

"So I'm askin' you to be the judge. Is this guy sitting between us a leg-puller just like me?"

A full smile beamed across the older man's face. In a vaguely southern drawl, he said to the pigeon feeder, "Well yes, he is a leg-puller. But he is not on your level. You, son, are a ball-buster."

"Hey, I don't know how to take that," the pigeon feeder said, a feigned grimace on his face.

"I think he meant it as a compliment," I said, "because a ball-buster outranks a leg-puller. It's like a full house beats a straight in poker."

"The man has explained it to you right," the older man confirmed.

"You guys are as good as me," pigeon man claimed. "I gotta get going 'cause I see a couple of my friends over on the other side of the fountain. Maybe I'll catch ya later."

"Have fun," I told him.

The pigeons, too, soon moved on, no longer having scraps of pizza as incentive to stick with us.

"Just you and me," I said to the older man. "We're empty nesters."

"Yep."

I placed my lapboard on my knee, and my writing pad atop, preparing to jot some notes.

"You're starting to write a story about him already?" His initiation of conversation surprised me.

"No. I *am* a writer, but I probably won't ever write a story about him, specifically. More likely, his behavior or something he said will be a seed for a thought, or some fictional character. I very seldom write about real people—unless the subject is very special to me."

"Did he say or do anything to give you a seed?"

"Yes. Actually, he did. He admitted that much of his behavior is a *put-on*—to stand out. To get attention. I've always thought that many of the people hanging around here are putting each other on, or even putting themselves on to stand out and get attention—or to be the same, and fit in with the scene. I use the phrase *posers*, but I don't claim to have originated it."

"And you?"

"What about me?"

"You trying to fit in with something?"

"Me?" I laughed. "I'm just glad I can fit in with *me*. There were times when I did try to fit in. We all did. You know, teenagers. And in my case, working in the business world. I certainly don't go out of my way to *not* fit in. But I don't go out of my way to fit in, either. Not at this point in my life. Maybe I'd have more contacts, and better contacts, in the publishing world if I did."

The man's forehead creased while he rolled my words around in his mind.

"How long ago did you work in business?" he asked.

"I left it ten years ago."

"The people you knew then—do they remember you?" he asked.

"Interesting question," I said, and thought about how to phrase my response. "It has several answers. In the case of a few very special people with whom I had, and still have, special relationships, the answer is yes. But as to the majority of people with whom I worked—even some whose backs I watched and troubles I counseled—within a year of my departure, they no longer had time to speak to me on the phone, or even respond to my emails. That doesn't really answer your question as to whether they *remember* me, though."

He looked at me purposefully.

"It answers the more important question—the one that, perhaps, I actually meant to ask," he said. *"Do they care anymore? Or, does it matter anymore?"*

I hadn't expected the topic of our interchange to turn to the endurance and spirit of how I am remembered by my former corporate colleagues. I concluded that it was related to something weighing on his mind while he was previously gazing straight at nowhere.

"I suppose you're right," I said, "though it may not always be as absolute as you express it."

"What do you mean?"

"It might not be that they don't care *at all* anymore. They simply care *less*. Time has marched on and other things have happened. Things are happening in the current moment, and other people have filled the place I used to fill. The memories of me might be the same, but they're no longer as immediate, no longer as relevant."

Once again, he took a moment to think about what I had said. He reached for his bottle of water on the ground in front of him, and I noticed the unusually large size of his hands. So wide, and so long. Then another look at his face, and it finally hit me. Everyone grows older, but how could I possibly not have recognized him right away? Me, of all people, not recognize *him.*

"I understand what you're saying, young fella," he said

"Young fella? It's been a couple decades since I've been addressed that way. Thank you."

"But, how did you feel when your ex-business friends stopped taking your calls or answering your emails? And how do you do feel about being less relevant?"

"First, how did it feel when there was no time for my phone calls and no response to my emails? It felt like crap. It felt terrible. I wasn't asking for their afternoon—just 'hi, how you doing, and what's going on?' If somebody didn't reply twice, I didn't try again. But not everyone was like that. I realized that there were people who truly did value our personal relationship after I was out of uniform, so to speak, and still do.

"And the question about being less relevant regarding what's going on today? That's just the way it is—it *has* to be. For some new kid who just started working at my old company, well, he never sat next to me in a meeting, never got any guidance from me, and very likely never heard my name except in reference to some historical contract. Colleagues from my time who are still there have been experiencing new things, and new people. They have those people *and* me to remember, in addition to me and what we did together. I would just hope that when they *do* think of me and our time together, their recollection is a kind and positive one. A fond one."

"What words would you hope they'd use to describe you?" he asked.

"Honest. Fair. Willing to stand-up for what I think is true and right. That would sum up what I think is most important that I'd hope they remember about me. Now, what about you, Mr. Question Man? What words would you hope people use to describe their memory of you?"

There was a lot of shifting around of his body on the bench until he was facing me, right elbow on the back of the bench, and one leg swung over the other.

"I always gave it my all," he said. "Always—two hundred percent," he answered, a cheek-creasing grin across his face.

"That's most important?" I asked.

"Oh, yeah."

"Not anything in particular that you achieved or did?"

"Your wish is to be remembered as honest and fair—personal qualities. You didn't choose a specific accomplishment to be remembered. You chose being remembered for how you went about doing what you did."

"You're right," I replied with a double head nod.

He helped me touch what I'd been trying to find a way to express in words. Do people care more about how others value them for their character traits, or for the milestones they've reached.

"Is this a subject that's been on your mind?" I asked my benchmate. "If so, you're not the first person."

He turned away from me, and then he turned halfway back, looking straight ahead. "You're a stranger. Talking about this sort of stuff with a stranger isn't natural for me."

"I understand. I talk *and write* about these kinds of things. These kinds of feelings. In fact, I have an article with me that I've written about Wilbur Jones, the greatest ballplayer I ever saw play, and the influence he had on my life. It's a personal thing, but I want the world to know about it." I looked at him. "Would you like to see the article?"

"Yeah."

I took it out of my bag and handed it to him. "I'd really like to know what you think of it. Read it out loud for me."

"Out loud?" he asked, looking up at me.

"Yeah. Please read it out loud for me. I'd like to know how it sounds when you read it."

"Okay."

"I was nine years old the first time I went to the ballpark and saw Wilbur Jones play, and I'll never forget it. He hit two home runs, stole two bases, and knocked in five runs. But it wasn't only his statistical feats of the day that were so memorable. I saw it all live instead of on TV, and saw him bigger than life—the way he stood in the batter's box, took a lead off first base or dashed around the bases. How he'd gracefully run into the dugout after the opposing team made a third out. Most of all, I felt the electricity generated by the way he played. Infinitely more than on TV, it could be seen in the ballpark how Wilbur Jones played the game—all-in, 200%, and with a sixth sense for the game.

"That was the day I became more than a team fan. I became a Wilbur Jones fan. I wanted to be like him. Having only average baseball talents, I couldn't be exactly like Wilbur, but I tried to mirror his example of putting total effort into whatever endeavor I tried in my life.

"We live in a nation that has historically been divided on matters of race, even if that divide has been lessening in recent decades. Many young white boys of my generation grew up cheering, admiring, respecting, and, in my case, loving Wilbur Jones. Those young white

boys grew up to vote, and have young children of their own to pass on the values that grew out of their life experiences.

"Each small drop of rain changes lakes, rivers, and oceans in immeasurable ways. One man made a change in our culture more significant than all the raindrops in Lake Erie."

"Thank you always, Wilbur."

He stared at the piece of paper in his hand, tears streaking down both cheeks. Neither of us said a word until he looked up at me.

"He'd like this article. I know he'd like it," he said, lower lip quivering.

"You say that with assurance. I bet you know him. Hey, if you do know Wilbur Jones, maybe you can do me a favor, and see to it that he gets this copy of the article. That would be great."

"Okay. I'll see to it."

"I need to be going, to meet a friend," I said, rising from the bench.

He rose from the bench, too, and reached out his big hand for mine, and looked me square in the eye. "Thank you."

I returned his smile with an emphatic nod, and grasped his big right hand. "Thank *you.*"

SON OF A BITCH, MEL

I used a White Castle hamburger eatery as my hangout when I first began writing many years ago. I sat for hours with a pen and pad and a half dozen skinny, greasy burgers garnished with oily grilled onions and a slab of pickle. Nobody was ever asked to leave White Castle. Now my unofficial office is a Panera Bread restaurant and bakery where I can sit all day in more comfortable quarters. I eat a bowl of soup, a healthy salad with an apple instead of bread, and take all the coffee or unsweetened iced tea I can drink over a three or four hour stretch, with one eye on watch in case my coveted only double booth becomes vacant.

There was a time that I considered renting a cheap office to write; however, having become a person that generally doesn't open an eye before 11:00 a.m., I wouldn't use the office in the morning. As my daughter pointed out to me, I have a good deal—ten or twelve dollars for an afternoon office with lunch included. What she didn't also consider is the value of being able to eavesdrop on other people's conversations, or merely observe their actions, as a source of potential stories or characters to be developed for stories.

I was sitting at my double booth, two tables away from the only table for eight. It was late afternoon, early enough that the seven-lady knitting group would not arrive for two hours, so the area would remain fairly quiet. Good time for creating.

I was two pages in when a man—early fifties, average height and build, wire-rimmed glasses, and gray hair—passed by and placed his tray on the next table to my right. We nodded to each other as regulars often do. I'd frequently seen him around Panera's the previous two months, but we'd never spoken. He was distinguishable for being notably indistinguishable, except for one thing—the scar running from behind his left ear down to the top of his shirt collar, maybe beyond. Oh, and the other thing; his left ear was slightly lower than the right. Not by a lot, but enough for me to notice that his glasses didn't sit evenly on his face. Like me, he was generally alone, but didn't have the company of a pen and writing pad. Just a newspaper, cup of coffee, and sometimes a piece of pastry or a bagel with jelly, suggesting he had a sweet tooth.

I know what you're thinking, and you're correct. This man was among the subjects of my observations. Because he had always been alone and there were no conversations on which to listen in, I could only observe and make up a character. I first cast him as Silvio, a former foot soldier in the Gambino crime family, now a bit too old to fill that job, and presently retired. But I scratched that role for him because he often received cell phone calls that caused him to go outside in the cold weather to speak. I then reassigned him as Steve Sachs, private investigator, who stopped by to relax and think. I could probably have kept going with imaginary roles for him if not for what happened next.

"Say, I see you here often," he said.

I looked up and nodded. "Yeah, I'm here often. You, too."

"Are you a writer?"

"Yeah, I am."

"That's what I thought." He pulled a chair over to my table and sat down. "Have you published any famous books?"

This is a frequently asked question, and one that I try to evade except when at a book signing. Nobody at Panera's, or most other places, knows my full name. I prefer that people relate to me as a person rather than as the celebrity author who's had nine top-ten best-selling books, after the typical initial years of being a struggling writer. When people interact with a celebrity they are either impressed or trying to impress, and the give and take between them is strained.

"I've published," I answered. "You probably never heard of any of my books."

"Oh." His shoulders dropped a bit. "You do a lot of your writing here. How long have you been writing?"

"In total, about twenty years now. The last twelve years have been full time. Before that I wrote only on Sunday afternoons."

"You quit your job and went for the gold ring."

"I went for what I really wanted to do."

He stood up, reached around for his tray of food at the next table, and started for the seat opposite me, asking, "Mind if I join you for a little while?"

He just had. "Okay," I replied with mixed feelings. On one hand, I'm compulsively curious about people, and I always like to be friendly. And maybe he's a private investigator named Steve Sachs. On the other hand, my concentration was being broken, and I felt as though I was being bulldozed.

"Do you write nonfiction? About the lives of real people? I can tell you stories from my life that I'd like someone to write about," he said.

I'd heard that before. Actually, it's become a common question for me in recent years.

"I don't do biographies," I answered. "In fact, the only nonfiction I write are essays tying my observations of human behavior to personal experiences."

"Then you can write about your personal experiences with me."

His persistence made me grin. I looked at his tray.

"First time you've ordered a salad," I said. "Usually just a cup of coffee and something sweet."

"You've been watching me?" he asked.

"I watch everybody. People call me Mitch. What do they call you?"

"Mel. Damn Mel. Son of a Bitch, Mel."

"What about the people that don't like you, Son of a Bitch, Mel? What do *they* call you?"

"The people that don't like me call me *Sir.* That's 'cause they're afraid of me."

"Uh-oh. So what should I call you?"

"Fuckin' Mel."

"Okay, Fuckin' Mel. But that might not naturally roll off my tongue in casual conversation, so how about me calling you *F.M.?*"

"Perfect."

"That's cleared up then."

"What are you writing now?"

"This? It's an essay."

"About?" he prompted.

"How we judge the behavior of people we like differently from the way we judge the behavior of people we don't like—even if it's the same behavior. This applies to politicians, or any category of people. But I'll explain it the way it comes out in fictional characters. Let's say the hero of a story is a good person the reader is rooting for, even if he has a few flaws. If that person does something wrong, he is judged less harshly than if another person does the same thing—and much less harshly than the antagonist of the story would be judged if he committed the same act. It's the nature of people to be more understanding when judging a person they like than one they don't like."

"And you figure that's true not just in politics, but with other people too?"

"Yeah, depending on the misdeed and the person's past history. A mass murderer won't be given a pass just because he bought a lot of Girl Scout cookies, but poor judgment in someone's personal life or a minor legal infraction would likely be forgiven if the person has had a reputation for good deeds."

"Oh. But what if the person's had a bad reputation, but he's never been *caught* for anything before?"

Is he pulling my leg? I thought. "In a court of law, reputation is not supposed to count, but in the subjective thoughts of people, including members of a jury, it does count. That's the overarching issue of what I'm writing."

"I'd like to be a writer," F.M. said.

"Why?"

"Say stuff. Tell about stuff."

"About your life?" I asked.

"Yeah, kind of." He paused, and looked down at the table. "Probably couldn't publish it though."

I gave him a bit of time to look back up at me, but he didn't.

"It would be trouble for you if you published it?"

He looked up and nodded.

"You can publish it as fiction, and change names, including your own."

"Ah, I don't know how to write stories, anyway."

"Maybe yes, maybe no. It's hard work. You have to like doing it. Or have a great purpose. And your present line of work is ... I didn't catch what you said."

That got me a short smile. "I didn't say."

"Of course not. I would've remembered."

"I'm in the service industry."

"Service industry. I'd need more than that if I were to write your story," I said.

"I didn't say my whole life story. I said I can tell you stories *from* my life."

"Oh, the abridged version."

F.M.'s cell phone rang, and he looked down at the number on its screen.

"Excuse me, I have to take this call," he said, getting up from the table.

I watched him walk outside to the parking lot.

I took a gulp from my cup of coffee. It had gotten cold and I wanted to get a refill, but I wanted more to re-engage with my essay. I did not begin tapping my pen on the table or pad, which meant I was quickly getting back into it and the words were flowing. After having written several pages and reaching a logical breaking point in the text, out of the corner of my eye I picked up Walter wandering about with a tray of food in hand. *Is it that time already?* I wondered. All the tables in the back, where Walter traditionally sat, were occupied. He stood fifteen feet away from my table, gazing at *his* spot, back turned to the front section which had eight empty tables, including the big conference table right in front of him.

I approached a young guy working on his computer at Walter's number-one table. I explained the situation to him, describing the white-haired old man wearing brown glasses, with a tray of food in his hand.

"Really?"

"Really," I confirmed. "Would you mind?"

"Okay. I don't care, if it makes a difference to him."

"Thanks. Someday, I'll be his age, and someday you'll be my age—and then his age. Thanks for understanding."

The young guy picked up his computer and coffee and walked toward the front of Panera's. I waved Walter over to his spot. He looked relieved when he got to his table, and expressed his thanks with his customary sweet smile.

"How are you today, Walter?"

"Good. That young guy didn't want this table anymore?" he asked.

"No. It was too busy back here for him—too much talk, and he couldn't concentrate on the work he was doing on his computer. He called me over to ask if he could switch tables with me, but I told him I was all settled in at my favorite booth."

"Oh. So I got lucky out of it all," Walter said. "I like to sit here."

"Yes, I know."

Walter lived at the Brandywine Seniors Home, two blocks away. He didn't want to have all three of his daily meals in the same place, surrounded by only old people.

"Who's your friend?" Walter asked me, nodding toward my booth.

"My friend?"

"The guy who just sat down at your table."

I turned. He was back.

"That's F.M."

"F.M., like J.D. Salinger? Is he a writer like you?"

"No, he's in the service business."

F.M. gave me a wave as though to say *I'm back. You can come back too, now.*

"Is everything okay, Walter? Are they treating you well down the block?"

"Everything is good. You should go back to your friend at your table, Mitch."

Walter and I bumped fists before I left his table. I taught him that a few weeks earlier.

F.M. was seated opposite me as I sat down at my table. Howie, the insurance salesman, was working his prospect near us. I often overheard Howie's sales pitch. He wasn't discreet. Because of my prior career, I understood financial matters and knew that Howie was pitching what was best for Howie rather than for his prospective buyers.

"Sorry for the interruption," F.M. said.

"Everything okay?"

"Yeah, yeah. Fine. Everything is fine."

"It must be cold outside."

"Kinda."

"You get a lot of calls that cause you to go outside in all kinds of weather to talk."

"I know lots of people," he replied with a shrug of his shoulders.

"Business people," I added with an intentional smile.

"Yes, of course," he said, his eyes meeting mine. "You were saying, before, about people judging what another person does based on whether they like or dislike the person doing it."

"Right. But that needs to be clarified. I said that someone's judgment of an action is partly based on how he otherwise views the person who committed the action—say, a bad deed. For example, I really like Billy Joel, and would probably tend to judge him a bit more leniently than I would someone I'd never heard of. If Billy got in a brawl and hurt someone, I'd probably try to rationalize why it happened, and why he wasn't really to blame. But I would judge him harshly if he shot and killed five innocent people."

F.M. sat quietly for a brief while, apparently absorbing what I said.

"Okay, say it's not a famous or rich guy who would never need money. It's a regular guy who steals money ... or sells drugs." F.M. said.

I repeated in my mind, *a regular guy who steals money ... or sells drugs.*

"I don't think you mean that exactly the way you said it—a *regular guy* who steals money or sells drugs. Do you? Don't you just mean that you want your example to be someone from the so-called neighborhood who is not rich or famous?"

"Yeah, yeah. That's what I meant."

"You're narrowing it down *some*. But even so, there are many shades of gray, depending on the specifics of the act—how much it hurt other people, what might have led the person to do it—and the positive things about that person that causes others to like him."

F.M. paused briefly, rolling his his upper lip in his mouth. "What do people like about you, Mitch?"

I laughed out loud. "That's a really hard question to answer. Could be that things I think people like about me aren't things they like at all. And I know that there are particular things about me that certain people like, but other people definitely don't like."

"Such as what?"

"That would involve rehashing and re-litigating, so to speak, old matters from my prior career. The details wouldn't add to what I think is the purpose of your question. So take it as true that different people react to certain character traits differently. But let's not go further away from what you seem interested in knowing."

"What do *you* like about you?" he tried, coming from another direction.

"Service industry? Now I get it. You're a shrink."

"Really. What do you like about you?"

"Sorry, I'm not going there. I'm not going to toot my own horn about positive traits that I think I have, and then wonder how often I live up to them." I stopped and looked at him. "What's this all about? Stuff from your psychologist?"

"Just talking about things. I'm interested. Figure you're a smart guy—a writer and all."

"I don't write about myself. Indirectly, I do. But not that way. I've included myself in stories about other people I've met, and in essays about my thoughts and beliefs. So I'm in the story if I'm telling it, and part of another person's experience. But it's not my intention to write about me."

"This is fun!" F.M. exclaimed, nearly bouncing in his seat. "I never get to have conversations like this," he added with a grin.

"How come?"

"I don't know."

"I'm glad you're enjoying it," I said.

"What kind of things do you usually do for fun?" he asked.

"Writing, listening to music, baseball, and going to the gym."

"Girls? You like to be with girls?" F.M. asked me.

"Yes," I replied with a laugh. "I like to be with girls. How about you?" I turned the tables on him.

"Yeah, I like 'em ... but, ah, something's not there for me anymore... I don't know."

"What do you mean?"

He looked around, clearly taking note of how close the tables were. "Not here. Not now... Listen, if you ever want to be fixed up with a really nice, good lookin' lady, Mitch, you just let me know."

"And?"

"And I'll see that it's taken care of... and the first time is on me."

"Because I'm a good guy? It'd be costing you money because someone would have to pay the girl."

"Like I said."

"Thanks for your offer, but I wouldn't want to get involved in that."

"You wouldn't be doing anything illegal 'cause you wouldn't be paying any money."

"Thanks, but I'll pass. I appreciate the offer, and appreciate that you don't make it to people very often."

"Never. This is the first time."

"I'm flattered. Now I understand why you have to step outside when you get a phone call. It's to talk to a customer or, uh, employee."

"They're not really employees."

"They're not?"

"No. That would make me a pimp. I'm not a pimp!"

I waited a few seconds. "What *is* the relationship?"

"It's very complicated."

"Okay," I replied with a nod of my head.

F.M. turned to Howie's client. "Hey! Mind your own business. I'm talking private stuff with my friend here. It's not for you to be listening in."

"Easy, F.M.," I said in a low voice. "The guy probably just turned his head to look at the salad in front of you."

"I wasn't really looking at you," *Mr. Client* said. "I've been sitting a long time, listening to a sales pitch, looking straight ahead. I needed to turn my neck a bit."

"Okay. Alright, don't look at me again."

"Hey, pal, you don't own this place," Howie said, throwing himself into a fire that had already been put out. "Don't go harassing people or I'll have you tossed out of here."

Uh-oh!

F.M. turned to Howie with the stare of a vampire at a fresh corpse.

The client pulled his chair farther away from the table, as though he might get up. I knew Howie was grandstanding for him. I also knew that F.M. might feel a need to live up to his claimed reputation, and beat the crap out of Howie, and so I worried what might happen next.

"F.M., getting back to what we were discussing," I began.

He got up from the bench seat opposite me and grabbed Howie's presentation papers.

"How would you like to see some shredding?" he asked, and slammed the papers back down, then sat again, facing me and across the aisle from Howie. "You know, you shouldn't be using this place as a fuckin' presentation theater. It's damn distracting and annoying to the rest of us who come here to relax."

"I have to go," the client prospect said. "It's getting late," he added, pushing his chair under the table.

"Let me know if you have any questions … I have your number. We'll talk," Howie called after him. "You ruined my sale," Howie said to F.M.

F.M. gave him another one of his stares, and I was concerned about what might be going through his mind.

F.M.'s phone rang. He looked at the number on the screen and took the call. "Hi, I'll call you back."

"I think you should take the call," I said to F.M. "It could be important. Howie, your client left; maybe you should leave, too."

* * *

I was sitting in my booth two days later, a cob salad with avocado to my left, a glass of iced tea on my right, and my pad dead center in front of me. My pen was tapping on the table—not a good sign. I was working on a different project. I like, even need to, alternate projects occasionally because my mood of the day might not fit the project I last worked on the previous day. I might yearn for rock 'n roll on Tuesday and the blues on Wednesday.

My mind was focused that day on how life is presented differently to people and, not just how it is unfair, but how some people handle the rougher waters by rising with it, and others stand still, watching and waiting for a tidal wave to overtake them.

I'd then been coming to Panera's for nearly two years, and gotten to know some of the young workers on a personal basis, as well as you can get to know people who are busy taking orders or preparing food or cleaning tables and refilling coffee urns. They are generally friendly. Yes, part of the job is to be nice to customers. However, some of them are exceptionally nice young people to whom I've grown attached and admire for working hard, while going to college or high school, to earn the money needed to purchase the special things they want to buy or go where they want to go in life. They strike a chord deep inside me, and when I ask them how their classes are going, I'm not merely making conversation. They remind me of someone I knew a long time back.

I began working at a large fast food restaurant near my home when I was fourteen. It was one of the best things I'd ever done. It taught me about hard work and laid the groundwork for always wanting to make the *best hot dog possible,* a phrase I employed when writing a paper for school, supervising an audit of a big corporation when I was working as a CPA, or issuing bonds for my corporate employer. I needed to do it the best I could do it. I saw in many of the friendly young Panera staffers the embodiment of *me*—forty-five to fifty years earlier.

After I'd written nearly six pages of the essay, a cup of coffee and a Danish pastry were placed down on the corner of the table. I looked up.

"Hey, Mitch," F.M. said, and sat down opposite me.

He sure doesn't believe in formalities, like "hey, mind if I join you?" Oh well, he is kind of interesting. Hope there are no near brawls today.

"How are you? I see you're back to sweet carbs today." I said.

"Yeah. I need them. Do you really like salads?"

"I do. Not that I wouldn't like to eat what you're eating, too. But if I did that every day, I'd blow up."

"What are you writing today?"

I laughed. "It's a different essay. I think you're itching to get into another philosophical discussion."

"Okay, tell me."

"I haven't sorted it all out yet. I've only written the beginning."

"Alright, maybe I can help finish it. Bounce things back and forth."

He's really something was my first thought. Then, *he's really hungry for something.*

"Okay, this is today's subject. Life is presented differently to people. What's presented to some to handle is harder than what's presented to others. This essay isn't about what's fair or unfair. It's about how some people handle rougher water by rising with it—meeting the challenge—and others stand still, watching and waiting for the tidal wave to overtake them."

F.M. gazed up and to the side for a moment. "Some people have nowhere to go, Mitch. And there are people who don't develop any instincts for survival until it's too late. Those instincts, when they do come, sometimes come the hard way."

"You say that as though it comes from deep down within."

"It does."

"Did a tidal wave ever come at you?"

"Many times. I think you're wondering what I did about it and how I ended up living the life I live."

"Yeah. Hanging out at Panera's—drinking coffee, eating unhealthy sweets, and ducking outside in bad weather whenever your phone rings. I wonder what tidal wave carried you to that life," I kidded him.

F.M. smiled. "My life didn't start out that way. We lived in the Bensonhurst part of Brooklyn, and, as a kid, I was the black sheep of my family for no reason. Somehow, I managed to go to college." He stopped and looked at me for a reaction to that. "Baruch College."

"That's where I went. What did you major in?"

"Accounting."

"Really? Me too. Who were your accounting professors?" I asked, thinking he wasn't that much younger than me, and it was likely he'd have had some of the same professors if he really had majored in accounting at the same school.

"I had Chaykin for Accounting 101. Let's see, uh, John Neuner for Cost Accounting, and uh … who was that tax professor? I can picture him … Dyckman."

Damn. I had all three of those professors, too. F.M. wasn't full of crap.

"Where did you work after graduating?" I asked.

"One of the large CPA firms just below the *Big Eight*—S.D. Leidesdorf. I was there for five years, and then took a corporate job in the controller's department."

"No tidal wave yet."

"Uh-uh, not yet."

His phone rang, and he looked at the number on the screen. "Ah." He answered, "Hello, it's me. Can you hold on a few seconds?" F.M. turned to me. "This might be take a while. You wanna come outside with me? Get some fresh air, walk, and continue talking when I'm off this call."

Probably without other people at a nearby table to overhear, is what I figured he really meant.

"Okay. It's a nice day. It'll probably do me good to stretch my legs."

* * *

F.M. animatedly spoke into the phone on the sidewalk with someone he twice called *Vic*. I saw a beautiful, smartly dressed brunette stride out of the nearby Starbucks and stop right next to F.M. He held one hand up to her in a *not now* motion. She poked his shoulder, and he made a pleading, beckoning gesture to me. With some reluctance, I approached them. He then walked sixty feet away to continue what seemed an important call.

"Damn Mel," the brunette said.

"Son of a Bitch, Mel." I playfully retorted.

She laughed heartily, her mood changing

"Why are you so angry with him?"

"I have an appointment."

"Yeah?"

"He has to arrange to get me there and he hasn't been answering my calls."

"I guess because he's been on some important call for a long time."

"I have to get to Manhasset. It's four or five miles from here. Do you have a car?"

"Not with me," I lied. "My car is in the repair shop."

The frown on her face changed to a smile and a nod to someone behind me. I turned for a glance. There was nobody other than Walter, and I bet he was wondering what I was thinking about her nod to him. Meanwhile, I was wondering what he was guessing about our conversation.

Finally, F.M. finished his phone call and approached the beautiful brunette and me.

"Mitch and Sara, I see you've already met. She's the one I had in mind for you, Mitch."

How do I respond to that? I thought. I didn't.

"I was trying to call you," Sara complained.

"Sorry, gorgeous. I couldn't help it."

"I have to be in Manhasset in half an hour."

"Sam?"

"Yeah."

"Okay. Don't worry. It's taken care of. Relax; you're not on the floor of the stock exchange." He put his arm on her back. "Fortunes aren't being won or lost. Are you chilling now?"

"Yeah." Her head tilted to the side and a small smile broke out in the corners of her lips.

"There you go, kid."

F.M. made a phone call, then suggested to Sara that she go back into Starbucks to wait for about ten minutes. "A beautiful woman standing outside of Panera's is gonna attract too many looks."

He and I began walking along the sidewalk of the small shopping center on the way to nowhere in particular.

"She wasn't what you expected … Sara."

"No. I have to admit she wasn't."

"I'm not associated with broken down druggies or drunks," he said.

We kept a strolling pace.

"The tidal wave. Right?" F.M. asked.

"You were the one talking."

"I was dating this chick for about five months—really liked her. Well, we took this trip up north to Canada, planning to visit her college friends in Montreal. Neither one of us had cars 'cause we were living in Manhattan, so we made it a bus trip. You know women—they pack too much. She asked me to stuff some of her things in my bags."

F.M. stopped walking, and looked around to check if anybody was near us.

"Our bus pulls up to the Canadian border checkpoint, the door of the bus opens, and so does the door of the baggage cabin below. To get to the point, somebody calls out my name. I step off the bus and see my suitcase on the sidewalk next to an excited German shepherd. They ask me if that's my suitcase. Well, it is since it has my name on the luggage tag, right? They tell me to open it. Okay. Half a kilo of heroin wrapped in what were supposedly gifts for my girlfriend's friends."

"And you told them whose things they were. Right?"

"She denied it."

"What about fingerprints?"

"Were none."

"None? Not even on the outside of the package she handed to you?"

"She kind of poured them into to my suitcase from her tote bag. Clever of her, huh?"

"You went to prison."

"Ten years ... and lost my license as a CPA. Nobody values the certification of financial statements by a convicted drug dealer, anyway."

"This is a true story?" I asked, looking him square in the eye.

"Fiction is your game, Mitch."

I absorbed what F.M had told me, wondering what to say, or ask.

"Ten years. It must have been rough. And in more ways than one." A very lame remark, but all I could think to say on the spot.

"In what way do you mean that?"

"Well, first of all, you were convicted and had your name ruined for something you didn't do. You were set up."

F.M. nodded.

"And then life in prison for ten years; I can only imagine from movies, television, and things read in papers. You must have put up with a lot of crap. What was it like?" I asked, still not one hundred percent convinced F.M.'s story was nonfiction.

"Everything you imagine, Mitch. It's much worse than that. And that's what I meant when I said that some people have nowhere to go, and that there are people who don't develop any instincts for survival until it's too late. Plenty of guys never made it out of prison either alive or anything like the same person they were before they went in, 'cause they didn't learn quick enough how to survive in that world. I did."

"Are you anything like the same person you were before going to prison?" I asked. "Your choice of words."

We kept walking till we turned past the big shoe store and were in front of the optician's shop.

"Part of me is the same person I was before prison. That part of me is still the same—when I'm able to use it."

I wanted to kid with him and ask which part was the same—the drumstick, the thigh, or the wing. But I didn't because F.M was in the process of getting close to some deep feelings. I waited for him to continue.

"I grew other parts 'cause I needed to."

"While in prison," I added.

"Yeah. They're still useful in the world I live in. Not that I go around killing people. But I don't let myself get hurt and I don't let the girls get hurt."

"Could you have gotten a white-collar job when you were released from prison? Your CPA license was revoked, but could you have obtained a job as an accountant, or even a well-paid bookkeeper?"

"You say you came from that world. Imagine me interviewing with you for an accounting job with my record. Besides, after being where I was for ten years, what kind of connections do you think I had when I got out?"

"I get what you're saying. A construction job?" I prodded.

"Do I look like a construction worker?"

"No."

"How about librarian, you're gonna ask."

"I looked at F.M., tilting my head from side to side in mock examination.

"Maybe with different style glasses."

"You think?" He grinned.

"What about the girl? Did you ever find out anything about the girlfriend who put the heroin in your suitcase?"

"No. She testified as a prosecution witness at the trial. Never heard from her, don't know where she disappeared to after that. Doesn't really matter."

"Truthfully doesn't really matter? What if she walked out that shoe store right now?

"I'd ask you to kill her."

"Yeah. So you must have all kinds of stories to tell," I said. "To write about if you want. Things both during and after prison."

"Oh, yeah. Some I couldn't 'cause it'd be too dangerous, and other stuff would be disloyal to people who trusted me, even now."

A code of ethics, I thought.

"Is that your real name? *Mel?*"

"Why're you asking that?"

"Just wondering."

"You're just wondering?"

"I figure if I put a character in one of my stories that lives the kind of life you currently live, that character would use a fake name when doing business. That way, if he's approached in the street by, say, one of his former *associates* or customers while he's with his mom, and is addressed by that name, he can brush it off as a case of mistaken identity."

F.M. shook his head and laughed. "Fuckin' Mitch."

"You can call me F.M., too."

"You're probably a really good writer."

"It's a matter of taste. I figured you're not really Mel."

"I'm Steve ... Steven Zaretsky. And you? Are you really Mitch?" he asked with a poke in my ribs.

"Yes, I'm really Mitch ... Mitchell."

"Mitchell what?"

"You know, nobody here knows my last name."

"Nobody here, or anywhere, knows my real first name," F.M. countered.

"I actually avoid sharing my last name," I said.

"Are you on the lam?"

"No. No, that's not it."

"So you think I'm gonna break into your home?"

I exhaled. "No, F.M., it's not about you—and by the way, I don't think I'll manage to switch and start calling you Steve—it's about me."

I paused, coming to grips with the level of confidentiality of the details that F.M. had just shared.

"Graye," I said. "That's my last name."

"Mitchell Graye." F.M. slowly placed my first and last names together. "Mitchell Graye."

"Yes, that's my name. Don't wear it out."

"Hey, there's a famous writer with the same name!" he blurted. "Right?"

"Yup."

"Bet you wish you were that Mitchell Graye."

I didn't answer.

"You're not. Right? He's a big-shot celebrity with lots of famous books. You're not him. You're not that guy."

"I bet your coffee is ice cold," I told him. "We've been gone a long time. They might have dumped our food in the trash."

"Mitch, are you that Mitchell Graye, the famous author?" he asked, standing in front of me, eyeball to eyeball.

"Can my answer be kept in strictest confidence? Like the kind of code you say you keep?"

"Yeah."

"Okay. Yes, I'm that Mitchell Graye."

"Wow. You don't seem famous."

"Thank you."

"Don't you like being famous?"

"Not really. Think about how people behave when they're around celebrities. They treat them like deities—or try to impress them. I want to relate to another person like we're both people. That's why there are no photos of me in my books ... and that's why nobody at Panera's knows my last name, or knows me as anybody other than Mitch, the journeyman author who comes in to eat a salad with a cup of coffee, and sits around and writes for a few hours."

"That matters a lot to you."

"Yes, it does."

"I think I get it. You know there are lots of times I feel like *nobody* knows me. I don't mean not know my name. I mean nobody knows *me*. Not their fault. I don't let myself show. I play *tough Mel*, doing the act I need to do in order to make it through the day of whatever life I'm living—prison inmate, sex salesman, booker and protector."

"Doesn't sound like you're happy with it."

"You know, I haven't really admitted it to myself in quite these words before, but I'm kinda lonely."

There I was, walking around Panera's parking lot, in a psychotherapy session with a former accountant/convict who's also a pimp—regardless of how he categorizes his occupation. The fact of the matter, I had truly begun to see F.M. as a three-dimensional person rather than a source of curiosity and entertainment.

"Lonely? Around beautiful, sexy women much of the time? All the sex you want."

"The novelty's worn off. Doesn't matter that much anymore ... or maybe I'm getting older."

"Who isn't? Tell me, please." *Now I'm a sex therapist. To a pimp.*

"It's mechanical. Not that I don't need or want it sometimes. But it's like it probably is for Sara."

I could have said *no it's not; Sara gets paid.* But it wasn't a good time for guy humor.

"I don't feel anything."

"But are you expecting to feel a connection with someone in that scenario? I have a sense that you might be feeling that about your relationships with people overall, not just paid or business-related sex partners. You said a moment ago that you're lonely. So maybe it's a lack of any real relationships with people in general."

"You know, until having conversations with you, I haven't really talked to anybody in the last twenty years except prisoners, cops, my girls, and customers."

"Well, then you've started on a new path to a whole new world."

We finally returned inside to the food on *our* table.

* * *

Early in the evening, I began to type the material I had handwritten during the afternoon. But my curiosity about F.M. was piqued, and I began searching the Internet for Baruch College yearbooks around the period of time I estimated he might have graduated. No luck.

I returned to my typing for half an hour till it was time for dinner. But instead of putting something in the oven, I called a long-time friend of mine from my prior career. Andy Bender and I had worked at the same company for five years before he moved on to take a position on the West Coast. That was something like twenty-five years ago, but we've stayed in touch a couple times a year.

"Hello. Mitch, is that you?"

"No. Someone broke into my place and is using my phone. Would you please call the cops?"

"How the heck are you?"

"I'm good. Lying low. You keeping the world on its toes?"

"It's the other way around. Actually, I wish I could speak to you for a long while, but Jennie and I are going to be picked up in about ten minutes by my daughter and son-in-law."

"I understand. Can I keep you just long enough to ask a question about someone you might have known when you worked at Leidesdorf before we worked together?"

"You working on investigative journalism now, Mitch? Prize novels have gotten boring?"

"Whatever. Did you know Steve Zaretsky at S.D. Leidesdorf?"

"Why would you be asking me a question like that?"

"Why are you asking why I'd be asking you that question?"

"Because it's strange to be asking, out of the blue, about a guy who died in prison something like twenty years ago. That's why."

"Are you shittin' me? I mean, I know you're not, Andy. It's just that it's not what I was expecting to hear. But then again, I did ask the question because I thought something might be off."

"Mitch, you sound like you're living out one of your novels. What's going on?"

"A guy I've been speaking to at the place where I hang out and write has confided in me that his real name is Steve Zaretsky, and that he had worked at Leidesdorf years ago. He also told me that he left Leidesdorf for a corporate position, and went to prison after being framed by his girlfriend for possession of a large quantity of heroin while crossing the Canadian border."

"Mitch, back in those years when a bunch of us were recent alumni of Leidesdorf, we heard about what was going on with other guys.

That sounds like Zaretsky's story—except that he's dead. He died in prison, gangland style. It's a sad story. I'm conveying what we heard back then. Unconfirmed with legal authorities."

"I hear you. Okay, I don't want to hold you up. You've got a deadline. Take care. We'll catch up soon."

"Mitch ... be careful."

* * *

The name *Steve Zaretsky* stayed on my mind the next morning, and I searched for it on the Internet wondering if an obituary would appear. Andy said he died twenty years ago, so it was a long shot. No results, as expected. *Why would there be an obit placed in the papers for a convicted felon who was killed in prison, and might not have had family wanting to claim him—or at least not wanting to advertise his demise and living relatives?* I next searched for the contact phone number for New York state prisons. After being transferred from one number to the next countless times, I finally reached someone who was able and willing to confirm that there was a convicted felon by the name of Steven Zaretsky that was imprisoned at Cayuga State Prison until the date of his death, July 4, 1983. The person either could not or would not give me the circumstances of Zaretsky's death. Befitting the scenario, I scrambled some eggs for breakfast.

* * *

It was quiet at Panera's when I arrived to continue work on my essays. My mind was distracted, and so the efforts weren't that fruitful. Sure enough, F.M. arrived nearly two hours later with a coffee and doughnut in hand, and sat down opposite me.

"Hey, Mitch. What's up?"

"Hi. Funny *you* should ask that."

"That's funny? So what are you working on today?"

I paused briefly. "A story about guys fighting in the Iraq War."

"You write war stories, too?"

"It's not so much about war as it is about the relationships between people, and the actions of survivors."

"A psychology kind of thing, like your essays."

"In some respects."

"So what happens?"

"One guy, I'll call him *Corporal A,* and his buddy, *Corporal B,* are sent over to Iraq together in the same unit, and they form a bond as a result of fighting and eating together, and sharing their life stories. There are lots of battles, and they watch each other's backs. But one day Corporal A's number is up. He gets separated from the unit, is captured and tortured to death by the enemy."

"Sounds rough. I thought you said this story isn't about war that much."

"Well, the brutality isn't described in depth. The battles are mentioned briefly in past tense. No gory scenes."

"So I guess that Corporal B is upset about his friend getting killed."

"Of course. It's his buddy."

"What does he do? Does he go around on a private mission killing enemy Iraqis in their sleep?"

"I haven't decided yet if he should respond violently. But what he definitely does do after he gets discharged from the military is use the name of Corporal A as his own. Corporal A won't know because he's dead. And having spent a good deal of time telling each other about their lives, Corporal B knows all about A's life, including how and why he joined the military."

There was a noticeable period of silence.

"So what do you think?" I asked. "About the scenario as the backdrop for the story."

"What's Corporal B gonna do with the name of Corporal A?"

"That's where I thought you might be most helpful. That's as far as I've gotten. But you've done a story like that, taking it much further. Here's a case where you have more experience than I do."

"What do you mean?"

"I mean, Steve Zaretsky died in prison twenty years ago. Don't freakin' deny it. I have it first from an old business friend of mine who was acquainted with Zaretsky years ago, and confirmed by prison authorities."

F.M. said nothing.

"I'm told that he was killed in prison. My intuition now tells me that you were his cellmate at some point."

Again, F.M. had no response.

"I told you my full name—the name I'm recognized by—something not known by anybody but my closest friends, and I did so because you told me so much detailed information about *your* life, including your *real name*. I hope I never regret having trusted you."

F.M. looked like a deer caught in the headlights of an oncoming car. "Steve Zaretsky did die in prison. And you're right; I was his cellmate. I'm sorry. I want you to know that I haven't told anybody about you being Mitchell Graye, the author, and I never planned to betray my word to you and out your secret."

"What was it all about? The masquerade? Being Steve Z, and attending Baruch College and becoming a CPA, going to prison because a girlfriend placed drugs in your suitcase and the whole bullshit story of being a make-believe person?"

"Of being a real person," F.M said, correcting me. "You create make-believe people. I couldn't do that."

"Don't bullshit yourself like that. You create fictitious people all the time—beginning with fictitious versions of yourself. Multiples versions. I mean, who the hell are you, really?"

F.M.'s face twisted, and his hands curled.

"Yeah, you're right. Maybe that's part of why I can't feel close to anyone. Remember I was telling you that sex isn't the same anymore? We kidded about getting older. But I really meant that I wished I could love someone. I wish someone loved me. Or even knew me. But, you know that's hard when ... well ..."

"You don't even know *yourself*," I finished for him. "Because you've spent so much time and effort conning people for years about *who* and *what* you are. Right?"

"Yeah."

"If you can be honest enough for a minute, why were you in jail, in the same cell with Steve Zaretsky?"

"Selling drugs."

Just what I second most didn't want to hear, murder being the first. But maybe it was just marijuana, I conjectured.

"What kind of drugs?"

"Cocaine."

"How did Zaretsky feel about being in a cell with a drug dealer after having been framed by his drug-mule girlfriend?"

"I didn't tell him. I said I held up a bank. Armed robbery. When you're in prison, it's better to appear that you did something tougher and more dangerous, anyway."

"The image thing."

"When it helps. You know, I was serious when I was telling you that people learn to do what they need to do to survive."

"Selling cocaine to survive?"

"That rubs you wrong. Well, I was young and stupid. And screwed up. What I said about being the black sheep of my family for no reason at all, that's true. Everything bad was blamed on me. I was the curse. I guess I actually became a curse. Having money in my pocket from selling coke, that made me feel good ... big. And it got me friends. Not real friends, I know. I mean I know now. Just like having sex with the women I have sex with today doesn't make me feel good, like I was sayin'. You probably think I'm full o' shit. That I'm making up more crap."

"Are you?"

"No, I'm not. I'd understand if you think I am."

"So why did you make up the stuff about being Steve Zaretsky, an accountant who got framed by a girl, and so on. Why'd you start sitting down with me and making an obvious effort to be my friend?"

"You really want to know? Okay. From the beginning, I saw you as someone who looked respectable and kind of deep compared to me. I wanted to get close to that. Then I enjoyed the conversations we were having. Nobody ever talked to me like I'm a normal person.

A real person. I know it's my fault because I've always been acting a part."

"Were you acting a part with me? You pretended you were Steve Zaretsky with his background."

"At some point I began to feel like I wanted to make *you* feel as though we had something in common. If I was Steve, the guy who I knew graduated from Baruch College as an accountant, and who talked to me about his teachers, you could feel closer to me."

"You didn't have to do that to feel closer to me. Not for my benefit. You were doing fine as yourself."

"Yeah?"

"Yeah."

F.M.'s phone rang and he looked at the number on the screen.

"Crap. I have to take this call, Mitch. Excuse me."

Once again, F.M. went outside to speak to his caller. I took a forkful of salad, a swig of coffee, and began to delve into my writing. My coffee had gotten cold. I decided to take advantage of the urns full of fresh coffee opposite the counter where staffers take customers' orders. Through the big window, I saw F.M. standing outside in a vacant parking space with the phone to his ear just before I turned to fill my cup with hazelnut coffee.

Three gunshots rang out! It was from outside, but many people inside Panera's reacted with audible and visible fear, including me. I turned back toward the window and saw neither shooters nor F.M. When my own panic subsided a half minute later, I looked more closely through the window, searching for F.M. That's when I saw him lying on the ground between two parked cars, in the same location I'd seen him standing, talking on the phone, only moments earlier. F.M. was on his side and he wasn't moving. I walked right up to the window and saw that his cell phone was lying on the ground next to him.

I hurried outside and knelt down over him.

"F.M., are you hit?"

"Yeah," he said, turning his head toward me.

I picked up his cell phone and called 911. After giving the details to the emergency operator, I noticed that F.M. was shivering. I took off the long-sleeved shirt I was wearing over a white tee-shirt and covered his upper torso with it, then took his hand.

"Hang on. An ambulance is on its way."

"You gonna catch cold without your shirt."

"I still have my tee-shirt on. I'm always warm. I'm fine."

"Mitch," he began, struggling with his words, "want you to know, I never told anybody your secret." He started to breathe heavily in and out.

"I know you didn't. Take it easy."

"This … what just happened … an old grudge. A vendetta."

"Who was it?"

"Not tellin' ya." F.M. coughed. "If I do, you tell the cops … then you're on a witness stand. Then they're after you. Then you're dead."

"Okay. Stop talking. Save your strength. An ambulance will be here soon."

"Mitch."

"What?"

"Thanks."

"You're thanking me for nothing. But you're welcome. Stay still and be quiet."

I turned my head and noticed for the first time that a group of people had gathered six or seven feet behind F.M and me. Standing at the front were Chris, Carlos, Andrew, and Lydie, Panera staffers that I knew fairly well. Chris's and Carlos's eyes both met with mine. There were also several regular Panera customers.

I turned back to F.M. as I felt his hand tighten on mine. He gasped a few breaths. I listened for an ambulance siren. There was none. A couple more gasps. I felt F.M.'s hand go limp. I placed my hand just in front of his nostrils. Nothing. I neither said nor did anything for the next half minute during which I stayed within my own thoughts. Then I removed my shirt from F.M.'s upper torso, placed it gently over his face, and stood up.

I heard a siren that sounded as though it was a few blocks away as I turned from F.M.'s body. A second siren, and a third. In what seemed like only seconds after, a police squad car pulled up in front of Panera's and two cops sprung out. Then a second squad car with two more cops. And finally, an ambulance.

A big, burly sergeant from the first car looked at the body in the vacant parking space.

"Why is the victim's face covered with a shirt? Whose shirt is that?"

"It's my shirt," I answered, stepping forward. "I first took it off and placed it over his upper body when he was still alive and shivering. After he died … it just seemed natural to cover him."

"You were with this guy when he died. You know his name?"

"I only know him from talking to him some inside at Panera's," I said, pointing toward the storefront. "I don't know his name … at least not his real name, I just knew him as *F.M.*"

"What's that for?"

"I don't know," I answered with a shrug.

"What's your name, sir?"

Shit, just what I need, I thought, *a headline in the papers that award-winning author Mitchell Graye witnesses death of man gunned down in front of Panera's.* "Why do you need my name? I didn't witness the shooting."

"Because you were the first person to reach the deceased and because you knew him in at least some way."

"I often served the dead guy his food, or took his order," Carlos said, stepping toward the cop. "Probably knew him more than this guy."

"Did you see what happened?"

"Through the window, I saw the guy go down because I was looking in that direction when the gunshots went off. But I didn't see anybody shooting. Nobody."

"What's your name?"

"Carlos."

"Carlos what?"

"Pavon."

"And I assume you work here."

"Uh-huh. Right."

"What shift?"

"I work three o'clock till eleven o'clock closing today. But it varies sometimes."

"Okay. Any of you other guys know the deceased, or see what happened?"

"I used to talk to him when I took his order," Chris offered. "Sometimes he was interrupted by a phone call."

"You possibly know who he was talking to?"

"No. He always went outside to speak on the phone. Never talked on the phone inside the store."

"Joe," the cop called to his partner who was working with other cops to restrict access to the crime scene, "be sure we hold on to the dead guy's cell phone."

There are going tobe a lot of unhappy johns, I thought.

"And what's your name, fella?"

"Chris Barreto. I've been working the same shift as Carlos today."

"Chris, did you see the shooting, or the guy go down?"

"No, I didn't. I was only meaning to let you know that I often spoke to the guy when I served him. I probably spoke to him as much as Carlos."

"Did he ever come in here with somebody else?"

"Not much. Couple of times a girl came in and went over to his table. Not for long."

"What did he talk about?"

"Uh … just stuff. Just to talk. Sports, my school, about the food."

"What did he usually order?"

I thought that an odd question.

"Usually a sweet pastry and a cup of coffee. Only sometimes a salad."

Chris got it right, and with that I melted into the crowd that had gathered, and slipped back inside Panera's. I returned to my table without a coffee cup, and sat down with my salad, pen and pad—my back to the front door. I played with my salad for ten minutes, then convinced myself that I needed to use one of the bathrooms, where I hung out for an extra-long time. After returning to the table, I packed up my pad and pens, put my jacket on over my tee-shirt, and pulled the hood up over my head. I put my black wire-rimmed reading glasses on and headed out the front door, dispensing with my usual good-night wave to whatever staff member might have been at the counter.

I walked quickly, but not too quickly, past the cops at the crime scene, breathing a sigh of relief when I reached my white Chevy and got in.

* * *

I think about F.M. from time to time. About his need to pretend to be someone more accomplished than he was in an unnecessary to attempt to be accepted by me. Me, of all people—someone whose goal is to fly under the radar so that I and people I meet can have more comfortable and real interactions. F.M. thanked me just before he died. I've thought about that, too. All I ever did for him was talk to him, like I do with so many people I meet when I'm not focusing on my work. I value that *thank you,* especially considering its timing, but something about it feels sad.

I was fortunate that my young friends on the Panera staff stepped in to tell the cops about how they also spoke to F.M., and even what kind of food he ordered. That gave me a chance to slip away. Yes, that was a good thing for me.

SECTION III

ESSAYS AND NONFICTION

SOMETHING BORROWED, SOMETHING NEW

I've been asked from to time how I go about writing a story. And if I know how it will end when I first begin. With very few exceptions, the answer is *no*. It's not until a certain point in time that I realize how a story will end—and I hope my readers are as surprised as I most often am.

Are my stories' characters actually real people that I've known? One or several traits of my primary characters might be those of a person I've known. For example, one character might have the arthritic limp of a real person; the speech pattern of another; the height, weight and receding hairline of a third; and the bad habits of still another. I resist the full use of a ready-made, real character because that would be uncreative and, more importantly, it would be unethical if the fictional character's actions were embarrassing to a real person.

The stories you have just read included characters that were inspired by people that I had singular or periodic brief interactions with and made a lasting impression on me. I borrowed recollections of those short encounters and added the product of my imagination, thereby combining *something borrowed and something new* to create a fictional character and story.

In the early morning hours of a January 1st in the mid-1980s (before caller ID), I actually did receive a phone call from a woman who had the wrong emergency number, and was making a desperate attempt to reach her psychiatrist. We talked for a long time until I was fairly sure she was not going to do anything rash—at least not that morning. Though she was not an Indian woman, and her problems had nothing to do with her parents or the person she would marry, the woman I spoke to that New Year's morning inspired the creation of Amala, in "A New Year," who thought she wanted to take her life when she began speaking to the fictional narrator. So the first two pages of that story were essentially nonfiction. I was inspired to create her as an Indian woman whose parents were insisting that she marry only an Indian man from a specific region of India because I was aware of a young woman, on a third hand basis, who once had that issue. I believed I could use it for purposes of both fiction and indirect commentary on parents placing such limitations on their children's choices. Every other detail of the story was made up in my mind.

Some readers ask me about the settings I use. Did I really spend time at those places, they often want to know. Because I periodically traveled for business, I had the opportunity to use my photographic visual memory to recall descriptions of scene locations in my stories, whether in Montreal, Toronto, Bermuda, an Amtrak train, or a location in my hometown New York City.

Like the fictional narrator of "Speak No Evil," I truly did hang out in the White Castle hamburger restaurant in Bayside, Queens during the late 1990s, downing some burgers and spending a few hours writing stories without being concerned that someone would ask me to leave. It's also true that an older woman in that White Castle often sat at a table doing nothing other than lining up a row up of lipstick cases, checking herself in a pocket mirror, putting everything away, and then repeating the routine again twenty to thirty minutes later. Like my *Mildred*, she spoke to nobody. I always wondered what her story might be. So I made up her story and it became "Speak No Evil."

I've always been interested in people and what makes them tick, and it's never been unusual for me to be listening to a total stranger telling me about the personal facets of his or her life. Whether on a park bench, a train, in a diner, at a gym, or a dance back when I was a teenager, an invisible sign on my forehead seems to read, "Go ahead, I'll listen." A very small percentage of people I meet or observe inspire a character in one of my stories, and I'm often asked why *some do* and most don't. It's because those that do made me feel a powerful emotion.

I had business to conduct in Toronto after the turn of the millennium, and stopped into Wayne Gretzky's bar and restaurant to have dinner one night. A couple nights later I stopped by again, and the bartender with whom I'd previously had a conversation asked when I was returning to New York. A woman in her mid-thirties overheard that, and asked me if I knew any famous people in New York who could get her on TV. Really. She believed that if I was from New York I must have known famous people. She wanted to appear on TV to tell her story because she had only six months to live. You're thinking this sounds familiar, and it should. It's the very beginning of "Not Near Halifax," and is the only part of that story that's true.

What the woman told me was sad. But I didn't get a chance to speak with her further because friends of hers drew her into a different conversation, and the bartender who served me my Diet Coke then drew me into sports talk. I never heard anything more about that woman. I made up the rest of the story, step by step, to create "Not Near Halifax." But it likely wouldn't have been written had I not met the real Tiara, whose situation made an impression and created an emotion for me. I thought about what that woman in the bar had said to me. I thought about it again and again. I imagined her feelings and, because I didn't know her history, I had to paint one.

Strong feelings were also evoked by an unusual young man who was a member of my gym fifteen years ago. He was approximately twenty years old and spoke a bit too loud, and in a slightly childlike manner. Though he was outgoing, few people spoke with him in the locker room. He was different—challenged. I found his relative immaturity engaging because he displayed exuberance when he shared a story or a thought. But I also noticed sadness at times, and I was certain that it resulted from the way most people treated him or brushed him off, not having the patience to talk to him. That young man was the inspiration for the mannerisms and spirit of Dennis in "Dennis And The Bad Guys," but the background of the fictional Dennis is entirely made up, as is the story.

When I was an adolescent and a young man, I hero-worshipped a particular black athlete I found especially inspirational. During the time I attended a local college in New York, he did a promotion at Macy's department store for a suit company and I cut class to see him and get his autograph. However, when I arrived I stood frozen, too in awe to approach and ask for his autograph. Time was up and the promotion handlers ushered my hero out of Macy's through an underground tunnel, into the street, and across Seventh Avenue to the front of Pennsylvania Station and a waiting taxi. I can recite his route because I chased him the entire way in a panic that I had missed my chance. Just as he was about to get in the taxi, I grabbed the door with my hand and blocked his entrance. "Please, can you sign this picture of you in the newspaper from when you hit four home runs in one game?" He did. I still have it.

I was passing through Pennsylvania Station one morning in the mid-1990s, and decided to stop into a shoe repair store for a quick shine. I caught sight of a familiar-looking black male, who appeared to be approximately sixty-five years of age, seated three seats to my left. I turned to get a better look, but avoided staring at him. I almost started to say *"Excuse me, are you him?"*

The man sure looked similar to my childhood-teenage-early adulthood hero, but I began to have my doubts. *Nah, it's not him. But what if it is him. I wouldn't want to insult him by not recognizing and acknowledging him—especially considering how important he'd been to me.* I was perplexed. You might think I'm kidding, but I'm not. The puzzle was solved when the man rose from his chair, gave a tip to his shoe shine man, and turned in my direction. It was definitely not *him*, and I was off the hook. On one hand, I was relieved that I didn't have to decide what to do, but I was disappointed that I wouldn't have a chance to ask for a second autograph from my hero.

It is assumed by most people, including me, that the majority of celebrities in their heyday wish they could walk down the street or sit and eat a quiet meal in a restaurant without worrying about being nearly assaulted by admiring fans seeking their autograph or wanting to talk to or touch them. I've wondered about how the same celebrities feel thirty to forty years after they've been out of the limelight. Do they then sometimes wish somebody *would* recognize them, and remember what they did—their accomplishments and contributions? And then I sometimes think about most of the rest of us—people who have never been celebrities. How much do they wonder if their work is remembered, was of value or carried on in some way.

When I became certain that it was not *him* in the shoe repair shop, my disappointment was offset by a feeling of relief, because if it had been *him*, I would have wanted the time for an opportunity to tell him how much he'd meant to me and that I still remembered him. My recollection of seeing that man in the shoe repair store and who I thought it might be, and the thoughts and feelings I described above, inspired the creation of the older black man sitting in Washington Square Park and the story, "The Eternal Legacy of Wilbur Jones."

"Billy Strum and Me," the shortest story in the preceding fiction group, was inspired by real-life attempts to meet Charlie Biddle, famous jazz musician (upright bass fiddle), in his Montreal jazz club and restaurant. Charlie always introduced the pianist and the drummer of his jazz trio, and then added "and me, I'm Charlie Biddle on the fiddle."

Charlie always looked so interesting to me, and I tried several times to get an interview with him by various means, such as trying to reach him before other fans during a break, asking a waiter to pass a note on a napkin, and leaving a phone message. I never got the interview. I didn't blame Charlie. I wasn't exactly the established press; he probably thought I was a nut.

After giving up on getting an interview with Charlie Biddle, I wrote "Billy Strum and Me," in which I make fun of my obsession of trying to guess people's life stories and situations. The fictional Mitchell Graye keeps bringing new versions of Billy's life story to Billy, hoping that one time Billy will say *yes, you got it right*.

Now you know some of my secrets, and the creative process of my fantasy world. A piece of real cloth from here, a string of thread from there, a wisp of white clouds, a flash of sun, and a piece of moon. Shape it. Pull on it. Reshape it.

Someday, you might get the feeling that a not-so-young male has been observing you for no apparent reason. His eyes might even seem to be glued on you except for when he takes a bite of a salad or sips on a Diet Coke. Before panicking and walking away, or calling a cop, check to see if he has a pad and pen with him. It might only be me, thinking about what your life might be—your past, what motivates you, and what makes you happy. And if we speak and you tell me your story, rest assured that I might use only a fiber of it, creating a story from *something borrowed and something new.*

MR. POTATO HEART

I was sitting in a Toronto bar, alternately dragging a burger through a puddle of ketchup and jiggling the ice in my Diet Coke. That's the sort of thing I do when I study people around me, eavesdropping on their conversations when I can hear them, and imagining their conversations when I can't. There were all kinds of people interacting but, my attention was focused on two guys. One of them was a middle-aged businessman type, and the other a mid-twenties baby-faced biker wearing a red-and-gold bandana. Their relaxed mannerisms told me that they had not just met, but were familiar friends. So I wondered what the role of each was in their relationship.

Unable to hear their words, I was forced to create the relationship of the older and younger man in my own mind. The older man, "Sam," was *big brother and mentor* to the younger "Ean," and they were bonded by a love of biking and a mutual history of being abandoned by their fathers when they were young children. Their relationship became the genesis of my story titled "Black Bull," named after the bar in which I created Sam and Ean. But there will be no previews here of "Black Bull." My intent is to share my observations regarding relationships between two people, and what's in it for both of them.

I believe that many relationships are vicarious, and that it is often the reason that opposites attract. Ean is a young man who is not yet established and on his feet in the adult world, and his association with Sam enables him to witness wisdom, experience, and success. In turn, Ean is a vehicle through which Sam is able to relive his youth, or use the tools of attained wisdom and experience to rewrite that period of life or experience it differently. And there is nothing wrong with this inasmuch as there is a benefit to both. An analogy would be a relationship between an older man and a younger woman—sexual aspects aside, it would likely provide an upper step on the ladder of knowledge, lifestyle, and security for one, and the *do-over* experience of energetic promise and possibility for the other.

You're snickering, and thinking that I never read the headline story in the *New York Post*, a number of years ago, about the Wall Street financial tycoon who lost everything because of insider trading tips he was accused of having given to his young porno-star girlfriend. "*That* sure ain't about promise and possibility," you say, laughing. "That's about D cups and the big O." Maybe. But who pays such a price for eight seconds? I suspect that it was also related to the vicarious experiencing of a life different from one's own through another person, but without giving up one's own life—at least not wittingly. Perhaps like taking a trip to a place where you could not, and would not ever want to live every day. But you think it's an interesting or exciting place to visit.

Have you read *The Bridges of Madison County*, or seen the movie version? My take on the motivation of the characters is different from that of most people. A middle-aged Italian woman married an American soldier during World War II, and lived with him and their two children for more than twenty years on the Iowa farm where he was raised. Life with her hardworking farmer husband in the conservative, quiet Iowa community provided security, but no fulfillment of her fantasies of romance, artistic expression, and footloose adventure. While her husband was away with their children at a county fair, a stranger came to town—a late-middle-aged photographer who had spent his life traveling the world on freelance assignments. He'd had romantic and sexual adventures with many exotic women, but never felt connected with a person or place. Such a connection could not be achieved inasmuch as it would require a life that would be totally at odds with his nature and lifestyle. Not surprisingly, his soul, like hers, craved what it did not have.

The farm wife and the roaming photographer both represented to the other the missing link in their own lives. While her family was away at the county fair, and there were no repetitious routines of farm work, child rearing, meal preparation, and mending clothes, the two had a four-day romantic and erotic affair. It was the fantasy she had dreamed about. Through him, she felt the adventures of his past life without experiencing its uncertainty and lack of cohesion. Through her, he felt a connection to *mother earth* stability without his having to be tied down to the drudgery of farm work twelve hours every day—because that need was already being fulfilled by her husband.

The crisis came when the farm woman's family returned from the fair. The photographer wanted her to leave with him, and she felt a great desire to do so. But she couldn't. The storyline was that she stayed due to a sense of selfless duty. Was that indeed the case? Okay, I know it's fiction just like my "Black Bull" story. But what would likely motivate real people in that situation in conscious or subconscious ways? Would the farm lady's inner instincts have been telling her that, if she did leave, she would lose the security she needed in her life and to which she had become accustomed—unless the photographer changed his life? And if he did change his life, would she lose her romantic image of him, and their affair? On the other hand, staying on the farm would enable her to always maintain the romantic image of her relationship with the roaming photographer, as well as maintain her stable though boring life, and her own legacy of "sacrificing" for her children.

She stayed on the farm, lamenting her self-sacrifice in a posthumous letter to her children. You can call me jaded, but my theory is that she chose the only way to hold on to her four-day fantasy and, in so doing, also hold on to her real world. The tragic irony was that her fixation on the fantasy interfered with the enjoyable aspects of her real world and did not allow her to express the joy of her fantasy played out.

How well did the farm woman and the photographer know each other? Certainly, they knew each other better than I knew Sam and Ean, to whom I never spoke and so created their relationship and life stories entirely from my own imagination. But how well did the farm lady and the photographer know each other as a result of a ninety-six hour relationship? I think it is very likely that each created an idealized image of the other to suit their specific needs. And given the fact that they were strangers with no shared past, both were emotionally virgin to the other. An empty slate on which to create a new image, allowing the process of creating what I call *Mr. Potato Heart.*

Many children have had a toy named Mr. Potato Head. It is a blank potato-shaped face with slits into which a child can insert various choices of eyes, nose, mouth, and ears. It allows a child to experiment, and create a facial image to suit his or her fancy. And I think that is what many people do with strangers, beginning with teenage years and onward.

The Mr. Potato Heart game is played with a blank heart into which romantic players can insert various attributes; these attributes might include sensitivity, warmth, industriousness, intelligence, and so on. Kind of like a personals ad. And the player chooses whichever characteristics his or her own heart needs at the time. I believe this is how people frequently assign characteristics to the emotionally virginal newcomers in their life. The irony is that the originator inevitably becomes angry with the real person (used as the *potato)* for not actually being the Potato Heart created.

I saw "Ean" unchaining his bike from a post on Queen Street, a year after I had written "Black Bull." He was easily recognizable due to his baby face and the very distinctive red-and-gold bandana he wore, added to the clue that he was unchaining a bike. I walked to within ten feet of him, halted, then moved forward until I was next to him.

"Excuse me, do you mind if I ask you a question?"

"What's that?"

"Do you hang out at the Black Bull?"

He grinned.

"I guess you probably do," I said with a laugh. He was a biker wearing a biker's jacket, and the Black Bull is so much a bikers' hangout that it has an unusual amount of bike racks outside. "Did I just ask a fish if it lives in water?"

"I think you did," he answered good-naturedly.

"Sorry, I didn't have my coffee this morning. The reason I approached you is that I recognize you from a time back—about a year ago when I was sitting in the Black Bull alone, kind of just watching people."

"You were watching me?"

"I watch lots of people. I'm a writer," I said, as though that automatically explained why I watch people. "Anyway, you were talking for a long time with a guy that looked around fifty and was wearing a suit and tie. Probably a businessman. I remember trying to figure out what the relationship was between you and him—a biker and a businessman."

"That must have been Charles. He's an insurance guy. Always trying to sell insurance to bikers—like car insurance. I remember getting his pitch in the bar back about that time."

"Oh … so he was prospecting you."

"Yeah."

"Thank you."

"No problem. Hey, what's your name? Maybe I'll see one of your books around."

"Mitchell," I answered, extending my hand. "Mitchell Graye."

"Sean, he said. Nice to meet you. Sorry I didn't have a better story line than an insurance salesman for you." He rode off with a wave of his hand.

I was slightly amused by the fact that the name *Sean* was so similar in spelling to the name *Ean,* and that he was a nice young guy, like my Ean. My big brotherly, mentoring *Sam* turned out to be profit-seeking, policy-pushing Charles. I had assigned the wrong attributes to Charles while watching him and Ean, and quietly playing the writer's version of Mr. Potato Heart.

I don't have to change the fictional Sam and Ean because they were created for fun, and with the desire to make them *seem real* to readers. I was playing the Mr. Potato Heart game as just that—a game—as children play Mr. Potato Head. When people play Mr. Potato Heart as part of their lives, they're setting up themselves, and *their potatoes,* for problems.

STEP ON A CRACK

I was sitting around my Bermuda hotel, thinking about the people I had talked with and what I'd learned from them. Since I'm not a golfer, nor a water sports enthusiast, there's not a lot for someone like me to do in Bermuda except think about stuff like that, and try to stich pieces of all the people I've met on this trip and others into some patchwork that makes sense to me. Otherwise, why collect those pieces?

Though my analysis is always changing, it is clear to me, at least as of today, that each human being has various needs that are in conflict with each other—or in conflict with the needs of another person. The interests of security battle the interests of curiosity, stimulation, and knowledge. And that is not a surprise to me. Most of us make choices as to which needs to satisfy beginning early in our lives. However, what intrigues me most today is the conflict of *legacies.*

Our legacy for others has to do with how we are thought of, both during and after our lives, by individuals, groups, or society at large. Our internal legacy is comprised of the private feelings about how one has lived life and the value of those feelings—a mixture of individually defined self-fulfillment and internal pride. The kind of pride that cannot be worn like a row of medals on one's chest for all to see.

At this point, you might be convinced that this narrator has spent too much time under the hot sun on a Bermuda beach, consuming excessive amounts of rum swizzles. You would be incorrect. I never cared for rum swizzles, and the less curious side of me seems content with Diet Cokes, a trait I should examine before I reach a point at which I'm unwilling to change. Still, my integrity—a sometimes very inconvenient component of my legacy to both myself and to others—requires that I admit to having spent a very long hot afternoon on Elbow Beach. Time went by because most of it was spent speaking to a very engaging young woman from Wales whom I have named *Amy.*

Amy had heard me inquire of people at the next blanket if there was a place where I could rent snorkeling equipment, and volunteered her own for my use. After my visit to the exotic fish at nearby reefs, I returned Amy's snorkel equipment and our conversation ensued. I was at first largely reeled in by the singsong lilt of her Welsh accent, a sound that I have noticed only amongst people from parts of the British Isles, Ireland, and Australia.

Amy was visiting a guy friend in Bermuda. She was a refugee of her parents who believed that she should make it easier on them as they got older by working at the family-owned pub instead of pursuing her chosen occupation as a hairstylist. After many arguments, she followed her own wishes. Amy became a hairstylist and began an unmapped journey of the Western Hemisphere. However, her choice was not without cost. She had to decide between her own self-fulfillment and her parents' approval of her, such approval being contingent upon their fulfillment. Judging from the vehemence of her feelings while telling me her story, it was clear to me that the cost of her choice was high. Nonetheless, she concluded that the cost was less than that of staying in the small town in Wales and spending the days of her life at her parents' pub, greeting their friends and patrons. So Amy chose her internal legacy.

Figuratively speaking, Amy had probably spent part of her life working hard to not step on a crack in the sidewalk. And then one day, she decided she was going to do it. *Purposely.* When I was a kid growing up in The Bronx, I had a certain period of preoccupation with not stepping on a crack in the sidewalk. I walked very carefully. The longer this ritual continued, the more important it became to stay the course and not break the rule. I believe it began when a respected older friend, a fourth grader, had advised me that bad things happen to someone who steps on a crack. He never explained why, and the longer I obeyed the rule, the less important it was to question it. I had become invested in the rule.

Amy had been invested in maintaining someone else's approval, as do many people who are dependent on others in either real or imagined ways. And she didn't dare break the rule until she experienced a conflicting greater need. Of course, her need to discuss her justification to intentionally step on a crack was also great—so it didn't come easy.

In many cases, people have invested so much of their lives avoiding stepping on a crack, that doing so is no longer an alternative—particularly when the person believes that the choice determines whether or not he will be viewed and remembered as good and righteous. What is at stake is one's legacy to the external world.

I've noticed that people who have walked many thousands of miles without stepping on a crack feel extremely threatened by *crack-steppers* because they challenge the value of a lifetime of devoutness. In a small percentage of instances, devoutness may be questioned by the non-crack-stepper himself and result in the most unsettling circumstances for a person. More unsettling than when the challenge comes from children or grandchildren. However, if a heretic has become a compulsive crack-stepper, and must do it for no explicable reason, or even fears bad things will happen if he doesn't, then there can only be a standoff. He will have become exactly what he has accused his predecessors of being.

YOU KNOW WHY?

(A True Story)

I was in seventh grade when my family moved from The Bronx to Flushing, Queens, just a stone's throw from the site that later would become the home of the New York Mets. I was the new kid in junior high school, but I made fast friends with Richie, a red-headed kid in my music class, as we practiced playing upright bass. One day, Richie made a very negative remark, mocking another kid for being Jewish.

I took a deep breath, then softly said, "Richie, do you know I'm Jewish?"

"No, you're not. You're kidding."

"I am."

"You can't be Jewish. You're my friend."

"Really. I'm Jewish," I insisted. His logic escaped me.

Richie was very embarrassed. But we stayed friends over the next couple of years. He began to run with a rougher crowd and, a few years later, he called a halt to a group of neighborhood bullies about to jump me on an empty street one snowy afternoon. It might have been accidental that Richie got to know me, but once he did, he liked me and it remained that way. But if he had known beforehand that I was Jewish, it's a good chance he wouldn't have wanted to be my friend.

I think about that experience and its ramifications from time to time. There are people disliking members of entire ethnic or racial groups even though they've never really known a member of those groups in any real way. I've always had a sense that there would be a lot less strife in the world if people took the opportunity to know and deal with *people* of different backgrounds as *people* on a one-to-one basis.

* * *

A couple years later, a few of my teenage friends and I often gathered at any one of the thirty yellow, red, or blue metallic picnic tables spread across the outside patio of a large indoor/outdoor eatery fronting an amusement park, close to where I lived. We'd check out the girls as they walked in or out of the restaurant, or we'd pop in the game arcade room when we felt itchy to drop a dime or two in the machines.

Inside the restaurant was a "relish bar" with all the fixings customers might want to add to sandwiches, hamburgers, and hot dogs—hot sauerkraut, pickled red beets, pickle relish, onions, mustard, and ketchup. We'd buy a hot dog for twenty cents, fill up a big plate with sauerkraut, then scamper to the outside terrace where our greediness would less likely be noticed. I didn't say never. Just less likely.

Sometimes we didn't go through the formality of buying a hot dog. We'd just grab a plate, fill it with free sauerkraut and maybe a bit of pickle relish, and move as quickly as possible without drawing attention. Usually, that would be when none of the managers were on the general floor of the restaurant.

We all lived in the neighborhood. It was 1960 and I was fourteen. No, wait a minute. At that age, every bit counted. I was fourteen and a half and my friends were either the same age or one to three years older.

My oldest neighborhood friend, Fred, got a job at the restaurant. The rest of us were envious that he had money to spend. And he was jealous that he was working while we were still free to hang out and screw around.

The managers eventually grew tired of us hanging out and screwing around there, and finally figured how to stop it; they hired Fred's friends and put them to work as well. They must have decided that the reduction in sauerkraut costs would more than pay our meager earnings of one dollar per hour. But the economic rubber would yet meet the road. I'll bet they didn't know how much free food and beverages we could chow down during our half-hour lunch and quarter-hour rest breaks.

I didn't get to serve food at the counter when I initially started working. My stripes were first earned as a busboy, pulling a heavy metal pail around the dining room to collect empty paper plates, cups, and leftover food from the tables. Then I'd wipe the tables clean and move on until the pail was full and ready to haul to the outside "garbage house," where the contents were heaved into larger bins, before returning to clean more tables. I also got to clean up the men's and women's restrooms. I could comment on which was consistently messier, but I am saving that for a more detailed sociological article.

At the age of fifteen I was proud when I was handed a set of hot dog tongs and elevated to counterman. But this story is not just about me. It is about friendships that developed at a unique place called the Adventurer's Inn, some of the people who worked there, and the unique atmosphere created by them.

I must remind you that it was the 1960s, with the civil rights movement in full swing; the black community had taken up the call to claim its own racial pride—while on the negative side there was racial strife in the streets of many cities.

Ten o'clock on a summer weekday morning was always a fun time when things were coming alive. Customers were being served eggs and pancakes from the grill that would soon be used to cook hamburgers. With the background sounds of '60s music cranking from the game arcade room, we'd start getting food stock out of the kitchen to store in the smaller refrigerators along the expansive eighty-foot customer serving counter.

I'd love it when the song "Blue Moon" by the Marcels was blasting over the loudspeakers; its lively beat had me moving fast. There was another reason I liked it so much. I never told the guys what the voices on that track brought to my mind. The bass singer made me think of Obie, the falsetto of Pierce, and though I never heard Leroy sing, I imagined that he would sound exactly like the lead singer if he did. So when I heard *Blue Moon*, I'd make believe I was listening to my friends in the kitchen. And me, a Jewish white kid from the immediate neighborhood who couldn't sing three successive notes in key, I imagined they'd find two notes I could sing in a cameo.

Around ten fifteen, Goldberry, a very stout black man in his sixties, would be cleaning up the game room and restaurant area, swinging his huge frame to the music and laughing. I'd wave to him, and happy Goldberry would dance a little more, calling to me, "Hey Slim!" (he called everybody Slim), then laugh and keep on with his thing. If Obie or one of the other guys came out to the counter, he'd call out the same thing. *And the band played on,* as The Temptations would have sang in their hit song, *Ball of Confusion.*

The small cash register behind the counter was used while breakfast was served and, as a way of assigning responsibility for shortages, only one person could take money from customers. During lunch there was a big line up of customers at the primary outside cash register station while food got cold. Sunday afternoons – forget about it – hot dogs got cold, ice cream sundaes melted, and customers' patience was strained to the max.

By ten thirty I would head back into the kitchen toward the three big walk-in refrigerators to start bringing things out to the small refrigerators at the counter. First thing I'd hear on the way in was Pierce singing some top hit song in falsetto voice, and laughing. He was an assistant baker with a workstation near the door. The things he most loved to do were sing, laugh, and make other people laugh, in no particular order. The fact was, he had a really good voice and with good luck might have made it in a singing group.

If I stopped to look at Pierce, it would surely result in a funny remark, or an exaggerated effort on a song and a big laugh. Shy he was not. Whatever Pierce did most likely made Obediah ("Obie") burst out in a loud bass laugh while he was preparing various meats in front of the big oven. I'd pass by him, and laugh at him laughing.

A left turn at the sinks toward the dessert table would lead me to Leroy, who by nature was more soft-spoken, with a big Hollywood smile. Whenever I saw Leroy, my instincts were always to say something to kid him, or casually bump or elbow him just to get a reaction. Totally actions of affection. He would either let out a small giggle, or feign annoyance and laugh. Leroy was a lovable teddy bear, yet he liked to exchange mischievous barbs with me.

Obie, the oldest of the three by approximately five years, was sometimes a bit more serious and, I thought, not as immediately accepting. But once Obie decided he liked a person, that was it— you need not ever prove yourself to him again.

One afternoon I had gone to the back storeroom to retrieve some paper supplies for the counter. I never liked going in there because I'd sometimes be surprised by a rat running across my feet. Once, a rat jumped from one shelf to another right past my face. This time, my surprise was finding Leroy on his break, curled up on a shelf of flat supplies. He was a little out of sorts and I was concerned.

"Hey, what's wrong?"

"Don't feel good."

"What is it?"

"Labor pains. My wife's pregnant."

"So doesn't *she* get the labor pains?"

"I have sympathy labor pains."

"Are you kidding me?"

"No. Really, it hurts."

"Do you want anything?"

"Yeah. Give me one of those soft flour sacks for a pillow."

I was only fifteen and for several years I believed him. Soft-spoken, yeah. But Leroy had laid down the gauntlet of private one-to-one pranks.

Joel, the daytime manager of the counter at the time I was hired, was an extremely energetic Jewish guy in his twenties. Though everybody respected and liked him, his obsessive cleaning and constant motion were both folklore and the butt of jokes amongst my neighborhood friends. It seemed as if he could slice a sandwich, wipe the counter, and sweep the floor in one motion—and be so happy doing it. It was actually a compliment that we made a joke about trying to imitate him.

When I was eighteen, Joel was promoted to General Manager of the Adventurer's Inn restaurant. Not a small thing for a guy still in his twenties. My memories of Joel relate not only to his humorous quirk of obsessive cleaning and speed. He was also a nice guy that others respected rather than feared, and he was honest with people. Thus, he set a positive tone. I wish I could say the same for a few of the people with advanced degrees I later worked for in the financial world. But either they didn't know how, or they were too full of ego to care.

It was common for Fred or Eddie and me to be sitting at a table in a corner on break and wave Leroy and Obie over when their break began. All of us would watch Pierce running a rack of fresh pastry goods over to the retail bakery, walking his walk, singing, and flashing his patented underhand wave. If that didn't make us laugh he'd crack a joke or pretend to slip. Meanwhile, at the opposite end of the restaurant, Ronnie, the German evening sandwich man, was probably explaining another of his favorite ways to satisfy a woman. Vic, an Italian guy who was like a utility player in baseball, was often the weekday afternoon sandwich man. If I merely said that Vic kind of lived in his own world, I wouldn't do justice to describing him.

Vic liked to clean the meat-slicing machine immediately after the busy lunch rush was over. That entailed taking it apart, soaking the parts in the sink, wiping them dry, and putting the machine back together. As sure as ice cream would melt while customers stood on line waiting to pay on a busy Sunday, a customer would come over to Vic shortly after he'd cleaned the slicing machine and ask for a corned beef or roast beef sandwich.

"Why don't you have a tuna salad sandwich?" he'd suggest. "It's really good."

"Nah. I' don't like tuna."

"Try the egg salad."

"I want the corned beef."

"Listen, I just cleaned the slicing machine," Vic would say with a hint of irritation. "Do me a favor and get something else. How about chicken salad?"

"I want corned beef!"

"Jesus! I told you I just cleaned the damn machine. Why do you have to have corned beef?" and he'd slam a towel down on the counter. "Damn!"

I witnessed this ritual every weekday for a whole summer and I was never certain whether he was serious or if he was entertaining either me or himself. Or Pierce, who I sometimes heard laughing from the other side of the door.

Not long after Vic's antics, Leroy would often meander out to the counter for some unspecified reason and settle close to where I was cleaning the post-lunch mess. He'd begin explaining to me some recently discovered power in that era of newly expressed black pride. I admit that I no longer remember specific examples, but the conversations went something reasonably close to this:

"I can run to first base in three and a half seconds."

"Really?"

"You know why?"

"Why?"

"'Cause I'm black," he said with a little crease at the corners of his lips.

"Really? That's cool."

The next afternoon, Leroy came back and, leaning against the counter, he had more news to share with me.

"I can lift two hundred pounds," he proclaimed, eyes wide. "You know why I can?"

"I'll have to think about that. Can you give me a clue?"

"'Cause I'm black," he explained in a higher-pitched voice accompanied by a wide smile.

"Really? Can I get to be black, or do you have to be born black?"

Leroy laughed, shrugged his shoulders, and headed back to the kitchen.

Next afternoon, he was pointing to somebody on a very high ladder cleaning the glass windows surrounding the restaurant.

"If I was at the top of that ladder and jumped, I wouldn't get hurt because I'd be able to fly away."

"So that's today's addition to your list of magical powers?"

"You know why I could just fly away and not fall to the ground?"

"Not a clue."

"Because I'm black."

"Listen up this time and pay careful attention before you try to fly off any ladders. Obie is black. Pierce is black. According to your theory, they can fly from the ladder. Now you, you big nut job, are *brown* and will just go splat on the ground. So if Obie and Pierce ask you to go flying with them—don't go."

Leroy's face formed a mock frown, he chuckled, then went back into the kitchen.

Not more than two days later, Leroy and I were working together serving breakfast. I was responsible for the small cash register behind the counter that morning. I had just scooped two portions of eggs and handed them off to Leroy to add the bread and potatoes while I tended to other things cooking on the grill. He handed the completed order to the customer, who gave him a ten-dollar bill. Leroy turned and headed toward the cash register, until I turned and stood in his way.

"What are you doing? You can't handle cash, Leroy." I looked straight into his eyes. "You know you're not allowed to handle cash. And you know why you're not allowed to handle cash? Because you're what?"

One knee on the floor was how Leroy ended up. He couldn't stop laughing. I thought we would both never catch our breath. I'd finally topped him with one he would never match.

That comment was funny because it was just between the two of us. I wouldn't have risked embarrassing Leroy if even one white coworker who didn't know us both very well was there. And maybe still not even with one who knew us well. Nor would I have made the remark in front of another black coworker, except Obie or Pierce, because it could easily have been taken as offensive if he didn't know how Leroy and I got along and joked around.

It's a matter of knowing people and their knowing you. There's a huge difference when people actually know one another on an individual basis. In the case of Leroy, Obie, Pierce, Ronnie, Vic, my neighborhood friends and I, and many others, we worked side by side, depended on each other, laughed together, had breaks together, and sometimes went to a ballgame together. I'm not going to use a stupid phrase and imply that my eyes didn't distinguish that Leroy, Obie, and Pierce were black—correction, Leroy was brown. It just didn't matter. They were the guys.

I'll fess up that even before the Adventurer's Inn there was no racist DNA in my genes, body tissue or soul. Even at a younger age, the notion of racial or ethnic prejudice made no sense to me, and when I heard stories about its harsh results I felt angry. Willie Mays was my idol, and in my boyhood mind, the black prince of the Polo Grounds was something special in an almost spiritual way. Each time he broke a record or pulled some unbelievable athletic trick out of the air to win a game it tickled me how it made laughable the foolish thinking of racial inferiority.

Examples of super-sports heroes and top-line entertainers are one thing. Really knowing "everyday" people makes a less exciting but deeper impression. It's probably easier to believe the stereotypes of different races and ethnic groups if you never really know any individuals in those groups on a personal basis. And that could happen when people live in neighborhoods that are racially or ethnically concentrated, whether the concentration is caused by forced segregation or the preference to live in areas totally populated by one's own group. And if the workplace also doesn't provide people with contact with others of diverse ethnic and racial backgrounds in more than a superficial manner, that's it.

The Adventurer's Inn workers were adult African Americans, Germans, Jews, Italians, Poles, Turks, Greeks, and a mix of young guys from the neighborhood. Though there were occasional individual differences and arguments about trivia, I never heard of even a single bad word said by one worker about another having to do with race or ethnicity. What caused conflict to part of the larger world was dealt with as a subject of humor among us.

I believe that it is not uncommon for people to use humor to express their solidarity in disagreement with actions they believe are wrong—by mocking them. What is the likelihood that a large number of people of diverse backgrounds would be of like mind regarding the matter of respecting people of other groups, and even liking them? Especially in the early 1960s. (Even if it was New York rather than a city less known for tolerance.) In a random group, not likely. What made the difference for this group? I'm certain it was because we got to know each other through close personal contact. When people deal with each other closely as *people*, they're more likely to see each other simply as *people!*

I graduated from college and married in the late 60s, but I continued to stop by to see my Adventurer's friends when I was in the neighborhood. If the place wasn't busy I'd just walk through the door to the kitchen like I owned the place, looking for the guys. Most people around knew me so I wasn't treated as a trespasser. Just someone coming home for a visit. In the mid-70s I became a father, moved to a nearby county, became consumed by significantly longer hours required by my profession, and my visits were not as frequent. In the late 70s the Adventurer's Inn was closed down.

It was 1982 when I found Leroy in the phone book and called. His daughter answered—the child his wife was pregnant with when he'd said he was having sympathy labor pains for her in 1961. His daughter was a student at LaGuardia College and was excited for her father that an old friend from the Adventurer's was calling. It was apparent that the era meant something special to him, too. We had a fun talk and arranged to meet up at lunchtime at the place where both he and Obie then worked.

When Joel left the Adventurer's around 1965, he was recruited by a customer to help run a rug-producing factory a mile or two down the road. Not surprisingly, Joel was extremely successful and ended up having a stake in the place, eventually owning it outright. Also, it was no surprise that Joel saw to it that Leroy and Obie landed on their feet when the Adventurer's closed by giving them better jobs than they had.

When I met with Leroy and Obie, they told me that Pierce had left the Adventurer's before it closed and was a baker somewhere else, and also that he was still the same happy-go-lucky guy. We had some laughs and they told me they were happy working in Joel's rug company. Obie mentioned that he now had weekends off; something he never had when he worked at the Adventurer's and wished he did so he could have played ball with his son. That reminded me of how Leroy, Obie, and Pierce had worked really hard for many hours at the Adventurer's to support their families, with dignity and with no complaints that I ever heard.

Time marches on, and though you think about people, life gets busy. Kids, bills, sixty-hour work weeks, physical problems. Years go by. Decades go by. But not a day went by that I didn't think at least once about Leroy, Obie, and Pierce. Our brief time together left an indelible impression on me for the rest of my life.

On New Year's Day, 2008, I thought it would be a great time to reconnect with an old friend and I did an Internet search. I was alone in my apartment and dialed Leroy's number. His wife answered. I told her who I was, how I knew Leroy, and asked to speak with him. She said she'd really like to speak with me and asked that I hold on so she could finish with the caller on the other line. When she returned to me I learned that Leroy had recently passed away. Obie had died a few years earlier. She gave me Pierce's phone number, but I was too sad for a couple of weeks to use it.

I eventually called Pierce and learned of his life's happiness and trials and tribulations during a number of conversations. Sometimes he was the same old Pierce who could make a person laugh continuously, and at other times he was quite serious. When this story was completed, I tried to reach Pierce to share it with him. His phone was disconnected. I knew the first name of one of his daughters and called phone directory information with no success. Ultimately, an Internet search informed me that he was deceased. *All three of them are gone now,* is the thought that kept sadly rolling through my mind. At least I had a chance to speak to Pierce a number of times.

I'm pleased, though not surprised, that Leroy, Obie, and Pierce remained close friends as long as Obie and Leroy were alive. Though the three were really very different from one another, there was something about them that always made it clear that they belonged together. A certain common thread. I couldn't think of one of them without then thinking of the other two. One of the things they had in common was the huge positive, and permanent influence they had on a white Jewish kid back in the 1960s. I only hope they each truly knew how much I appreciated them. And I regret that they did not stay a greater part of my life and I of theirs. For sure, the greater loss was mine.

Not many people can ever be in a position like John Kennedy, Lyndon Johnson, Martin Luther King, Jr. or Bobby Kennedy and have an effect on the texture of society on a grand scale. However, merely by being the kind of people they are, some people accomplish the same thing because they are ambassadors of goodwill to one person at a time. Collectively, that could be huge.

The Adventurer's Inn no longer physically sits on the side of the Whitestone Expressway in the Flushing neighborhood in New York. I don't like to look at the building that's taken its place when I pass by because it doesn't seem right to me. In my mind the Adventurer's still sits on that spot. I can still see myself behind the counter listening to the song *Blue Moon* and imagining that it's really the voices of Obie, Leroy, and Pierce. Goldberry is finishing his cleaning routine, doing his funny dance. Pierce is singing and laughing at his bakers' workstation, and Obie is letting go with his big bass laugh. I bump into Leroy as I pass through the kitchen and he feigns annoyance, then laughs and breaks out in his big smile. They will always be there in my mind that special way.

For the most part, it was fun to reminisce; however, it was emotionally difficult to write certain parts of this story, typing on a blank page what has been in my heart all these decades. But I now feel better for having finished it. I just wish Leroy, Obie, and Pierce could have read it.

ABOUT THE AUTHOR

Mitchell Graye was raised and still lives in the New York City Metropolitan area where he has held a variety of positions during his career in the financial community.

When not applying his analytical skills, Mitchell enjoys being a people watcher and has been a student in various psychology courses because he is intensely interested in what makes people tick. His keen observation of human behavior comes into play in developing the interactions of his compelling characters.

Mitchell Graye has also written *Return To Go,* a novel published in 2007, and *The S*heep Rise *Up,* a novel published in 2013, and a sitcom pilot.

Made in the USA
Middletown, DE
04 April 2021